ALSO BY KAY CHARLES

THE MARTI MICKKLESON MYSTERIES

Ghosts in Glass Houses

OLD BONES AND NEW GHOSTS

MARTI MICKKLESON MYSTERIES
BOOK TWO

KAY CHARLES

One Ghost Another Ghost

Copyedited by Lily K Coy-Johnson

ISBN: 979-8-9896759-0-6 (eBook)

ISBN: 979-8-9896759-1-3 (Trade Paperback)

Old Bones and New Ghosts / Kay Charles—1st Edition

One Ghost Another Ghost: January 2024

www.kaycharles.com

For all those who ~~nagged~~ asked
for another Marti book
with special thanks to
Doug Anderson and Valerie Burns

CHAPTER

ONE

Marti Mickkleson, family black sheep and newly minted interim director of the Mickkleson Foundation, tried to focus on the matter at hand.

Mom held the reporter in thrall. Emily from *The Gilmore Girls* could learn a thing or six from her. Full-strength Margaret Alberta Dibble Mickkleson was impressive, not to mention scary.

However, the girl hovering in the corner behind Mom was intriguing. As far as Marti was concerned, intriguing beat impressive every time.

"Battlesborough County has been good to the Mickklesons, and it's time we gave something back. Try one of the pink ones." Mom handed a plate of cookies to MaryEllen Pernelli. The reporter purred.

The Girl flickered and disappeared.

A fat marmalade cat leaped to the arm of the tastefully upholstered sofa and settled in next to Marti. His purr hit chainsaw level. The rumble wasn't the reporter after all.

"Is that..." Rather than the fawning voice MaryEllen used on Mom, the two words dripped with distaste. The unfinished question was the first the reporter directed at the Mickkleson daughter formerly known as "Marti Cray-Cray."

Ginger-Boy flicked his fluffy tail.

"Bernard." Marti scratched his chin. The rumble escalated to jet-on-the-runway level. "We don't talk about his past." She'd taken in the enormous orange cat when his previous human was arrested for murder. Mom was opposed, to put it mildly, to furry creatures residing in Bickle House, the family citadel. When Marti reluctantly agreed to help set up and oversee the Foundation, one of her stipulations was Bernard be allowed to live in the office. Mom wasn't pleased but declared it better than having him mucking up her valuable heirlooms. Not her exact words, but if Marti's alternate plan, leaving Bicklesburg and taking the cat with her, had any effect on her mother's acquiescence, Mom would never admit it.

"Interesting name," MaryEllen said.

"He came with it." Not completely true. Bicklesburg's sole veterinarian told Marti Ginger-Boy's name was Barney, but she'd decided he deserved a bit more dignity. He had, after all, saved her life. He saved her mother's too, but Margaret Mickkleson wasn't about to award him any medals.

"My great, great uncle was a Bernard," Mom said. "It is a name with gravitas."

First Marti'd heard of any Uncle Bernard in the family tree. She'd ask Grandma Bertie about him when she had the chance. It was hard to believe Mom would make up ancestors for the cat's benefit. Maybe she was softening.

The Girl was back, hovering behind MaryEllen. Of all the ghosts Marti had known—and she'd met many in her thirty-two years—only two had flickered and wavered like the Girl. Both had blinked out and disappeared for good to wherever it was the dead went when they weren't hanging around bothering her. Grandma Bertie, who, being dead for over thirty years herself should know, called it "crossing over" but was reticent on the details.

Where was her great-grandmother, anyway? The spirit of Alberta Marcile Ferguson had been with Marti her entire life. The old spook nagged a lot but also provided moral support when Marti needed it. At the moment, she needed it, and Grandma Ghostypants was nowhere to be seen.

"Marcile? Ms. Pernelli asked you a question." To the untrained ear, Mom's silky tone could be construed as parental pride. It told Marti the interview was a test. One she was in danger of failing. Big time.

"I'm sorry. I was thinking about Bernard."

MaryEllen Pernelli tilted her head, widened her eyes, and said, "Poor dear. He came to you in a trying time."

The reporter's attempt to appear sympathetic was past the danger of failing. It was an all-out fiasco. Of course, "Pernelli" and "sympathy for a Mickkleson" were incompatible terms, even if MaryEllen was a Pernelli-by-marriage. Marti assumed she was. Her appearance didn't bear the Pernelli stamp, and genes ran strong in that family.

"Ms. Pernelli asked about overhead. There are rumors the Mickkleson Foundation is a scam, somehow meant to increase the family coffers." Mom brought the discussion back on track. The events of five months ago were off-limits. Mom's goals with the Foundation weren't entirely altruistic. The Foundation was an opportunity to repair the Mickkleson reputation and do good at the same time. The *Gazette's* editor had agreed to the stipulation, even if the reporter hadn't. All the same, the rules would be adhered to. Mom would make sure of it.

The Girl disappeared again. At times, Marti was jealous of the dead. This was one of those times.

"You can't really blame them. The only salaried employee is a Mickkleson, and Mrs. Mickkleson, you own the building we are sitting in. How much rent does the charity pay you?"

Mom arched her elegant eyebrows.

Marti took it as a sign she was supposed to answer. Examination time just got real. She stopped petting Bernard and folded her hands in her lap. If nothing else, Mom might give her points for ladylike deportment.

"My salary is a token one dollar per year, and ownership of the building has been transferred to the Mickkleson Foundation. Although we occupy this office rent-free, all rent paid by the other tenants goes directly to the Foundation. All legal work is being done by my sister, pro bono." Marti left out *much to my brother-in-law's dismay*. "So, you can see, although the family is involved in all facets of the charity, none of us benefit in any way. Financially, that is. Helping those in need is its own reward." No need to mention the possibility that funding good works for the local population might wipe out the memory of her late father's sins, both proven and alleged.

Mom beamed. Marti hoped her delivery of the lines didn't sound as rehearsed—over-rehearsed—as it was.

"How lovely," MaryEllen Pernelli said. "Funding?"

To Marti's relief, Mom fielded the question. She could have handled answering but continuing to be nice to a Pernelli was another matter. Not being born into the clan didn't buy the woman any grace. Anyone who willingly became a Pernelli had to be worse than those for whom Pernelli-hood was a birthright.

"Initial funding was provided by family money, both Mickkleson and Dibble. The Dibbles, I'm sure you know, were my people. Eventually, we hope to receive bequests from the other leading families of Battlesborough County—"

All three of them, Marti thought.

"—and possibly donations from local business owners. However, the Mickkleson Foundation will always remain a private operation devoted to helping county residents in need."

"I'm covering the groundbreaking for your son-in-law's new shopping center," MaryEllen said. "He's quite the up-and-comer. It's good to see a local boy make good. Is he a donor?"

"Peter currently has no involvement in the Foundation. His growing business concerns keep him busy enough," Mom said.

RachelAnne's husband, to whom the word nonprofit was anathema, had campaigned hard for a role, as long as that role didn't involve parting with his own money. He was smart enough not to push his mother-in-law too hard, or maybe just smart enough to be afraid of her. For Marti, he had neither respect nor fear. She'd avoided him since she agreed to be part of Mom's project. Giving away the family money was a feel-good project for Marti. Annoying Peter was a side benefit.

Helping with the Foundation not only gave her the warm fuzzies, it would keep her out of trouble while she served out the six months she was required, by the terms of her father's will, to stay in Bicklesburg in the bosom of her family and behave herself. She only had one month left, but she had a history of screwing things up at the finish line. Helping her mother with the Foundation would go a long way toward convincing her sister she was a responsible adult, another requirement for gaining access to her trust fund.

RachelAnne threw her full support behind Mom's plan. Marti credited her sister with the best of motivations, although Rachel-Anne-the-lawyer might view it as a way to keep a semblance of control over the family coffers. The Judge put everything in her mother's name before he died and no legal charges could be brought against a dead man, but there was still a chance of civil suits. RachelAnne assured Marti that somewhere a lawyer was trying to talk someone into suing the Mickkleson family, and it would be expensive no matter what the outcome.

Marti doubted Peter's desire to be involved had anything to do with philanthropy. The only good he'd done for the world was fathering her niece and nephew, and the credit for them went to RachelAnne.

"And Marti, what qualifications do you have for the position of Executive Director of the Mickkleson Foundation?"

"Interim director." Marti hadn't committed to staying in Bicklesburg.

"I would have thought your sister would be the more likely candidate," MaryEllen said.

Born and bred or not, the reporter definitely had Pernelli skills. With one little statement, she managed multiple digs. She knew—the whole town knew—Marti never finished college. Instead, she spent her senior year in her second and final stay at The Birches, a storehouse for the troubled offspring of the rich. She hoped it was her final stay. If she gave in to impulse and threw the plate of pink iced cookies at the woman, she might end up back there. Shock treatment wasn't fun. Also, it would be a waste of good cookies.

Maybe the reporter was pumping for information about Marti's ten years of self-exile from Bicklesburg, a subject as off-limits as what Mom called "the recent unpleasantness."

Either way, MaryEllen Pernelli reminded Marti just how different she was from her baby sister, the ever-perfect Rachel-Anne—*one word please, capital A, and don't forget the E at the end*—former homecoming queen, current lawyer, mother of two adorable children, and heiress apparent for Mom's mantle of Queen of Bicklesburg.

The sisters had one thing in common, and it wasn't to be sold short. They were both raised by Margaret Alberta Dibble Mickkleson.

"I am my mother's daughter," Marti said. She channeled her mother in voice, posture, and every fiber of her being. If her mother wasn't alive and sitting next to her, she would have believed she was possessed by Mom's spirit—and possession had never been one of her ghostly problems. Margaret Mickkleson should be proud. MaryEllen Pernelli should be terrified.

The reporter wasn't. If Marti was feeling charitable, she might have considered the crinkling around MaryEllen's eyes laugh lines.

They were crow's feet and made the woman look like an in-progress dried-apple doll.

"So, you've been assisting your mother from afar all these years?"

Until recently, Mom's main occupation—other than being The Judge's wife, a more than full-time job—was sitting on and often chairing the boards and fundraising committees of a dozen nonprofit and charitable institutions. Marti's last job was flipping sort-of-beef patties on a Burger Buster grill.

"I'm sure I'm capable of earning every penny of my salary," Marti said.

"Oh, dear. Look at the time." Mom rose and extended her hand to the reporter. "I have another appointment, and I believe my daughter also has matters to attend to."

No room for quibbles, the interview was over.

"Cookie for the road?" Marti offered the platter to the flustered reporter. The power of her mother's command voice never ceased to amaze her. When directed at a Pernelli instead of at her, it was awesome.

"No thank you. The piece should be ready for next week's edition." MaryEllen Pernelli gathered her things and made her escape.

"We'll discuss this at dinner," Mom said. Marti's name was on the newly printed letterhead, but Mom was, as always, the boss.

"You know she's going to make things up, write whatever she wants, right? She's a Pernelli." Marti had a sinking feeling she'd failed her exam.

"Don't worry. I have final approval before it runs." Bernard wrapped himself around Queen Margaret's ankles. She shuddered. "Have you begun interviewing potential assistants? You need to get that taken care of. And make sure she—or he—has no qualms about cleaning up after a filthy cat."

Marti didn't bother to walk her mother to the elevator. She stood at the office door and held in her laughter until Mom was safely inside and the elevator door closed. She scooped up the cat. "Thank you, Bernard. I owe you one. Another one."

He looked pretty proud of himself, but he was a cat. Arrogant was his normal expression. Maybe the orange fur covering her mother's rear end wasn't intentional. It was just what cats did. Bernard did it particularly well. It looked lovely against Mom's navy dress.

CHAPTER

TWO

MARTI SETTLED in at her desk. *Her desk.* She couldn't get used to sitting behind the oak monstrosity, chosen by her mother, rather than standing in front of a steaming grill flipping heart-attack burgers at the ding of a bell. Any job that came with a desk that size required the use of a brain, and some days, especially those when she dealt with her mother for any significant amount of time, she wasn't sure she had one. At least not one capable of coping with anything more taxing than semi-automated-burger-land.

It wasn't only the desk. It was the entire room. The behemoth of a desk sat in front of large windows which offered a view of downtown Bicklesburg or would have if the desk wasn't situated with the windows at Marti's back. Her view was a pair of wing-back chairs in front of the desk and a large oval conference table, surrounded by eight matching chairs, beyond them. Until Bernard moved in, fresh flowers, replaced as needed, graced the center of the table. After the third morning of cleaning up pieces of broken vases and torn and scattered flowers as soon as she arrived, Marti decreed the centerpiece was only for official functions. It was her first executive action.

So far, the table had only needed flowers once. At the first official meeting of the Mickkleson Foundation Board of Trustees, Mom sat at the head of the table, and Marti at the foot. Margaret Mickkleson's six carefully chosen acolytes lined the sides. A tasteful arrangement of iris and roses sat in the middle. The gathering wasn't a memory Marti cherished. Although her mother assured her the table would make an excellent work surface when not in use for meetings, Marti had yet to use it.

Dark wood bookshelves lined one side of the office. Waist-high antique wood filing cabinets, all empty except the one where Marti stashed Bernard's food supply, lined the other. When she asked why filing cabinets in the age of computers and why all the dark wood—she would have preferred something light and modern—Mom said something about a sense of dignity and history. Marti knew better than to argue with her mother.

She did ask for a coffee maker and refrigerator, and she had to admit, her mother came through there. A small refrigerator disguised as an old-fashioned safe replaced two filing cabinets. Above the safe, a counter held a small sink and the coffee station of a coffee lover's dream. Beans would always be freshly ground. She could make coffee by the pot or the cup. She could make espresso, lattes, or cappuccinos, courtesy of De'Longhi's finest. If she had a hankering for French press or pour-over, Mom had that covered too. A temperature-controlled electric kettle sat next to a gleaming stainless steel French press, a glass Chemex, and a selection of fine teas. There was something for everyone.

When Marti asked if it came with a barista, her mother replied, "Isn't food service part of your resumé?"

"I stayed away from coffeehouses and bars. I preferred not to combine my hobbies and my work," Marti said.

"Maybe you should add that to the qualifications for your administrative assistant."

Marti didn't know if her mother was joking. Margaret Mickkleson wasn't known for her sense of humor.

Mom was right about one thing. Marti needed to wade through the stack of resumés sitting in front of her, interview the likely candidates, and hire an assistant. So far, most of her new job involved filling out forms for setting up the legalities of the Foundation or doing PR work. Her sister helped with the former, and her mother led the charge on the latter. When the newness wore off—about the time the real work began—they would likely get bored and leave her on her own.

Hiring an assistant was the first task the two respectable Mickkleson women had left entirely up to her. She needed to get it right.

No pressure whatsoever.

The first candidate was young and had no work experience but had recently graduated from the county Vo-Tech high school with a major in business administration services. Marti put her resumé in the maybe pile.

The second resumé was riddled with enough errors to be unreadable. The problems were worse than typos. Marti made a note to look into funding basic literacy skills classes, put the resumé in the sorry-not-sorry pile, and picked up the next one.

Dawn Pernelli Gunderson.

"Unbelievable," she said.

Dawn Pernelli, the personification of all things Pernelli, bullied and tortured Marti all through their school days, starting on their first day of Kindergarten. Dawn was the first to use the despicable nickname "Marti Cray-Cray." Certain Bicklesburg residents, and not all of them Pernellis, still used it—most behind her back, a few to her face. Her family weren't the only ones who considered her ability to see and converse with the dead a mental illness rather than a gift.

The tormenting didn't stop with adulthood. Marti'd run into Dawn a dozen times since her return to her hometown. Each time, Dawn managed to work the word "crazy" into the conversation, and not in the "wow, it's crazy good to see you" sense. A decent person would have left high school behind long ago. Dawn Pernelli wasn't a decent person.

Neither was Marti. She tossed the resumé, unread, into the sorry-not-sorry pile.

And picked it up again. What qualifications could Dawn possibly have to make her think Marti would hire her?

She'd spent the last eight years as a Walmart cashier. Considering her job history, Marti wouldn't hold that against anyone. It was honest work. One semester at Lakeview Community College, no note on what she studied. The dates attended were right after they graduated from Bicklesburg Area High School. The attempt at higher education was probably hard on Dawn. No Marti to kick around. No longer a big fish in a small pond.

"Poor baby," Marti said.

The rest of the resumé detailed Dawn's high school career. Cheerleader. Homecoming court—listing that one took cojones. Had she forgotten the time Marti caught her in the girls' restroom furiously erasing and changing the names on the ballots? National Honor Society. Really? Marti didn't remember Dawn being all that bright in any area other than dreaming up ways to torture her.

If it was anyone else, she would toss the resumé into the maybe-maybe pile. Since it was Dawn's, she wanted to shred it and kill it with fire.

There was no way she could consider hiring Dawn. She didn't trust her. She didn't trust herself not to kill her old nemesis if confined with her in the office for more than an hour. Make that fifteen minutes.

The Pernelli power lay in their mouths. If she didn't call Dawn in for an interview, every Pernelli in town would have something to say and would say it to anyone willing to listen and a few unwilling, too. The Pernellis were a large, over-extended, and close-knit family. They weren't only part of every facet of Bicklesburg life, they kept creeping into Marti's life. MaryEllen Pernelli, reporter. Winter Adams, one of Mom's night nurses during her recent illness, now part-time housekeeper at Bickle House, was a Pernelli even if she didn't bear the name. On Marti's return to Bicklesburg, the first person she saw was a Pernelli. For all she knew, Pimples, overlord of the So-nutt-ee Donut drive-thru, had a resumé in the stack in front of her.

In Bicklesburg, gossip was gold. Starting up the Pernelli rumor machine wouldn't make things any easier for her or the Mickkleson Foundation. Mom would never admit it, but the Pernellis were a more powerful force in town than the Mickklesons.

She started a new pile, the I'd-rather-have-root-canal-than-deal-with-it pile.

For all she knew, a dozen Pernellis had applied for the job. She stuffed the remaining resumés into a manila folder, stuck it in her desk drawer, and looked up.

The Girl stood in front of Marti's desk, the closest she'd gotten. Like a feral kitten torn between fear and the need to make friends, she edged a little closer each day. Also like a feral kitten, the moment Marti acknowledged her, she fled. Grandma Bertie was of the opinion the Girl wasn't used to being seen by the living, but she flinched from Grandma too, and they were both ghosts. Marti had met Caspers, friendly spirits. She'd met Eeyores, sad spirits. She'd met Cantankerous Old Coots, whom she assumed were as awful alive as they were dead, and General Pain in the Butt Ghosts. Grandma Bertie, Queen of the Eye Roll, often fell into the last category.

She'd never met a Scaredy-Cat Ghost until the Girl.

"I don't suppose you've seen my grandmother around, have you?"

The Girl disappeared, and Grandma Bertie took her place. Fair trade. At least Grandma spoke to her.

"Maybe she read a lot of ghost stories while she was alive and thinks that's what she's supposed to do," Grandma said.

"Could be," Marti said. The massive belled legs of the Girl's jeans, like her gauzy shirt, were heavily embroidered. Marti thought she'd spotted cork platform sandals peeking from beneath the ragged hem of the jeans. Either she died in the 1960s or early 1970s, or she was a big fan of the fashion of that era. She'd barely seen the Girl's face, usually hidden behind the fall of her long, straight, center-parted hair. The few times she caught a glimpse, she couldn't tell if the Girl's expression was murderous or terrified.

"Just keep talking to her, she'll come around."

Marti wasn't sure she wanted to put in the effort. "Where have you been?"

Grandma couldn't have wandered far. If she strayed more than a football field's length away from her great-granddaughter, an invisible bungee cord snapped her back to Marti's side. The same thing happened when Marti got too far away, the reason her teenage attempts to escape the company of the old ghost failed.

"Talking to Janice Heedly."

"Ugh." Marti's third-grade teacher wasn't Marti's biggest fan while alive, and nothing changed after her death. Mrs. Heedly roamed the park in the center of town, known as the Green to the locals. The office was located in one of the buildings, old as the town itself, surrounding the Green. Close enough for Grandma to visit her friend, as long as they stayed on the office side of the gazebo.

"Show some respect," Grandma said. "Janice needs to talk to you."

During the Mickklesons' recent troubles—Marti found herself using her mother's term for the chaos wrought by her late father —Mrs. Heedly had been a fine source of information. She had free rein of the Green and no issues with eavesdropping on the living or relaying anything she heard to Grandma. She did have issues with Marti. They couldn't stand each other.

"*Needs* to talk to me? If she *needs* to tell me something, can't she pass it on through you? I like that arrangement."

"It's important."

"I have work to do." Marti pulled the manila folder from her desk drawer and opened it. She didn't recognize the name on the first resumé. That was a good start.

"Peter's breaking ground on his new strip mall tomorrow."

"So what? Peter's always up to something." RachelAnne's husband had inherited his father's used car dealership and was intent on parlaying it into a business empire. As long as he stayed out of Marti's way and didn't treat her sister and niece and nephew badly, she didn't care what he did.

"It's in what used to be called Henrietta's Hollow."

"It still is until Peter's through with it. Mrs. Heedly wants to give me a lesson in local history?" Marti knew the place. With a name like Henrietta's Hollow, of course it had a ghost story attached to it. In this case, a typical woman in white urban legend. She doubted it was true but had never visited the field and had no idea if it was actually haunted. She made it a rule never to search out ghosts if she could help it. Enough found her on their own.

She tossed one resumé onto the I-can't-make-up-my-mind pile and picked up the next. Faustyn Anguish sounded like a likely candidate. Lots of administrative assistant experience, but none of it with nonprofits. She wanted to see the person attached to the name. He had to be a survivor. His resumé went into the definitely-interview pile.

"Janice says when they start digging there's a good chance they're going to turn up a body, and she knows who it is."

"Lalalalala. I can't hear you."

THREE

NO SIGN OF SNOW, either in the air or the forecast, but the wind cut through Marti's jacket. No sane person would choose to eat their lunch on a park bench on the Green on a windy day in March. Marti sat down and pulled her sandwich from her bag.

When she gave in to Grandma Bertie's hounding, she'd planned to eat in the gazebo in the center of the park, but it was occupied. The two people in the gazebo swing were either huddled together for warmth or making out. They probably didn't want company any more than she did.

She sat as far away from the gazebo as the Green allowed. She would listen to Mrs. Heedly and let Grandma do all the talking. She was the only one who could hear either of them, but on the off chance she needed or cared enough about her former teacher's story to contribute to the conversation, she didn't want witnesses.

She had her phone, which she used more often as a smoke-screen for fake calls to the post-living than for real conversations with the living, in her pocket to be used as needed. Her batiked cotton scarf was more a fashion accessory than a source of warmth, but considering the wind, it wouldn't look odd if she used it to cover the lower half of her face. Anyone who noticed her sitting alone wouldn't see her lips moving. They would notice her. Mickkleson watching was a popular Bicklesburg sport. Since she was the oddball daughter, she was worth extra points.

Of course, she couldn't eat her lunch through the scarf, and despite devouring all the leftover pink iced cookies, she was starving.

The wind didn't ruffle Grandma or Mrs. Heedly's hair. Mrs. Heedly's steel gray helmet was probably wind-proof when she was alive. Marti buttoned her inadequate wool blazer, unwrapped her sandwich, and shivered.

"Are you quite ready?" Grandma said.

Marti raised her peanut butter and banana sandwich to her mouth. "Shoot," she said and took a bite. The banana was a tad over-ripe for her taste, but the sandwich was one of her favorites.

"That looks disgusting," Mrs. Heedly said, true to form.

Marti wanted to point out that for a ghost who wanted a favor from the only living person she could ask, disapproval wasn't the way to go. She kept her mouth shut and chewed. Talking with her mouth full would only attract more criticism, from Grandma if not Mrs. Heedly.

"I don't know where to begin." More than the wind had ruffled Mrs. Heedly's feathers. Her voice shook. She wrung her hands like the maiden in a Victorian melodrama.

"Just tell her what you told me." Grandma gave her friend an encouraging squeeze. Marti wanted to puke. "My granddaughter is very smart, you know."

Mrs. Heedly looked doubtful.

Marti stayed quiet. She didn't care one way or the other if her former teacher talked. If she didn't, Marti could get back inside where it was warm faster.

"When I was much younger, I taught at the high school. Algebra and Civics."

The pairing of subjects made no sense to Marti, but she hoped

Mrs. Heedly had been better with teenagers than she was with eight-year-olds. She doubted it.

"Go on," Grandma said.

"Teachers, especially women teachers, were paid even worse back then than when I left teaching—"

When you keeled over and died, Marti thought.

"—and I'm sure worse than today. I took in a boarder. A student teacher from down at State. She was a young woman with...ideas."

Marti stuffed the end of her sandwich in her mouth. The replies running through her head shouldn't be let out.

"She thought she could change things. She came to me with stories about...things that shouldn't be talked about. I told her I would speak to the students involved, but that wasn't what she wanted."

Marti's phone rang, her sister's ringtone. She pulled it out and hit ignore. RachelAnne would have to wait until she was back in the office. Her warm office, where she couldn't go until Mrs. Heedly finished her story.

"Are you listening to me?" Mrs. Heedly used the same tone she used twenty-four years ago asking Marti the same question.

Marti pulled her scarf up to her nose and stuck the phone in her pocket. "Get on with it. I'm freezing."

"Be nice, or you'll be a lot colder," Grandma said.

An empty threat. The dead couldn't harm the living, but they could make things darned uncomfortable by passing through them. Even a casual brush against an arm caused chills. A pass-through caused internal icicles. Grandma had never purposely used the ghost freeze on her, and never would. Or Marti didn't think she would. Under cover of her scarf, she stuck out her tongue.

"I saw that," Grandma said. "Go on, Janice."

The clatter of breaking glass came from her pocket. Rachel-Anne had left a voicemail.

"Susan Silliphant was her name. Did you ever hear anything so ridiculous? She wanted to go to the school board. The police. I told her some things needed to be handled privately. Too many good names would be dragged through the mud."

"Was one of those names Mickkleson?" Marti had to ask. Until recently, the family name was Scotchgarded and stainproof. No matter how much mud was slung, none of it stuck. Thanks to her father's shenanigans, those days were gone.

"Not everything is about you," Mrs. Heedly said, "or that family of yours."

Grandma glared at Marti. Clearly, she was expected to shut up and listen. She tried to look interested.

"Susan and I argued. She said she knew what she had to do and left. Her car was found here, parked on the Green, but no one ever saw or heard from her again. You haven't seen her, have you?"

"Not that I know of. When did this happen?"

"A long time ago. I don't remember." Mrs. Heedly shifted her nonexistent weight from foot to foot.

"You don't remember? A young woman—your roommate— vanishes, and you don't remember when it happened?"

"March 14th, 1972, and she was my lodger, not my roommate."

"Why didn't I ever hear anything about this?" It was before Marti was born, but vanishing young women were the stuff of small-town legends, and Bicklesburg was fond of their local tales.

"I remember," Grandma said. "I heard she burned her bra and ran off with some young man to join one of those hippie communes. I was jealous."

"That's what people said. Her skirts were very short, so most people believed it," Mrs. Heedly said.

"So why are you telling me this? Grandma said something about a body. Did she kill someone before she left town?"

"She never left. I think Peter Rudawski or whomever he has working for him is going find Susan Silliphant or what's left of her in Henrietta's Hollow."

Which explained why Mrs. Heedly asked if Marti'd seen the missing woman.

"And why do you think that? Have you seen her?"

"No, but..."

If Marti didn't know better, she would have sworn there were tears in Mrs. Heedly's eyes. The dead were incapable of tears. Body language was a different matter. Mrs. Heedly hunched her shoulders and hugged herself as if she'd been punched in the stomach. Misery radiated from the old ghost. Marti couldn't bear to look at her.

Over in the gazebo, a third person joined the canoodling couple. The newcomer was dressed against the cold—over-dressed. The faded green parka was more fit for a raging blizzard than a March day, even a windy one. Its fur-trimmed hood lay on the man's—or woman's, Marti couldn't tell which—back. A bright red knit hat covered their head.

Grandma made soothing noises and urged her friend to continue her story.

Mrs. Heedly wailed.

Marti never imagined the stern and unyielding woman as a drama queen, either alive or dead. Whatever she had to say, she needed to get on with it. Marti was freezing.

The couple unclinched. One of them handed something to Green Parka.

"My sister saw her." Mrs. Heedly might not be able to shed tears, but her voice was choked with sobs.

Green Parka pulled a small package from inside his—or her— coat.

Bicklesburg wasn't quite the center of wholesomeness and propriety the Chamber of Commerce liked to think it was. She was witnessing a drug transaction, and it was none of her busi-ness. "Your sister?" she asked.

Sirens drowned out Mrs. Heedly's answer. All three of the town's police cruisers screamed up to the Green, and Bicklesburg's finest invaded. The trio in the gazebo scattered. In a ballet-like move, a mountain of a man took down Green Parka. Billy "Big" Fysh, former high school football star and current chief of police, hadn't forgotten how to tackle.

One of Marti's two standard New Year's resolutions was "avoid the police." That one was easier to keep than the other. She usually broke "be nice" before Martin Luther King Day.

"I need to go," she said. One resolution had to stand. She rose and walked calmly toward the street. No reason to hurry and attract attention. Big wasn't her biggest fan to start with. No reason for him to know she was in the park or saw anything.

Grandma and Mrs. Heedly flanked her.

"You need to listen," Grandma said.

Marti didn't answer. She stopped at the curb and looked both ways. The speed limit was low around the Green, but it paid to be careful.

"Listen to me!" Mrs. Heedly grabbed Marti's arm.

Tried to grab it. Her substance-less fingers sunk into Marti's arm and stayed there. Icicles shot up to Marti's shoulders. "L-l-l-l-et-t-t g-g-g-go."

Mrs. Heedly released her. "They showed her Susan's body and said 'This is what happens to little girls who tell lies.'"

MARTI FINISHED her first cup of post-lunch coffee. She'd made more headway on coffee consumption than resumé review. They all sounded alike after the eighth or ninth. She couldn't keep her mind on the task. Faustyn Anguish and a woman named Sandra Booth were still the only definite interviews. Neither were Bicklesburg natives, which probably wasn't a coincidence.

This is what happens to little girls who tell lies.

Mrs. Heedly had used those exact words every time she punished the young Marti for telling tales. In third grade, Marti's tales of ghosts roaming Bicklesburg were responsible for eight out of ten of her exiles to the hallway. The other two were usually due to her smart mouth.

Marti's stories hadn't been lies. Most of them, anyway. She'd heard the tales from the spirits themselves. Not that all of them could be believed. The dead lied as readily as the living.

Sure, she embellished a few, playing up to her audience. The story that gave Dawn Pernelli nightmares and brought her loud-mouthed mother to the school demanding "they do something about that insane girl even if she was a Mickkleson" might not have been the beginning of Marti's troubles, but it was certainly a catalyst.

Hungry for friends, her eight-year-old self didn't realize she was marking herself as the weird girl. The crazy girl. As if being the eldest daughter of the pinnacle of Bicklesburg aristocracy wasn't enough to set her apart, the incident with Dawn—which Dawn, already a bully, deserved—resulted in Marti being sent to her first therapist. The therapist was followed by a psychologist who was followed by a psychiatrist. The latter had the power to medicate her—and when she turned into a wild teenager, arranged her first trip to The Birches.

Ghosts weren't real, therefore Marti couldn't see and speak to them, therefore she was either a pathological liar or suffering from a mental illness. Grandma Bertie assured her neither was true, which didn't help a whole lot since no one else could hear the dead woman. Her parents believed she was both. When punishment didn't cure the first, they sought treatment for the latter.

After her last trip to The Birches, Marti took matters into her own hands. She ran away and hid.

Ten years later, her father, the late Judge Thaddeus A. Mickkleson, found her. She felt he owed her an apology. He'd been dead for weeks. Death didn't change people, and The Judge never believed in apologies.

He did manage to talk her into going home.

Adult-Marti knew better than to blame her troubled youth on Mrs. Heedly and Dawn Pernelli, but she didn't want to adult. She'd had more than enough of adulting in the past few months.

What she hadn't had enough of was coffee. Never enough coffee. She contemplated making another cup. Maybe a latte this time. Too bad the cookies were gone. She could use a cookie or two or a dozen.

"What do you think? More coffee, or more coffee?" she asked her audience.

The Girl vanished.

"I promise. This is my last cup. Today."

Bernard blinked and yawned.

"What are you going to do about Janice's problem?" Grandma said.

"What problem? She told me a story. An outlandish story. The kind of story she used to punish me for telling. What am I supposed to do?"

"She wants that young woman identified. She wants her returned to her people so they can give her a proper burial. She wants Susan Silliphant's family to know what happened to her."

"I thought she ran away and became a dirty hippy or something."

"That was gossip, not fact."

"In the off chance Mrs. Heedly's not...delusional..." Marti wouldn't use the despicable c-r-a-z-y word. She'd had it hurled at her enough. "...the police will deal with it. They have ways of identifying remains, even ones in the ground for what, over fifty years?" Bicklesburg's finest wouldn't be up to the task, but some state agency would take over and do what needed to be done.

"They might figure out who it is, but odds are they won't figure out what happened to her. This town is good at burying the past."

"What do you want me to do about it? "

"Find the answer. You've proven you're good at this."

"Huh?" Marti was confused. Until recently, all she was good at was flipping burgers and hiding from her family.

"You solved the McDonaghs' murders. You rescued your mother."

"I got lucky. I almost ended up joining you in spooky-spooky beyond-the-grave-land." Bernard switched his tail, and she picked up the cat. "Yes, you helped."

"Aren't you the least bit curious?"

She was but wasn't about to admit it. "Why is this so important to Mrs. Heedly? Is this one of those must-be-solved-so-the-dead-can-rest things?" Marti didn't have a clue why some ghosts stayed earthbound while others went wherever they went. She'd asked, but Grandma was always fuzzy on the details, either because she didn't know herself or didn't want to tell.

"Eh. I think Janice just likes the Green. She'll probably be there until the earth falls into the sun or whatever."

Marti went back to her desk. Bernard leaped from her arms and sashayed across the desktop, stopping to knock the sorted stacks of resumés to the floor. Maybe he knew something she didn't. Maybe she should spread the applications across the floor and hire the one Bernard slept on.

The long-haired cat hacked.

"Uh-oh." Not a good sound. Marti dove but wasn't quick enough to rescue the targeted resumé before he puked up a hairball. "Yuck." She pulled the paper from under him. He stretched and stalked away.

"Dawn's," she said. "He is a clever boy."

"Stop changing the subject," Grandma said.

"I didn't. Bernard did." She *was* curious about Susan Silliphant, her disappearance, and any part her third-grade teacher may have played in it. When Mrs. Heedly said the young teacher had "ideas", she spat the word as if she was saying "herpes." Marti wondered what those ideas were. She had a feeling she would have liked the missing woman.

The Girl peeked around the door to the office. For a change, Marti could see her face. Minor progress on the befriending-the-stray front.

"Your name doesn't happen to be Susan Silliphant, does it?"

Ghost-girl's eyes widened. She squeaked and vanished.

"She really needs some special effects, a puff of smoke or something, when she does that," Marti said.

"Are you going to do anything for Janice?" Grandma said.

"If it's the only way to shut you up." Marti let out an exaggerated sigh. It wouldn't do for Grandma to think she'd gotten her way too easily. If the project somehow went south and got Marti into trouble, as things had a way of doing in her life, she could blame Grandma Bertie for getting her into it. Wouldn't do any good with the living, but it would make her feel better.

She opened her laptop and typed "Susan Silli" into the search box. As soon as she got to the second "i", Google supplied the "phant". She wasn't the first to search for the name.

"Whatever did we do before the Internet?" Grandma hovered over her shoulder.

"I have no idea."

The top two hits were a real estate agent in Florida. From her picture, much too young to be the woman Marti was searching for.

The rest of the page was filled with what was, unless women named Susan Silliphant made a habit of vanishing, exactly what she wanted. The Bicklesburg hive mind might have written her off as a runaway, but Susan's family never stopped looking for her. Nor did they ever find her. The student teacher, while not Judge Crater level, was on the list of famous missing persons.

Which didn't mean she was dead. Marti had hidden from her family for ten years in the days of digital trails and Homeland Security. She hadn't bothered to change her name or otherwise compli-cate her life with a false identity. Of course, her family hadn't looked for her all that hard. Number twenty-seven on her list of family-induced resentments to overcome. She was working on it.

Becoming a new person was easier in 1972. Katherine Ann Power went underground in 1970 and stayed hidden for twenty-three years, fourteen of them on the FBI's most wanted list for bank robbery and murder. If she hadn't turned herself in, she might still be a teacher, restaurateur, and upstanding citizen living in small-town Oregon. Susan Silliphant could be a mild-mannered mother or grandmother in an upscale suburb anywhere in the country. According to a few websites, she was. According to others, she was living in sin with Elvis in a Malibu beach house.

About eight years ago, *America's Most Mysterious Missing Persons* did an episode on Susan's vanishing act. Marti hadn't seen the show. In those days, the only televisions she saw were hung above bars and tuned to sports. The show was in large part responsible for Susan's popularity with conspiracy theorists. The web pages and blog posts reporting sightings of her dining with Elvis or speculating on alien abduction were all dated after it aired.

"Ooooo. We should watch that," Grandma said.

"Maybe," Marti said. If she looked hard enough, she could probably find it online or on DVD.

The Silliphant family ran a website devoted to finding their missing progeny. It hadn't been updated for a few years. Photos showed a smiling young woman, nicely dressed. Conservatively for the times, even if her skirts were a few inches above her knees. Attractive in a wholesome girl-next-door way. Likable. Definitely not the office haunt. She reminded Marti of the young teacher in an old television show—Karen Valentine in *Room 222*, that was it.

A quick Internet side trip told her the show first aired three years before Susan went missing. Before Marti was born. Thanks to the wonders of cable television, she'd seen it when she was a teen. Maybe during one of her incarcerations at The Birches.

"I loved that show," Grandma said.

"Me too."

Other than a few tidbits about Susan's childhood, Marti didn't discover anything Mrs. Heedly hadn't already told her. Less. None of the news clippings or sites mentioned the argument the two women had before Susan left or any reason for it. Investigators at the time found no signs of foul play, just a perfectly parked abandoned car. Susan Silliphant had evaporated.

"Did you know Mrs. Heedly's sister?"

"Janice and I weren't friends before I passed," Grandma said. "We didn't move in the same circles when we were alive."

Teenaged Marti'd gone to her former teacher's funeral—the old bat nearly had a second coronary when Marti struck up a conversation with her—but didn't remember any family other than a few distant cousins. She found Mrs. Heedly's obituary on the *Bicklesburg Gazette* website. For years, they'd only put out a print edition once a week, but they kept a strong online presence including back issues.

Those preceding her in death include her husband of 27 years, Stanley; her father, James Monahan; mother, Marilyn (Stryker) Monahan; and stepmother, Lenora (Watkins) Monahan.

No "She is survived by" list. No mention of a sister, living or otherwise.

"Looks like the obit writer—or somebody—forgot her sister," Grandma said.

"Oh, crap." The obituary writer wasn't the only one who forgot sisters. Marti'd never listened to RachelAnne's voicemail. Forgetting one's sister was easier than one might think. Even a sister as unforgettable as RachelAnne. Marti pulled out her phone.

Marti? Pleath call me ath thoon ath you get thith...oh, it'th not Mom or the kidth, tho don't panic.

Not good. Her sister's childhood lisp, the reason "Marcile" was shortened to "Marti" rather than "Marci," only showed up when RachelAnne was upset or angry. Seriously agitated, like a twelve on a scale of one to ten. Or when Marti intentionally pushed her baby sister's buttons. She hadn't done that for weeks.

RachelAnne didn't sound angry. She sounded sad. Mournful. Like she'd lost her puppy. Except she didn't have a puppy. Relieved her sister added the disclaimer about Mom and the kids, Marti hit "Return Call." She'd tell her sister she forgot to take the phone off "Do Not Disturb" when the morning's interview was over. She wasn't quite the pathological liar her parents—and everyone else—once believed her to be, but teeny-tiny fibs came in handy for navigating the pitfalls of Mickkleson-world.

She didn't need to fib. RachelAnne didn't answer. Marti left a message of her own. "I just got your message. Hope everything is okay. I'm about to leave the office." She might as well. She'd pretty much killed the whole afternoon falling into the black hole of the Internet. "I'll call you again when I get home."

"What was that all about?" Grandma asked.

"I don't know, but RachelAnne'th lithping."

"Uh-oh," Grandma said.

CHAPTER
FOUR

MARTI UNLOCKED THE LEXUS. Grandma was already in the passenger seat.

"Took you long enough," Grandma said.

"I had to feed Bernard, then the elevator stopped at every floor."

"You could have taken the stairs."

Marti normally would have run down the stairs from the fourth floor, but the elevator was waiting when she left the office. She took it as a sign and figured it would be faster. She was wrong. She hoped *that* wasn't a sign of anything.

She buckled her seatbelt and stuck her key in the ignition. Her ancient Taurus, best described as a rolling trash bin, had given its life getting her back to Bicklesburg. Her first month back, she drove her mother's little Audi TT, a car she loved with the same passion she hated her late father's school-bus-sized Lexus. The Lexus was ostentatious, much like its late owner. The Maggie-sized child seat in the second row of seats didn't explain why a man whose two children were grown and gone needed three rows of seating. When Mom took her baby back, Marti's choices were drive the Lexus or buy her own car. Although her brother-in-law kept trying to put her into one of his pre-owned vehicles—he never said "used car"—she wasn't yet ready to take that step.

She could afford it. The first portion of The Judge's bequest was hers no matter what. She got it just for showing up in Bicklesburg. She was five months into her prison term—probationary period—whatever. Her father'd stipulated she remain in the family cradle for six months to access the trust fund he set up for her. The really, really large trust fund. If she lasted out the final month, she could buy a Porsche or a Lamborghini, a house or two, and maybe a yacht. She wouldn't buy any of those things—possibly a small house—but she could. After ten years of scraping by on minimum wage or less, she was amazed and more than a little uncomfortable with the idea she might be able to afford luxuries.

First, she needed to get through one more month of proving to her sister she was reliable and responsible. Four more weeks without screwing up or running away. There were precedents for her doing both, and if she did, it was another well-used vehicle for her. When she got the first part of her inheritance, she thought she could live for years on it. By the time she let her sister talk her into an iPhone, refurbished her wardrobe with clothing not from Goodwill, and bought herself a laptop, she realized two things. First, at a higher standard of living than she'd grown accustomed to, the money wouldn't last as long as she thought. Second, she was tired of living hand to mouth and wanted that higher standard of living, which was why she treated herself to a MacBook Pro rather than a budget-line PC.

"RachelAnne didn't say what was wrong?" Grandma waited until they were well on the road, away from the ever-present risk of small-town spies before speaking. Marti seldom answered her when there was a risk of being seen talking to herself.

"She said Mom and the kids were fine. The only other thing she said was to call her as soon as possible."

"Peter?"

"She didn't mention him."

Her sister had married a watered-down, cut-rate version of their father, and as far as Marti could tell, wasn't aware of it. Marti had her own daddy issues, but that wasn't one of them. What really bothered her was the way Peter treated her sister. No matter how badly The Judge behaved behind his wife's back, he treated her with respect to her face. Peter didn't bother. And, he referred to spending time alone with his kids as "babysitting." That really got her goat.

Peter was no more fond of her than she was of him. She thought his biggest problem with her was The Judge left money to her but none to RachelAnne—or him. There was some for the kids, but Peter couldn't get his hands on it. He didn't get—or if he did, didn't care—that the Judge's reasoning was that her sister could take care of herself and he doubted Marti had that ability. A lot of the time, she doubted it too.

"He's probably gotten himself into some kind of trouble. It was only a matter of time." Grandma had no use for Peter Rudawski either.

"I'll try to call her again as soon as we get home." The Lexus had a Bluetooth phone hookup, but she hadn't bothered to pair her phone with it. She didn't like talking on the phone and saw driving as a good excuse to avoid it. "We're almost there."

She wasn't worried about Peter. She was worried about RachelAnne. Their relationship was rocky, but they were still sisters.

BICKLE HOUSE SAT at the end of Albion Court, a wide tree-lined boulevard ending in a cul-de-sac, known to everyone except the US Postal Service as the Avenue. Built by the town's founding family, Bickle House was home to Bicklesburg's current royal family, or what was left of it. The King was dead, Mom was still Queen, but Marti felt more like peasant than princess.

No matter how many times she made the drive up the Avenue, her childhood home looming ahead intimidated her. Luckily, she didn't have to make it often. She turned into the alleyway running behind the three houses—mansions, as far as she was concerned, although her mother considered the word crass—which lined the east side of the street. She passed the Albion Court Security office. If he could have, her father would have gated the Avenue. Failing to find a way to pull that off, he created a private army to protect the residents from the general population.

"I wonder if your young man is working?"

"He's not my young man." Dmitri Doyle, briefly her high school boyfriend, was in charge of ACS. Thanks to her father, their long-ago relationship ended badly. They'd maybe flirted a bit since her return—or he might have. She was so bad at the game she usually failed to notice what was happening. He was hardly her "young man."

When he wasn't working, he lived in a small apartment on the upper floor of the former carriage house occupied by the ACS office and sometimes hung out in the downstairs control center during his off hours. She shared a beer or two with him there after the weather turned too cold for them to sit outside. She'd never been upstairs. For some reason, having Dmitri living on the Avenue made the place less frightening.

He was in no way a factor in her decision to stay. It was a temporary decision anyway.

"I haven't even seen him in months," Marti said. Just after the first of the year, Dmitri talked RachelAnne, who'd taken over for The Judge as head of the Albion Court Residents' Council, into giving him an extended vacation or sabbatical or something. Marti didn't know where he'd gone and hadn't heard from him. Not so much as a postcard. According to her sister, he'd been back for two weeks. He hadn't called her. Definitely not "her young man."

"Maybe he's waiting for you to call," Grandma said.

"We're just friends and that might be pushing it," Marti said.

"Friends call friends."

They reached Bickle House. RachelAnne's Subaru blocked the path to the garage.

"Looks like you won't have to call her," Grandma said.

Back door, open. Back door, open.

"Shut up, Harriet." Marti closed the door, silenced the electronic voice of the security system, and was nearly knocked off her feet by two pint-sized missiles.

"Aunt Marti!" Thaddeus Aaron Mickkleson Rudawski, named after his Mickkleson grandfather and great-grandfather, let go of her first. He preferred to be called T3. It was his superhero name. "And how was your day?" Seven years old and—as far as his doting aunt was concerned—off-the-charts smart, he went back and forth between adult-in-miniature and superhero-in-miniature. She adored both versions.

His little sister hung on and peeked around Marti's legs at Grandma Bertie. "Hey-yo, yady," she said.

According to T3, Maggie didn't have a superhero name because no one knew what her superpower was.

Marti knew and had known since the first time the toddler pointed at Grandma Bertie and said, "Who's that yady?" Her niece was the biggest reason she was still in Bicklesburg. The trust fund would be nice, but she'd survived without her family or their money before and could do it again. She had to admit, despite their differences, that she loved her mother and sister. Leaving didn't have to mean cutting them out of her life again.

She had a sneaking suspicion they'd all love each other more from a distance anyway.

Maggie's superpower meant she would need a friend. A living friend. One who understood. One who would make sure the little girl wasn't labeled cray-cray.

One of Marti's first kindnesses was not telling her niece the "yady" was her great-great-grandmother. Talking about Grandma Bertie got Marti in trouble from the time she learned to talk. Maggie still talked to and about Grandma, but she called her "the yady." Marti had a hard time believing her sister hadn't caught on, but RachelAnne's only reaction was to correct her daughter's speech. *Lllllady, Maggie. Lllllady.*

Her sister managed to exist inside her own little bubble. RachelAnne ignored unpleasantness until it jumped out and smacked her up alongside in the head, which explained how she was able to stay married to Peter.

"Kids, go watch TV." RachelAnne and Mom sat at the island counter in the center of the kitchen. Mom sipped from a delicate china cup adorned with daisies. The familiar cat-pee scent of valerian meant the matching teapot held Mom's special tea, which she blended herself. RachelAnne held a glass of red wine.

Not good. At least her sister was no longer lisping.

"We're seeping here tonight." Maggie stuck her thumb in her mouth.

"Slllleeping, Maggie. Slllleeping. Both of you—TV. In the family parlor. Now." RachelAnne took more than a sip of her wine. "And Maggie, take your thumb out of your mouth. You are almost four. Time to stop that."

"This does not bode well," Grandma Bertie said.

Maggie obeyed her mother—the thumb part—and leaned against Marti, who scooped up the little girl and hugged her.

RachelAnne drained her glass, reached for the bottle, and refilled it far past the tasteful "pour to the bell of the glass" mark.

Very not good. Her sister didn't drink much at any time—that was always Marti's department—and never before six. It was just past four-thirty.

"Nana too," T3 said. "The ponies are on!"

Mom raised her eyebrows, and RachelAnne nodded. Mom patted her younger daughter's hand. "Lead on, my pretties!"

Maggie squirmed, and Marti put her down. The kids tore out of the kitchen, Mom in pursuit.

Marti had first thought her mother's fondness for the neon-bright animated ponies was a sign of early dementia. Turned out it was just a manifestation of Grandparent Syndrome. Mom had a severe case. "Nana" bore no resemblance to the strict and unyielding woman who raised Marti and her sister, although every time she called her grandchildren "my pretties," Marti imagined Margaret Hamilton and her flying monkeys. With the new Margaret "Nana" Mickkleson, it wasn't the Wicked Witch of the West who was in charge. It was the monkeys.

Nana-Mom's monkeys didn't fly. Marti hadn't seen them fly. If any kids could, they were her niece and nephew. There was a good chance she had a bad case of Doting Aunt Syndrome herself.

At the moment, she needed to put on her Caring Big Sister hat. It wasn't one she wore naturally, but she had been trying to make it work, and not only because RachelAnne had the final say on whether or not she was fit to gain access to her trust fund.

She moved Mom's teapot and cup to the sink. "Oreos?" She checked the canister marked "Flour," where the holy cookies were stored. It was empty.

Marti had raided the stash the night before but left half a bag uneaten. Maybe a third of a bag.

"I ate them for lunch," RachelAnne said.

Things were grim, indeed. "What did Mom have to say about that?"

"I let her have a couple."

Marti eyed the bottle of wine.

"Get yourself a glass," RachelAnne said.

Marti did, and RachelAnne poured. She stopped at the halfway mark, then filled her own to the brim.

Marti sat down across from her sister. Small talk was as good a place as any to start. "Where's Winter? Did you send her home early?"

Bickle House always had a full-time housekeeper, and when Mom found herself in need of a new one, willing and suitable applicants proved hard to find. Winter Adams and Georgia Harrison, who'd been night aides during Mom's illness, were hired to work alternate weeks. Marti liked Winter despite her being a Pernelli. She was good with Mom and worked hard. Besides working at Bickle House, she still worked for the home health aide service two nights a week and sometimes babysat for RachelAnne.

"With any luck, lying dead in a ditch somewhere."

Marti choked. Red wine in the nose was not pleasant. Her sister subscribed—other than when Marti was the subject—to the "if you can't say anything nice, don't say anything at all" theory.

"Sorry." RachelAnne handed Marti a napkin.

"Are you going to explain?" She wiped her face and dabbed at the wine splatter on her dress.

"That'll leave a stain," Grandma said.

"She and Peter..." RachelAnne didn't need to continue. The pain in her voice told Marti all she needed to know.

Little sister had married a Daddy clone in more ways than one. The Judge and Sheila McDonagh's long affair had been an open secret. Even Mom knew although she kept her knowledge to herself until after The Judge's death. RachelAnne had been, as far as Marti could tell, the only person in a thirty-mile radius who didn't know.

"Are you sure?" Marti vibrated. Seeing red wasn't just an idiom. For all their differences, RachelAnne was her baby sister and no one should hurt her. "By the way, the anger you hear in my voice? It's not directed at you."

"I know." RachelAnne attempted a smile and failed miserably.

"Do you want to tell me about it, or shall we just drink?"

RachelAnne talked. She'd received an anonymous letter. She ignored it. She received more. Although she tried to ignore them, she couldn't stop thinking about them. She couldn't bring herself to show them to her husband. "Things have been...stressful between us for a while."

Marti had seen signs of strain in the Rudawski marriage but figured it had to do with The Judge not leaving anything—other than responsibility for her fruitcake big sister—to RachelAnne. Mom would make that right eventually, but Peter was impatient.

"The one I got this morning was different. Or maybe it was just the proverbial straw on the camel's back."

"What did you do?"

"I looked at his laptop and phone. He's really bad at passwords. They were both the same. I got it on the third try." There hadn't been much on his laptop, but his phone showed a history of calls to and from Winter. "And there were texts. Sexts. With photos."

Listening to her sister wasn't doing anything good for Marti's rage level. "Did you confront him?"

"He said I was imagining things. Making it up. Acting crazy. He said I was just like—"

"Me."

"He said my whole family."

"But he meant me. I'm the crazy one. He needs to die a thousand horrible deaths."

"Fire ants. Hot pokers up the wazoo," Grandma said. "I'll start a list."

RachelAnne had devoted her entire life to being the anti-Marti. She was the well-adjusted teen, the straight-A student, the popular-but-nice girl. She graduated from Vassar, married—although not to a man her parents would have chosen—and produced two lovely grandchildren. She went back to school and became a lawyer. She wore perfect clothes and the perfect amount of makeup. She had the perfect haircut and the perfect manicure.

Usually. At the moment, she was chewing on a thumbnail. Her mascara was smudged. A hair or two was out of place.

Only recently had Marti begun to understand that the role RachelAnne played in the Mickkleson family was as hard as her own. Peter knew exactly what he said to her sister, and he said it on purpose.

"I didn't tell him I looked at his phone or that I copied everything I could from it."

RachelAnne was a smart one.

"I take it you and the kids will be staying more than one night?" Marti dumped the end of the wine into their glasses.

"Probably. I don't know what to do." Tears ran down Rachel-Anne's cheeks.

Marti didn't say anything. Maybe that behemoth she was driving would come in handy. She could use it to run down her brother-in-law.

"Hung, drawn, and quartered," Grandma said. "And not necessarily in that order."

CHAPTER

FIVE

THE KIDS always ate dinner early. The Oreo lunch and red wine afternoon took their toll on RachelAnne. When T3 and Maggie made hungry noises, Marti decided to feed everyone. The kids were thrilled with spaghetti and meatballs.

Mom dug in right along with them. Old-Mom would have never permitted red sauce from a jar and meatballs from the freezer, but either age, widowhood, or grandparenthood—or all three—had mellowed her. That, and on the weekends, with no housekeeper on duty, she and Marti had to either cook or eat out. Neither of them liked to cook and both were bad at it. The two things were probably directly related. New-Mom had lower standards, but she'd never admit it.

RachelAnne opened another bottle of wine.

"Maybe you should go easy on that," Marti said.

"Bite me," her sister said.

"What does that mean?" Maggie asked.

"It means she loves me," Marti answered. Maggie didn't appear convinced.

RachelAnne had assured her the kids hadn't heard anything.

She confronted Peter at his office while they were at school. T3 was in first grade and Maggie, preschool.

"No, Nana. This is how you do it." T3 sucked a strand of spaghetti into his mouth. The kid was good. He managed to get marinara on both his nose and chin.

Mom imitated him but only got the red stuff on her chin and the front of her silk dress. She giggled.

"Curiouser and curiouser," Marti said.

"Huh?" T3 said.

"Nothing." Marti would stack her trip down the rabbit hole, aka her return to Bickle House, up against Alice's any day. The changes in her uptight mother—especially when she was in Nana mode—beat mere Jabberwockies for weirdness.

Maggie stared at her grandmother and didn't say anything.

Spending the night at Nana's house was exciting, but the kids knew something was up. For one thing, it was a school night, and their overnighters were always on weekends. For another, Mommy was staying too. Last, kids always knew. Marti had known whenever her parents were on the outs although they never so much as raised their voices in front of her. She assumed her sister knew too, but maybe not.

RachelAnne ignored the mess her kids and mother were making. She picked at her food, more interested in her wine than pasta.

"You know who's a good noodle slurper?" Marti said. "Your mother."

"Show us, Mommy," Maggie said.

"I'm not hungry tonight." RachelAnne pushed her plate away, picked up her glass, and left the room.

The rest of them finished their meal in silence.

DINNER FINISHED and faces wiped clean, the whole crew adjourned to the family parlor. Mellowed or not, Mom still insisted they call the comfortable, informal room filled with cushy furniture, an overflowing toy box, and a gigantasaurus-sized television by the old-fashioned name. Totally at odds with the hushed formality and uncomfortable museum-piece furnishings of the rest of the house, save for the top-of-the-line modern kitchen, it was the only room that was changed during Marti's absence. The arrival of grandchildren had a lot to do with that.

RachelAnne curled up in the corner of the couch and made herself as small as possible. Even the colorful afghan pulled up to her chin looked sad. It didn't take an expert in body language to know she was miserable.

Maggie crawled under the blanket, crooked one small arm around her mother's neck, and stuck her thumb in her mouth.

T3 dug around in the cabinet by the television, came up with a DVD, ran to his mother, and waved it in her face. "You like this one," he said.

"It's my favorite."

Marti didn't think RachelAnne had a chance to see the cover, but T3 dashed over and stuck the disk in the player.

"Has someone died?" said a small girl in a violet taffeta dress, circa late 1800s.

Marti had been so wound up with the living occupants of Bickle House, she'd never given a thought to the absence of the long-departed ones. Edwards, butler to the original Bickles, took care of Amity, granddaughter to those same Bickles. Or made her feel cared for. It wasn't as if the deceased had a lot of physical needs. It was unlike the two of them to make themselves scarce for so long.

"Who let this riffraff in?" Amity fluttered a painted silk fan in front of her face.

Marti was no fashion historian, but she knew Amity's skirt was too long and her bustle too large for an eight-year-old child.

Grandma Bertie had explained that ghostly style reflected the way the departed saw themselves—or wanted others to see them. Amity looked very grown-up.

"Zip it," said her companion. The formal older man wore a dark suit from an earlier era. Edwards's attire hadn't varied during the time Marti had known him, which was her entire life if not his.

"Not yet, but we can hope." What Grandma's outfit said about her, Marti hadn't a clue. Maybe she saw herself as a cross between a parrot and a peacock with a little lioness thrown in for good measure. Maybe her wild print minidress was inspired by the Girl. On the other hand, she lived through the 1970s. She would have been a little old for miniskirts, but that didn't mean she hadn't owned and worn the same outfit when she was alive.

T3 started the movie.

"Movie night!" Amity plopped herself in the middle of the floor.

"This one is the bomb." Edwards joined his charge.

"Be quiet. I can't hear," Maggie said.

"You're the only one making noise," her brother said.

"No fighting. Fighting equals no movie." RachelAnne stayed nestled in her cocoon, but her Mom-voice was the first time all evening she sounded like herself.

They settled in and watched Antonio Banderas be out-secret-agented by his movie kids. T3 knew all the dialogue and chanted it in unison with the actors and often in unison with Amity. At regular intervals, Maggie told them to shush. About halfway through the movie, RachelAnne's snoring joined the din.

Mom spent more time watching Marti and Maggie than the screen. Not for the first time, Marti wondered if her mother knew just how much her granddaughter and oldest daughter had in common.

Everyone, the living and the post-living, cheered at the end. Everyone except RachelAnne. She was out. T3'd turned up the volume for the last twenty minutes so they could hear the television over her snoring.

"Time for bed." Marti snagged the remote from her nephew and turned off the set.

"I'll take them," Mom said. "Upstairs. Pajamas. Then I'll read you one book, and it's lights out."

"Two books? Pleeeeease, Nana," T3 said.

"Okay, but that's all." Nana was a pushover.

"Can the yady come?"

"Llllllady." RachelAnne sat up. "And the lady is your Aunt Marti."

"I certainly can." Grandma Bertie knew which yady the little girl meant.

"I think I'll stay with your Mom. Nana has things under control."

After a flurry of kisses and hugs, Mom, Grandma Bertie, and the kids headed upstairs.

"Three books?" T3 was quite the little negotiator.

"We'll see." Mom was noncommittal, but Marti figured T3 would talk her into six before he was done.

"I want another movie," Amity said.

RachelAnne yawned. "What time is it?"

"I believe it's time for all good children to hit the sack," Edwards said.

"Just after eight," Marti said.

"Get real." Amity stuck out her lower lip and stomped her foot. So much for the grown-up dress. The little ghost, if Edwards could be believed, was as spoiled in life as she was in the afterlife. Marti wondered if the butler, who had a fondness for any and all slang he'd heard since his passing, ever regretted the effect of his vocabulary on his charge, but Amity did have a point. Ghosts didn't sleep.

"Really? Feels like midnight." RachelAnne yawned again.

"Real as a heart attack, which is exactly how I bit the big one." Edwards hustled his sulking ward away.

"It's the wine. Even Antonio Banderas couldn't keep your attention," Marti said.

"I'm going to bed. I've had all I can take of today."

"Night." Marti left out the "good." She didn't think her little sister would have a good night for a long time.

WHEN MARTI SET up a Netflix subscription and her mother discovered she could watch the ponies any time, Mom was so thrilled she offered to pay the monthly bill. Marti told her to consider it a gift. The streaming service was cheap enough RachelAnne couldn't call her fiscally irresponsible. Marti wondered if Mom's fondness for the cartoon—not only when her grandchildren were around—was a sign she hadn't fully recovered from her "little illness." At times, Marti felt like the sanest and most responsible Mickkleson, which wasn't much of a recommendation for the others.

She subscribed to the service solely for the ability to binge-watch shows she missed during her TV-free years. Some of them were even worth the fee. Netflix earned its next payment by carrying the entire three-year run of *America's Most Mysterious Missing Persons*. She scrolled through the seasons and searched for the Susan Silliphant episode.

"Thought you weren't interested in sleuthing," Grandma said.

"I'm not. Just curious. And smug doesn't become you."

"Janice will be eternally grateful."

"Does that mean she'll move on to her eternal rest?"

"Don't get snotty with me, young lady, or I'll—"

The chimes of Big Ben rang—and rang and rang and rang. Someone was leaning on the front doorbell. Her security-conscious bordering-on-paranoid father had installed cameras throughout the Mickkleson property. They fed into monitors and televisions throughout the house. Marti clicked the remote.

The big screen filled with four views of her brother-in-law on the doorstep.

"What's he saying?" Grandma said.

"I'm not a lip reader." Marti hit the volume button.

"RachelAnne! I know you're in there! Let me in!" Peter was not happy.

"Crap." She could ignore him and hope he gave up and left sooner rather than later.

He stabbed his finger at the brass lion head in the center of the door, a doorbell disguised as a traditional door knocker, and Big Ben pealed again.

If he kept it up, he'd wake the kids—and RachelAnne. None of them needed the aggravation.

She didn't need the aggravation. She answered the door anyway.

"I want to see my wife." Peter's physical resemblance to her father was remarkable, with one difference. Marti had been terrified of The Judge. Her brother-in-law was just a pathetic little man, a pale imitation of her domineering father.

"Are you drunk?"

"Get RachelAnne out here. I know she's in there." He didn't slur his words, but he didn't sound completely sober either.

Marti stepped onto the porch and pulled the door shut behind her. If Peter got any louder, RachelAnne would hear him. Then Marti would have to kill him. "She's in bed. You can talk to her tomorrow."

"She has my kids and I want them back." He stretched his lips into something that might have been intended to be a smile.

The theme from *Jaws* played in Marti's head. "*Your* kids?"

"She's not breaking up my family." He got louder with every word.

"From what I heard, *you're* the one doing that."

"She left."

"And you had nothing to do with it?" Marti fought to keep her anger under control. She was a hair's breadth away from nuclear meltdown.

"She left. You know what? You can have her, but I'm taking my kids. I'm getting a lawyer. A better one than she'll ever get. She'll never see them again."

Marti's rage did an about-face, from inferno to arctic. She stiffened. She drew herself to her full height. The theme from *Jaws* blasted into her head.

She reined in her emotions.

Sharks didn't get angry. They went for the kill. Part of her hated herself for what she was about to do, but the rest of her rattled pompoms, jumped up and down, and cheered *Go, Marti! Go Marti go!*

"Peter Rudawski. Those children are Mickklesons, and you are not. You are nothing. This is Bicklesburg. Battlesborough County. Home of the Mickklesons. If *you* ever want to see them again, you'd better shape up and play nice. Go home. Now. You may speak to my sister tomorrow if—and only if—she chooses to speak to you." For the second time in less than twenty-four hours, Marti channeled her mother.

"Impressive," Grandma said.

Peter's already flushed face went purple. He took a half step back and raised his fist.

"You bi—"

"Is there a problem here?"

She hadn't seen Dmitri arrive, but she was glad he had. She hated being rescued, but she hated being hit worse. Or the idea of it. No one had ever hit her.

"Yes," she said. "Dirtbag here needs to leave."

"You bet there's a problem," Peter said. "I want my wife and kids."

"Sounds like you need to do some cooling off." Dmitri was

calm. Too calm.

If she was a shark, he was a...she didn't know what. A super-shark or something. The silky smoothness of his voice didn't hide the danger. She wouldn't want that tone directed at her. She hoped Peter heard it and knew enough to be afraid.

"Stay out of this, Doyle. It's family business." If Peter was afraid, he didn't show it.

"Have you been drinking?"

"I asked him the same thing," Marti said.

"He's obnoxious enough sober." Grandma Bertie gently laid her hand on Peter's shoulder. He shivered.

"RachelAnne! I want my kids!"

Gently wasn't cutting it. Grandma dug in her fingers.

"R-R-RachelAnne! G-g-g-g-get d-d-d-own here!" Peter shuddered and went pale, but Grandma failed to cool his rage.

"She's not coming out. You are not going in," Marti said.

He stuck his face up to hers, as close as he could get. He was four inches shorter than her. The nose-to-nose impact was lost. The effect was comical rather than intimidating.

Marti pursed her lips in an attempt to stifle the giggle she felt coming on.

"Don't you laugh at me! You are not—" Peter swayed and winced.

Dmitri's grasp on Peter's shoulder had more effect than Grandma's had.

Peter tried to shake off the larger man. Dmitri spun him around and pinned his arm behind his back before he—or Marti —knew what was happening.

"I like your young man," Grandma said.

"Where are your keys?" Dmitri said.

"Why should I tell you?"

Dmitri made a slight movement, and Peter gasped.

"In my pants pocket."

"Marti?" Dmitri didn't loosen his grip on Peter.

The last thing she wanted to do was touch the slimy little toad, but in the interest of getting rid of him, she stuck her hand into the pocket of his khaki pants and pulled out his key ring. A roll of cash held together with a red rubber band fell to the floor.

Marti picked it up. "Classy," she said.

"Give that back, you b—OW. Stop that."

"Stop what?" Dmitri was the soul of innocence.

Marti shoved the money back into her brother-in-law's jacket pocket. No way was she reaching back into the slimeball's pants pocket.

"Time for you to go home and sleep it off." Dmitri frog-marched his captive to the red sedan parked at the curb and stuck him into the passenger seat. Marti didn't recognize the car, but it had dealer plates. Her brother-in-law drove loaners from Rudawski Motors and changed them weekly.

Peter started to get out. From the look of it, Dmitri said something, but Marti couldn't hear him. Peter settled back into the seat, but not quietly. "The groundbreaking is tomorrow! You tell my wife she'd better be there, standing by my side and looking happy! There'll be press!"

Press? Seriously? Maybe MaryEllen Pernelli. Only the *Gazette* would care about his little strip mall. No matter what Peter did, he was a huckster at heart, always looking for free advertising.

Dmitri slammed the car door, gave her an exaggerated salute, went to the driver's side, got in, and drove off.

"Your young man is looking good," Grandma said.

"He's not my young man." Grandma had a point. Wherever Dmitri had gone on his mysterious sabbatical, it hadn't done him any harm.

Marti wondered how he planned on getting home. Rachel-Anne's house was a long walk from the Avenue. The wind hadn't let up, and the temperature had gone down along with the sun. The walk would be cold and miserable.

She could take the Lexus—or the TT since Mom was in for

the night—and follow him.

And risk another run-in with Peter.

Dmitri had her phone number, even if he hadn't used it for months. He had other friends. Friends he probably talked to since he got back. Friends he probably called while he was away. Friends who probably got postcards that said *Wish you were here.*

If he needed a ride, he could call one of them. She was going to bed. Like her sister, she'd had more than enough for one day.

"Double crap." The heavy mahogany front door didn't budge. She'd locked herself out.

"Whoops," Grandma Bertie said.

"I don't want to hear it." Her grandmother could walk right through the door, and anything else for that matter, which was no help to Marti. Ghosts opening doors and moving objects was an invention of those who told stories. Spirits couldn't open doors or rustle curtains. Number one on the list of why she wasn't afraid of the dead—other than the ghost freeze thing. That could make one miserable.

"You can ring the doorbell," Grandma said.

She could, but that would mean explaining to whomever answered why she was out there. The longer her sister and mother lived in ignorance of Peter's visit, the better.

Dmitri was in civvies rather than his ACS uniform, which meant he was off duty. He must have been hanging out in the office and seen Peter arrive. Maybe whoever was on duty saw her shivering on the doorstep and would bring her the ACS key.

It was Monday. Richie was working, and he was half afraid of her. Maybe three-quarters. She hadn't been at her best the first time they met.

"I'll have to go get the ACS key," she said.

The front door opened.

"That was impressive," Mom said.

"Told you," Grandma said.

"Locking myself out?" Marti stepped inside.

"You and Peter. Not to mention, Dmitri's knight in shining armor act."

"You saw?" Marti wasn't sure how she felt about her mother witnessing her Mom-on-her-high-horse act, but it made one less person she had to tell about Peter's visit. She'd intended to downplay the story in the telling. She still would, to RachelAnne.

"In high definition, on the family parlor television. I came down to see what all the fuss was about and there you were. I don't think your sister needs to know the details. We'll just tell her Peter stopped by after she went to bed."

"Absolutely." Marti only agreed with her mother on about one thing a week, and she had no problem playing that week's yes-ma'am card for RachelAnne.

"However, you will need to talk to the security office and make sure they save the video."

"Why?" She wasn't sure she wanted video evidence of her turning into her mother.

"For her lawyer. I'm hiring Philippa Berryman."

Marti recognized the name. Battlesborough County wasn't Hollywood or New York by a long shot, but from what she'd heard Berryman could go up against any big-time divorce attorney and walk away with everything. Or, her client would and Berryman would get her cut. Philippa the Piranha was expensive and guaranteed things would get nasty.

"RachelAnne hasn't decided what she's going to do."

"She will."

Marti wondered what made her mother so sure. After all, she'd stuck with The Judge until death did them part, despite Sheila and who knew who else. She decided she didn't want to know. "I'm going to bed."

"It's ridiculously early. I don't know what's wrong with you girls. I'm going to watch a movie."

"Whatever." Marti'd had more than her fill of family time for one day.

SIX

"Good morning, sleepyhead." RachelAnne had no business sounding perky first thing in the morning, especially considering the amount of wine she downed the night before.

First thing for Marti. RachelAnne was already dressed in a trim navy suit, her hair artfully tousled, her make-up perfect. Everything about her grooming said competent young professional.

Her brittle smile said *woman on the edge.*

"And good morning to you too," Marti said. If her sister was playing Little Mary Sunshine for the benefit of the kids, who sat in the breakfast nook, she'd play along.

"Want some Chocolate Cinnamon Oaty Puffs?" T3 was exuberant, but he always was when he had sleepovers at Nana's.

Marti's stomach turned at the thought of the sugary cereal. Not that she was opposed to it in general. She just considered it a midnight snack, not breakfast.

"No thanks." She headed for the coffee.

"What are your plans for the day?" RachelAnne said.

"I thought I'd go into the office. If nothing else, I need to check on Bernard." Marti's presence in the office wasn't required full-time, but she needed to finish going through the job applications. If she didn't hire someone before they got fully up and running, she would have to show up every day. Besides, she didn't want to hang around the house with her mother. "Need me to do something? Run the kids to school?"

"I'll do that on my way in, but since Mom doesn't have any help coming in..." RachelAnne's cheerful mask threatened to crack.

Marti figured her sister wasn't about to cry over the milk and cereal T3 and Maggie had spilled on the table. And the floor. And the seat cushions. "I'll clean up." If she could, she'd clean up Winter Adams. And Peter. "I take it you're going to work?" If anyone deserved to take the day off, it was RachelAnne. She wasn't going to argue. Whatever got her sister through the day.

"I took yesterday off. I can't afford to miss another day."

Thanks to The Judge, RachelAnne's planned career in the Public Defender's office ended before it got started. Benjamin Bowman, The Judge's best friend and Mickkleson family attorney, was ready to move into semi-retirement. He had no children of his own and considered his best buddy's daughter the next best thing. He brought RachelAnne into his law office. Her sister said contracts, wills, and torts weren't as exciting as she'd hoped defense work would be, but then excitement wasn't all it was cracked up to be.

It hadn't dawned on Marti that money might be an issue with her sister. She found it hard to believe Bowman paid her by the hour. RachelAnne always had more expensive tastes than Marti, or she indulged them more. She and Peter might not have been as loaded as Mom and The Judge, but they did well for themselves. Peter was one of the area's leading businessmen. Or so he said every chance he got.

Maybe it was a dig. RachelAnne seldom let any resentment at The Judge's bequest slip out. Usually around the same time she let other things slip. Things that had Marti wondering about her sister's marriage before she left Peter. But her sister was human. Marti would have been suspicious if their father's monetary snub didn't bother RachelAnne at all.

She could offer financial help. She had more than she needed —or would have soon. RachelAnne might take it as an insult. It was hard to tell with her. One thing Marti was sure of. If she brought it up in front of the kids, RachelAnne would skin her alive.

"Thad. Maggie. Go wash your faces and hands. We need to get a move on." RachelAnne didn't always adhere to her son's "my name is T3" ruling.

He didn't correct his mother. He and Maggie jumped out of their seats and took off. They were good kids, but they were kids. Immediate obedience meant RachelAnne's perky act wasn't fooling them. Their mother was stressed, and they knew it.

"Listen, Rach. RachelAnne." Her sister hated it when Marti shortened her name. "If you need money—" Her sister went rigid.

She shouldn't have brought it up.

"I'll let you know. I need to get going."

The kids returned, backpacks in hand. T3 had milk on his face. Marti hoped it was only soggy Oaty Puffs stuck in Maggie's curls.

In dulcet tones, Harriet announced the opening of the back door, and RachelAnne and the kids went out to face the world.

It wasn't that Marti had forgotten to give her Peter's message about the groundbreaking ceremony. She just hadn't bothered. She was thinking about attending it herself. Not as a substitute for her sister.

"You look like you need another cup of coffee," Grandma Bertie said.

"I don't suppose you know what time Peter's ridiculous road show is?"

"Not a clue."

Once she got to the office, she'd make a few calls. If Mrs.

Heedly was right, maybe she'd find Susan Silliphant's ghost lurking in Henrietta's Hollow. She could use a distraction. Some days, dealing with the dead was easier than dealing with the living. It was looking like one of those days.

∼

MARTI PULLED the folder of resumés out of her desk drawer and stuffed it back in. She'd already procrastinated by playing with Bernard as long as she could. If she could find out what time the groundbreaking was, she might be able to put off dealing with job applicants until tomorrow.

"What are you looking at?" As soon as Marti spoke, the Girl disappeared.

"Nothing," Grandma said.

"I wasn't talking to you." Maybe she'd just hire Faustyn Anguish on the basis of his name and be done with it.

"Be nice to her. She's like a scared kitten."

"Whatever," Marti said. She dug out her cell rather than using the phone on her desk, found Ashley Fysh in her contacts, and hit the little phone icon next to her work number. The former Ashley Carlyle was briefly the closest thing Marti had to a friend in high school.

Back when Ashley called herself Raven, she, her boyfriend Oliver, Dmitri, and Marti were a Goth quartet. They reveled in being the weird ones, being different together, being the cooler-than-cool outsiders—right up until they stumbled on The Judge in a place he wasn't supposed to be. Oliver and Dmitri finished high school in a state juvenile detention facility thanks to what Marti still believed were trumped up, if not totally faked, charges. After the boys were sent away, Raven went back to being Ashley, ran for student council, and cut Marti from her life.

Raven-Ashley grew up to become the manager of the Bicklesburg First Seventh Federal Bank, married the police chief's brother, and was, once again, the closest thing Marti had to a living friend.

Other than Dmitri. Who hadn't talked to her for months. Rescuing her from Peter didn't count. That was his job.

The Bicklesburg, as it was known to the locals, was Marti's bank, the Mickkleson family's bank, the Mickkleson Foundation's bank, and according to Peter, an enthusiastic investor in his latest scheme. Marti had the number for Ashley's direct line.

She answered on the second ring. Good. She wasn't with a customer.

"Hey, it's Marti."

"I was just about to call you." Ashley was the only non-animated character Marti knew who sounded exactly like Betty Boop.

It had to be a handicap in the banking world.

"Business or personal?" With any luck, whatever Ashley had to say would lead gracefully into what Marti wanted to ask. She wasn't good at social niceties.

"Personal." Betty Boop sounded sad.

"You first," Marti said.

"Your office looks out on the Green, right? Did you, um, see anything yesterday?"

The Bicklesburg sat on the Green, but the manager's office was in the back, sequestered from the outside world.

"I don't think—oh! Around lunchtime?" With everything else going on, she'd forgotten the excitement in the gazebo.

Ashley's sigh whistled across the virtual phone line. "It was Oliver."

The cops hauled away three people. Marti didn't know which one was Oliver, but she wasn't surprised. Dmitri became an upstanding citizen after their release from juvy-jail. Oliver remained in and out of trouble. Mostly in.

"You need to stop worrying about him," Marti said.

Ashley was happily married to a high school teacher, but for some reason had either a soft spot for or a guilt complex about the boy she dated nearly fifteen years ago.

Marti'd told her repeatedly to let go of the past, "do as I say, not as I do" advice. As hard as Marti tried not to feel guilty about her father's misdeeds, she couldn't help but wonder which came first, the chicken or the egg. If not for his time in detention, Oliver might have grown up to be a dentist or a podiatrist or something respectable. He'd never been the brightest bulb in high school, but it *could* have happened.

"I know, but I heard Winter Adams bailed him out. Did you or the Foundation or your family have anything to do with that? If so, I wanted to say thank you. He won't. Neither will his mother."

Oliver's mother was a Pernelli, the only Pernelli with a solid reason to hold a grudge against the Mickklesons.

"Winter and Oliver are some kind of cousins or something. Maybe it was a family thing."

"They do protect their own. So you're saying it wasn't you?"

"By yesterday afternoon, Winter Adams had nothing to do with the Mickklesons, nor us with her."

"I heard something about that. How is RachelAnne?"

"As well as can be expected." Of course Ashley had heard. Bicklesburg didn't have a grapevine, it had a faster-than-the-speed-of-light broadcast system. "That's sort of why I called. You don't happen to know what time Peter's dog and pony show is, do you?"

"I was supposed to attend, but I'm sending my assistant. Why?"

If Ashley was scheduled to put in an appearance, Peter was telling the truth about the bank backing him. He'd asked her mother, but she'd given him a run around about money being tied up with the Mickkleson Foundation. He would never have dared approach The Judge.

If Ashley was bowing out and sending an underling, Marti's warning that Peter shouldn't go to war with her family was not unfounded. The Bicklesburg supported local businesses and invested in the town's economy but would be cautious about pissing off one of their biggest customers. Old money was better than iffy money.

"RachelAnne was supposed to be there. I don't *think* she will go, but on the off chance she does, I'd like to be there for moral support." Not exactly a little white lie. Chances of her sister showing up were about the same as Marti's chances of marrying into the British royal family, but if she did, Marti would be present to do the sisterly thing. "If she's not going, I don't want to call her and remind her. I'll hang out by myself in the back and try not to heckle."

No point mentioning Susan Silliphant or Mrs. Heedly or the Mickkleson Foundation's office ghost. Ashley had outgrown her teenage fascination with death and the dead. Marti let her friend think that was all behind her, too. She liked having a friend. Two friends, if she counted Dmitri. Call it a friend and a half. If she wasn't careful, she'd be voted Most Popular at their next class reunion.

"You'd better hurry. It starts in fifteen minutes. Harold just left."

"Crap." She had just enough time to make the sideshow but not enough time to do any preliminary scouting of the site for roving spirits. "Thanks, Ashley. I'll talk to you later." She cut the connection.

"Come on, Grandma. Field trip."

Despite its romantic name, Henrietta's Hollow was an untouched meadow overflowing with nature to those being kind and a vacant lot begging to be developed for those not so kind. Peter was among the latter.

Marti maneuvered her mother's TT across the bumpy ground

destined to become a parking lot. T3 usually rode a bus to after-school care in the same building as Maggie's preschool. When Winter finished her day at Mom's house, she picked them both up and ran them home. If both Peter and RachelAnne were late, she stayed with the kids until one parent or the other got home.

Since that wasn't happening anymore, Mom would pick them up until other arrangements were made. The TT's backseat was no bigger than a thimble, and Maggie's booster seat was in the Lexus. Mom took the monster SUV. Marti got the deep-blue sports car. Margaret Mickkleson had never picked her own daughters up from school, but getting to drive the sweet little car went a long way toward burying any resentment Marti might have harbored.

"Looks like we made it in time."

"Thanks to your race car driver act," Grandma said.

"Fun, wasn't it?"

"It's a circus. A pathetic circus." Grandma Bertie wasn't talking about Marti's driving. Peter had done his best to create a carnival atmosphere. His best wasn't good enough.

Calliope music crackled and blasted from speakers attached to the front corners of a trailer. The name of a construction company was emblazoned on the mobile office building. Marti didn't recognize the name. They weren't local. She assumed the music was a recording. The building wasn't big enough to hold a pipe organ, and if Peter'd managed to find the real thing, he wouldn't have hidden it away. A creepy-looking clown held a bouquet of helium-filled balloons. Each bore a grinning caricature of her brother-in-law's face.

"That man will put his face on anything that doesn't move," Grandma said.

"Apparently, he'll put it on a few things that do move too," Marti said. "That's what got him in trouble. Look, there he is."

MaryEllen Pernelli chatted with the little toad next to a roped-off area containing some kind of gigantic digging machine.

It might have been a backhoe, but it looked bigger to Marti. Excavator? Was that a thing? Whatever it was, she hoped it was symbolic and her brother-in-law intended to symbolically break ground with a ribbon-festooned spade. If he operated the digger-thingy himself and spotted her, things might not end well. The machine reminded her of a Tyrannosaurus Rex.

Two men, one dressed in jeans and shouldering a video camera and the other wearing an ill-fitting suit and a pink tie, lingered nearby. The camera bore no television station call letters or other identification. Peter probably hired them. At a recent family dinner, he'd gone on and on about "video news releases." When Marti brought up fake news and the downfall of civilization, RachelAnne kicked her under the table.

The *Gazette* was the only legitimate press present, and they hadn't even sent a photographer. MaryEllen had a camera slung around her neck.

"At least he didn't hire an elephant," Marti said.

"He might have drawn a bigger crowd," Grandma said.

Peter'd gone to a lot of trouble for minimal turnout. Harold Binks from the bank chatted with a woman in a dark power suit and high heels. Or chatted at. He was doing all the talking. She was talking on her phone. Marti didn't recognize her, but she got props for negotiating Henrietta's Hollow in heels. Two men in black suits and dark sunglasses stood off to the side. Aside from the clown and the press, both real and fake, that was it.

No ghosts. No Woman in White. No Henrietta. No Susan. No one in the field had that special shimmer, the one that told her they weren't among the living. She couldn't explain what it was. The dead, although solid enough—to her—looked different from the living. She always knew, sometimes before they did, they'd left the realm of the living.

Unless she was missing something. Or someone.

"How do you feel about mingling?"

"You mean eavesdropping," Grandma said.

"That too. Scout around. See if the Hollow has any permanent residents. I don't see anyone, but you might. See if you can find out who the Men in Black are. I've always suspected Peter might be an alien."

"I love that movie." Grandma left the car.

Marti decided she might as well get out too. Unlike Grandma, she had to use the door, which should have been simple. And would have been if she hadn't caught her jacket on the door, tripped, and landed on her butt on the ground.

A meaty hand appeared before her. She grasped it and pulled herself to her feet.

Billy "Big" Fysh Jr. earned his nickname honestly. In high school, his size and ability to mow down and smash opposing football players brought on comparisons to a big green superhero. He'd grown larger in the ensuing years. He'd also followed his father into the role of Bicklesburg police chief. The town hired their chief, but Marti had no doubt if the post was elected like the county sheriff was, Big would have been a shoo-in.

"You okay?" he said.

"Yeah. They call me Amazing Grace, but only behind my back." She couldn't tell if his expression was distaste or confusion. He either didn't get her sense of humor or didn't like her. She'd bet her entire annual salary on both.

"Thanks." She brushed the dirt off her rear end. "Are you expecting trouble?" He was in uniform.

"Just doing my part. Supporting the local business community and all that. Surprised to see you here."

"To tell the truth, me too." She wasn't about to explain. She had reason to believe he still thought of her as "Marti Cray-Cray" and there was no reason to live up to her despicable nickname.

"Heard you had some trouble of your own last night."

"Nothing I couldn't handle." Word traveled fast. "With Dmitri's help." Dmitri must have told Big about Peter's visit. The two of them, separated by the vast chasm of the teenage social order in school, developed a friendship bordering on bromance during her decade away from Bicklesburg.

"You tell RachelAnne if anything—and I mean anything—happens that shouldn't, don't hesitate to call us. You too, for that matter. We'll have a car out ASAP."

"Will do." The thought of Peter being led away in handcuffs cheered her up.

"I mean it." Big no longer looked confused. His face was as stern as his voice.

"I do too."

"Welcome!" Peter wore a yellow hard hat and shouted through an orange and turquoise bullhorn. His suit was well-cut and expensive, but his tie matched the rent-a-reporter's. If the clown quit, Peter was dressed for the job. "If you folks will be patient for a moment or two, we'll be underway before you know it." He ducked under the rope and exchanged words with a man, also in a hard hat, fussing with something on the T-Rex-Digging-Machine-Thing. Hard Hat Man stepped over the rope and stalked away.

"Peter's not going to try to operate that beast, is he?" Big said.

"Good gawd, I hope not."

"Shall we?" Big offered her his arm. She took it, preferring to think of it as a friendly gesture rather than a concession to her clumsiness.

"Into the madding crowd," she said. Not quite right, but it would have to do. She was bad at small talk but well-read.

"Huh?"

"Never mind." Getting literary references wasn't Big's forte. Nor was getting her sense of humor.

The bargain basement Bozo made a beeline toward them, two balloons in his outstretched hand, stopped, opened and shut his mouth, made an about-face, and took off.

"Do you think it was you or me?" Marti said.

"Could be either, but my money's on me."

"Lots of criminal clowns in Bicklesburg?"

The calliope music came to an abrupt end.

"Welcome to the birth of Rudawski's Henrietta Square, an investment in Bicklesburg's future and a nod to its past." Peter's bullhorn squealed. Marti flinched.

"Right on cue," she said.

"I thought it was another strip mall," Big said.

"It is."

Peter introduced Hard Hat Man as the head of the construction company and rambled on. He may have hired a bad speechwriter, but he sounded like he was making it up as he went along. She tuned out at "the growth of the growing Bicklesburg's growing economy and superb shopping places to shop."

"Let's move some dirt!" He climbed onto the T-Rex's haunches and crawled into the windowed cab atop the beast.

MaryEllen Pernelli and the rent-a-reporter backed away from the rope.

"He is going to do it," Marti said.

The big machine rumbled. The monster's enormous head swung. Even though she and Big were a good twenty feet away from the action, Marti took a step back.

Big laughed.

"Self-preservation instinct," Marti said.

"He's not doing bad."

Big was right. After a few false starts, the machine's maw broke ground and took a bite of earth. Peter smoothly raised the load and dumped a sprinkling of dirt next to the shallow hole.

The onlookers clapped.

"He didn't get much," Marti said.

"He's going back for seconds," Big said.

"He's an attention hound."

Peter managed a second load, a good-sized one, without mishap.

"He should quit while he's ahead," Big said.

"Have you ever met my brother-in-law?"

"The men in black are investors. Which doesn't mean Peter's not an alien," Grandma Bertie reported.

Peter buried the mechanical jaws in the ground and came up with a serving sized to satisfy even him.

"Don't know who the woman in heels is. She and Harold sound like old friends, or Harold thinks so." Grandma said.

The big earth mover dumped its load next to the crater.

"But all of the guests are alive and accounted for," Grandma said.

MaryEllen Pernelli screamed and grabbed her camera.

"Maybe not all of them," Grandma said.

"Wow." Marti thought the grinning skull sitting atop the mountain of dirt would be much darker. If Mrs. Heedly knew what she was talking about, it had been in the ground for close to fifty years.

"Things sure have gotten interesting around here since you came home," Big said.

"He didn't mean that as a compliment," Grandma said.

CHAPTER

SEVEN

MARTI MANAGED a few more hours in the office. The Girl made herself scarce. Grandma went to the Green to fill Mrs. Heedly in on the events at the Hollow.

"You could come with me, you know," Grandma said.

"You know everything I know. Besides, I need to finish this." Marti pulled the dreaded manilla folder from her desk drawer.

Grandma gave her the evil eye. "See that you do."

With only Bernard for distraction, she made it through all the resumés.

She decided to interview the teenager from the Vo-Tech, Faustyn Anguish, and Sandra Booth, the only applicant with any nonprofit experience.

And, just for grins and giggles, Dawn Pernelli.

"Maybe I am nuts," she said.

Bernard blinked his big green eyes. It didn't look like a denial.

She sent emails offering each an interview and stuck the remaining resumés back in the drawer. If she hired one of the four, she'd have them write a polite thanks-but-no-thanks note to the rejects. If she didn't, she would reconsider letting Bernard choose her new assistant.

"Time to close up shop."

Bernard flicked his tail and turned his back on her.

"I love you too," she said.

At home, she found Mom and the kids parked in the parlor in front of the TV. It was prancing ponies time.

Edwards and Amity were nowhere to be seen. Marti'd had a relatively ghost-free afternoon. She hoped it wasn't a sign of the apocalypse.

"Where's RachelAnne?" she said.

"Kitchen," T3 said.

"Practically perfect prancing ponies!" Mom and the kids sang along with the animated horses. Rainbows exploded on screen.

"I think I'll join her."

"I'll stay here," Grandma said and joined the others in song.

"Et tu, Brute?" Marti mumbled.

"What?" Mom said.

"Nothing."

Marti and RachelAnne made dinner. Rather, RachelAnne made dinner. Marti watched and handed her sister pans and utensils on command.

"I didn't know you could cook," she said. Her sister was a woman of many skills.

"My family would starve if I didn't."

Marti'd stuck her foot in her mouth. She should have known. A man who considered spending time with his kids "babysitting" wasn't likely to consider feeding them his job.

"Get me the pepper grinder," RachelAnne said, "and don't enjoy this too much. You're doing the cleanup."

"No problem." Marti dug in the cupboard and came up with the pepper. She handed it to her sister and turned on the small television built into the wall above the counter. "News? Unless you want to watch the ponies."

"Channel seven. I like the weatherman."

Marti didn't argue. The WBOT weatherman was kind of cute. Adorable, even. He looked a lot like Dmitri.

The six o'clock news was just beginning. "The festivities took a gruesome turn out in Battlesborough County at the ground-breaking ceremony for Rudawski's Henrietta Square, a planned shopping center in Bicklesburg." The vivacious blond anchor's demeanor was at odds with the image behind her. A skeletal arm encased in bangles—they looked like plastic, no biodegrading there—stuck out of the dirt.

"Turn it off," RachelAnne said.

"Wait." Marti hadn't told her sister she'd gone to the ground-breaking. The bracelets on the bony arm looked familiar. She tried to remember where she'd seen them or something very like them. Probably in one of the junk shops or retro-style clothing stores she adored.

They would have been popular and cheap jewelry around the time Susan Silliphant disappeared.

"Roving reporter Bradley Bates was on the scene." The blonde and the bracelets were replaced by the man in a pink tie and Peter's digging machine.

The rent-a-reporters had sold their footage to the local station. Peter considered any publicity good publicity.

Marti got a better look at the skull. It looked like a grinning Halloween decoration, not the real thing. She didn't learn much from the news report. They didn't have much to report.

Bates managed to get a statement of sorts from Big. "We will be shutting down construction while the remains are removed and investigated. Mr. Rudawski has promised his complete coop-eration."

The leprechaun by Big's side nodded in agreement. Peter looked like he'd swallowed a spider.

"Oh, he's going to be pissed." RachelAnne looked like she'd swallowed a double-dip Rum Raisin and Rocky Road ice cream cone. "Hand me the oregano."

Make that a triple-dip with cookies and cream on top.

RachelAnne went back to cooking, humming all the while. Marti half expected her to break into song and do a two-step.

Dinner was delicious.

MARTI LOADED and ran the dishwasher but left the pans soaking in the sink, as good of an excuse as any to spend some quality time with her niece and nephew before they went to bed.

"You are the Raging Troll. Mags and me are the heroes and must save Mommy and Nana," T3 said.

Mommy and Nana sat on the couch. Neither looked in need of rescuing.

"Oh, no! Save us!" RachelAnne didn't look up from her phone.

"Help!" Mom turned a page in her magazine.

Marti's designated role consisted of sitting cross-legged on the floor and growling while T3, assisted by Maggie, tried to subdue her.

Her niece's main responsibility appeared to be giggling. She did a bang-up job of it. She giggled more when Marti grabbed her, but that was probably due to the tickling. Marti discovered, in her adjustment to aunthood, she was what T3 called an "Awesome Monster Tickle Machine." She planned on adding the title to any future resumés.

Amity watched from the sidelines. Marti kept a close eye on her. Her scowl didn't bode well.

"Get her!" T3 commanded.

Maggie the Giggling Minion dived for Marti's lap—and so did Amity. Marti rolled the living girl away and ended up with a lap full of ghost girl.

"That's mean!" Maggie said.

"Play nice or it's bedtime," RachelAnne said.

"Amity Bickle, you know better." Grandma Bertie pulled Amity to her feet.

The ghost girl flounced from the room, not bothering to use the door. Edwards followed.

"Sorry, Miss Marcile," he said.

"Are you okay?" Mom didn't sound concerned.

"F-f-f-f-ine." Marti wasn't fine, but explaining wouldn't help.

"That's it," RachelAnne said. "Baths, then bed for both of you." She corralled her kids.

"Way to go, Mags," T3 said.

Maggie stuck her thumb in her mouth. Marti had no doubt her niece saw her mother's disapproving look—it was hard to miss —but the thumb stayed.

RachelAnne picked up Maggie's favorite doll from the floor. "Don't forget Amity," she said.

Maggie pulled out her thumb and said, "Her name is Dawn."

"R-r-r-really?" Marti said. Like Marti as a child, Maggie had named her favorite doll after the little girl only they could see. Over the past months, Amity's jealousy at Marti playing with her niece and nephew had grown. Her natural brattiness had grown with it. Maggie was angry at Amity, so renaming her doll wasn't a surprise, but why on Earth did she have to choose *that* name? "C-c-can't you c-c-come up with s-s-something else?"

"Whatever," RachelAnne said. "Upstairs, both of you. Aunt Marti needs to finish cleaning the kitchen."

MARTI HAND-WASHED THE TOP-OF-THE-LINE COOKWARE, which wasn't permitted in the top-of-the-line dishwasher. She emptied the dishwasher and generally wiped down the kitchen.

There'd be no Winter in the morning and Georgia wasn't due until next week. She'd end up doing it anyway. A few months back in Momland and she'd already become spoiled by the presence of household help. Not that she'd been any great shakes at looking after herself. Laundry once a week and dust—or move—once a year suited her nicely.

The kitchen was as good as it was going to get. She dried her hands and headed back to the parlor. If no one else was there, she'd watch the show about Susan Silliphant. Maybe they'd do an update if she'd been found.

Once they figured it out.

She was the only one who knew the likely identity of the skeletal remains, and it wasn't like she could go running to Big and tell him. *Hey! Remember Mrs. Heedly, our long-dead third-grade teacher? Well, she told me...*

Wasn't going to happen. Carrying tales from the dead would only enhance her Marti Cray-Cray reputation. It was what earned her the nickname in the first place. She and Big had been almost friendly that afternoon. If she was going for that Most Popular crown, no point in ruining it. They'd run a DNA test or something on the bones.

America's Most Mysterious Missing Persons wasn't going to happen either. Mom and RachelAnne were stretched out in front of the television watching something she didn't recognize. Amity and Edwards were back.

"She promises to behave," Edwards said. Amity stuck her tongue out at him.

Marti still couldn't get used to the sight of her uptight mother lounging with her stocking feet propped up on a table.

Mom wasn't drinking her stinky tea. She cradled a brandy snifter. Two empty glasses sat on the end table next to the sofa along with a bottle of Rémy Martin. The good stuff.

"Is snifter number three for me, or are you expecting company?"

"Help yourself." RachelAnne wasn't drinking.

The evil voice in her head screamed *it's a trap*. Part of her still believed her sister wanted to trip her up and find a reason to deem Marti unfit for access to the money The Judge left her.

When she first returned home after The Judge's death and found Bickle House in an uproar and RachelAnne in charge, her sister had possession of the key to their father's liquor cabinet. The one with the good stuff. She never relinquished it. If she was going to use it, having her around might be a good thing.

"Maybe later," Marti said. Not because of evil voice. If they all drank enough, they could have a drunken girls' night. Frightening thought. Drunken girls' nights were fun—and funny—for television sit-com families, but the Mickklesons were not a television sit-com family.

She joined her sister on the couch. Next to the Rémy, in case she changed her mind.

The woman on television seemed to be speaking to a spirit. Someone's beloved grandmother. Grandma, Edwards, and Amity were between her and the screen, so it was hard to see.

"What in the world are you watching?"

"*Ghost Whisperer*," Mom said.

"You have got to be kidding." Another show she'd heard of but never seen. Never wanted to. From what she knew of it, it hit a little too close to home. Netflix might turn out not to be such a good idea after all.

"It's ridiculous," Grandma said.

"I don't want to go toward any stinkin' light," Amity said.

"If you don't start behaving yourself, I'll send you there myself," Grandma said.

"Zip it," Edwards said. "I want to hear this."

"She's just like you." RachelAnne laughed.

Mom didn't. Neither did Marti.

"It was a joke," RachelAnne said.

"Wish I'd had a grandmother like that." Marti attempted to lighten the atmosphere.

"I like her," Grandma Bertie said.

"Ha," Mom said. "None of your grandmothers were that nice. On either side of the family."

The ghost rustler woman wasn't at all like Marti. Miss Sensitive had people who believed in her ability and valued her for it. She bet Miss Ghost Mutterer's parents never sent her away or medicated her. No shock treatment for Little Miss Friend to the Recently Deceased.

On television, an angry ghost made the lights dim. "Can I do that?" Amity said.

"No, dear. The living just like to blame us for things they can't figure out on their own," Grandma said.

Mom stuck out her glass. Marti refilled it. "RachelAnne?"

Her sister shook her head. Too bad. If RachelAnne imbibed, Marti might give in and have one too.

"They got the ghosts all wrong," Marti said.

RachelAnne laughed. Mom didn't.

None of Marti's ghosts asked her for help. Other than her father. And Mrs. Heedly. And possibly the Girl.

Maybe she should pay attention to Little Miss Spirit Rustler.

One of the dearly departed laid a hand on the cheek of his grieving love. She smiled. Marti shivered.

The show came to a sappy end. Ghost problem solved. People problem solved. They could all live and not live happily ever after.

Mom picked up the remote, and the screen went black.

"Now that we are all together, we need to talk." No more lounging. Mom sat ramrod straight, both feet on the floor. She used her command voice. Margaret Alberta Dibble Mickkleson, Queen of Everything, Ruler of Her Daughters and anyone else who crossed her path, was in charge.

Marti wanted to melt into the couch cushions. She desperately tried to remember everything she'd done wrong—by her mother's standards—in the last twenty-four hours.

"First, Marcile. You need to do something about that hair."

"I just had it cut!" A month ago. Queen-Mom brought out the

insecure thirteen-year-old in her, who wasn't all that different from the insecure thirty-two-year-old she was.

"Marti's in trouble! Marti's in trouble!" Amity hadn't learned the Charleston that passed for her Happy Dance while she was alive. The dance came decades after the little girl's death from influenza. Marti blamed Edwards. For the Charleston, not the death.

"You now represent this family, and you need to look like it. If you like, I'll make an appointment with Jean-Paul for you."

"I'll take care of it." No way was she going to her mother's stylist. Not that he did a bad job. Ashley went to him, and both she and Mom always looked stunning. It was the principle of the thing.

"Do that." The corners of Mom's mouth twitched.

Marti knew she'd been manipulated, but if her hair was her mother's only issue, she was okay with it.

"Next, RachelAnne. You need to decide what you are doing. You are welcome to stay here, but I will not allow you to wallow."

Marti hadn't noticed her sister wallowing. She thought RachelAnne was, other than her justifiable Oreo and red wine binge, doing remarkably well.

"I'll take some of that brandy now," RachelAnne said.

Marti poured a little into a snifter and handed it to her sister.

"I have contacted Philippa Berryman," Mom said. "She is willing to represent you, and I am willing to pay her fees. Of course, she can't do anything until *you* contact her."

RachelAnne's hand shook. Her drink sloshed. She took a healthy slug and choked.

"Watch that stuff. It's strong." There was a time when Marti enjoyed seeing her baby sister in the hot seat. In the past, when it seldom happened, she'd taken her small joys where she could.

In truth, she still felt a tiny thrill, but she felt guilty about it. She must be growing up.

"It's made to be sipped," Mom said.

RachelAnne set her brandy on the coffee table.

Just a teeny-tiny thrill. Just a little guilt. Someday she might grow up, but today was not that day.

Mom put her empty glass down next to RachelAnne's unfinished Rémy. "Now, about Philippa."

Okay, a big thrill. She was a bad sister. She couldn't be expected to flip a switch and turn off years of conditioned response.

She could try. She would make little Miss Goody Two-Shoes Ghost Murmurer her role model. "Mom—"

They were interrupted by an angry T3. "Mommy! She was calling you and you didn't come!" He held his sobbing sister's hand. "I think she had a bad dream."

Marti was relieved to see Amity still in her place on the floor. She didn't have anything to do with the state Maggie was in. How much of the grown-up conversation had the kids heard?

RachelAnne picked up her daughter.

"Daddydaddydaddy," Maggie sobbed.

"Oh, honey. You can see him tomorrow." RachelAnne hugged Maggie.

"We talked to him this afternoon," T3 said.

"When?" RachelAnne packed a lot into that one word, most of it anger.

"He called."

"When was this? I didn't hear the phone," Mom said.

"You were sleeping." T3 stuck out his lower lip.

"I was not."

"You were snoring." T3 spread his legs, planted his feet, and set his fists on his hips. He was in superhero stance—and not enjoying the interrogation. "He said to tell you we want to come home."

"Why didn't you tell me he called?"

Marti had only seen RachelAnne truly angry with her kids once. They'd hidden in the Bickle House attic. After two hours of searching, Marti was calling Big when the kids showed up and shouted "Surprise!" RachelAnne exploded.

Her sister's current anger wasn't really for T3, but there was no way for him to know that.

"He said you are being silly and it is time for you to get over it."

RachelAnne swore. T3's eyes got big. Marti seethed. What kind of a jerk said things like that to a seven-year-old?

"I don't want Daddy to get hurt." Maggie buried her face in her mother's neck.

"It was just a dream. Daddy's fine." RachelAnne handed Maggie to her grandmother. "See if you can stay awake. I have something to take care of."

"RachelAnne—" Marti stopped herself before she said "calm down." In her experience, telling people to calm down had the opposite effect. "Breathe."

"Marti? Stuff it." RachelAnne left the room.

T3 started to tear after her, but Marti grabbed him.

"I shouldn't have told her," he said.

Back door, open. Back door open. The room wasn't all RachelAnne had left.

"It's not your fault," Marti said. "She just needs some air."

A cheery voice rang out, thrilled beyond credibility about a trip to the zoo.

"Mommy yeft her phone," Maggie said.

Neither Marti nor her mother bothered to correct the little girl's speech.

"How about if we all go upstairs and read a story?" Marti said.

"I want Mommy." Maggie dissolved into tears again.

"I want Nana to do the funny voices," T3 said.

Marti had never listened when her mother read to her grandchildren. Margaret Mickkleson doing funny voices might make up for abstaining from the brandy. "Good plan," she said.

RachelAnne's phone rang again.

"I'll take the kids. You find that damned thing and turn it off," Mom said.

"Nana, that's a bad word," T3 said.

"Only Daddy's ayyowed to say that."

"Alllllowed," Nana-Mom said. "Let's go."

Marti located the phone as it finished its third ring. "I wonder if RachelAnne would notice if I changed her ringtone?"

"I think she's got enough changes in her life at the moment," Grandma Bertie said.

The zoo song blasted a fourth time.

"Do it," Grandma said.

The screen said POLICE calling. Marti answered it instead of hitting the mute switch. "Yes?"

"Mrs. Rudawski?"

"This is her sister Marti. Can I help you?"

"Oh."

Dead air.

"Hello?" Marti said.

The caller cleared his throat. "Sorry, ma'am. This is Rodney Carpenter. I'm looking for Rach—Mrs. Rudawski."

Baby Face Rodney. Richie's big brother was slightly less intimidated by her than his little brother was, but then he was a cop rather than a security guard. He had a gun. And he'd never seen her shouting at ghosts. Richie had, although he hadn't seen the ghosts.

"She's not available at the moment. I'll have to do."

"Ummm, it would be better if I could talk to your sister."

"I don't know where she is. It's me or nothing." Enough with the polite.

"It's her husband."

She hoped Peter had been arrested. She didn't care for what.

"We have him here at the station."

Dreams did come true. "And?"

"Someone needs to come and get him."

"Let him rot."

"That wouldn't be such a good idea."

"Is he okay?" It dawned on her that something serious might have happened to him. Her feelings were mixed.

"He's not hurt."

"Spit it out, Rodney."

"Look, can you come and get him? Somebody needs to. I could throw him in a cell, but he hasn't really done anything. Word will get out. Your mother won't like it."

"My mother doesn't like a lot of things." Rescuing Peter from the police station wasn't on her top ten, or even top one thousand, list of things to do.

"Look. I know he and RachelAnne are having, um, problems," Rodney stammered, "but we promised to call her."

Word traveled fast. She imagined him blushing.

"She doesn't like him coming home in a patrol car," he continued. "Neither does your mother."

Bless the small-town social order.

"I'm not my mother." But, Peter was T3 and Maggie's father. Maggie. *I don't want Daddy to get hurt.* He couldn't get hurt at the station, could he? He was safer in police custody than he would be in hers.

He was a prick, but the kids loved him. *Crap.*

"You'd better tell me what's going on," she said.

Rodney had found Peter sitting in the gazebo on the Green, crying like a baby. He was beyond three sheets to the wind, more like six or seven.

"DUI?" Marti said.

"Nope. He doesn't know where he left his car. He's unable to tell us what he's currently driving."

"I'm still not sure why I shouldn't just leave him there." Other than the kids. And Maggie's nightmare. Kid-logic was special. If Maggie somehow found out her father asked Marti for help—and

Marti wouldn't put it past Peter to tell her—and she'd said no, her niece would be angry. Or worse, disappointed.

She should have had a brandy, or two or three. She would have had a good excuse to say no. "I'll come and get him."

"Thank you." Rodney's relief was evident.

It didn't make sense, but she chalked it up to another one of those small-town things.

She found crayons and paper in the toy box and scrawled a note for her mother.

Had to run out. Will explain later.

M.

She stuck it under the Rémy. Mom was sure to see it there.

She considered her note, took her crayon, and squeezed the word *love* above her initial. She was still getting used to this we're-a-happy-family business.

P.S. Took the TT.

Mom wasn't going anywhere.

CHAPTER

EIGHT

"Do you want to tell me where we're going?" Grandma Bertie said. "I only got to hear one side of that conversation, you know."

"We, believe it or not, are going to get Peter from the police station."

"This had better be good."

"Will you settle for mildly amusing?" She filled Grandma in.

"That is kind of funny, but why aren't we just leaving him there?

"I don't know. Somehow, Rodney talked me into it."

"They couldn't have taken him home? Our booming metropolis has what, three? Four patrol cars now?"

"Rodney said RachelAnne doesn't like him being delivered in a cop car."

"So this has happened before?"

"Apparently." Despite their improving relationship, her sister still kept a secret or two. No big surprise. Secrets were a Mickkleson family tradition. Marti had a few herself.

"You are a marshmallow."

Was that pride in Grandma's voice?

"Keep your eyes on the road and don't give me that look," Grandma said.

Marti turned onto the square and reined in the TT. Rodney was probably on speed trap duty when he found Peter. The headlights that had been in her rearview mirror since she pulled off the Avenue followed. They didn't look like cop car lights. She assumed Margaret Mickkleson's TT—and its driver—were ticket-proof but was in no mood to find out otherwise.

She crept around the Green and turned off the square. The headlights followed. There were other things than the police station on the side road. The fire department. Churches. The cemetery. It didn't have to be a ticket-writing cop behind her. Just in case, she kept the TT a mile below the speed limit. When she hit her turn signal, the other car's blinker flashed in her mirror.

She pulled into a parking spot in front of the Municipal Services Center. The car behind her pulled in next to her. A small red SUV. Not a police car.

Marti glanced at the driver and did a double take. Winter Adams. What was *she* doing there?

Except she wasn't there. As soon as she saw Marti, Peter's little friend backed out and took off.

"I'm having second thoughts. Let's just leave him," Marti said.

"We're here. We might as well go in." Grandma Bertie said. "While you're rescuing Peter the Not-so-Great, I'll have a little chat with Eustace."

"One-Eye?"

"Don't call him that. He hates it."

The legendary Eustace Cunningham was once the Law in Bicklesburg. He gained his nickname when he lost an eye to either a barroom brawl or a bride with no patience with his fondness for pretty women who weren't her. The story varied depending on who told it. It varied when One-Eye told it. His disappearance was never solved, and over a century after his death, he still considered himself a member of Bicklesburg's finest. Like most old dead guys, he considered Alberta Marcile Ferguson the bee's knees.

"You are an incorrigible flirt," Marti said.

"Don't be ridiculous. I'm going to ask him if they've identified Susan Silliphant yet. I'm asking for Janice since you don't appear to be doing anything."

"I don't think it's her." Marti remembered where she'd seen the gaudy bracelets. Thought she remembered. She needed to be sure before she said anything. "If we're going to do this, let's do it."

PETER SLOUCHED in one of the plastic chairs lining the outer walls of the reception area. Too bad. It would be fun to see him in a cell surrounded by big hairy biker-type dudes. It probably only happened that way in movies. Still, it was a good fantasy.

He didn't look up. She walked over and kicked his foot. If he'd been anyone but Peter, she'd have felt sorry for him. Pale blotches bloomed under his spray-on tan. His highlighted hair stuck up in spikes sharp enough to make an aging punk rocker proud. His eyes were swollen and bloodshot. He wore the same tasteful suit he'd worn at his big-top show—she assumed RachelAnne picked it out—but it was rumpled and dirty. The pink tie was gone.

"What are you doing here?" His slurred words and hoarse voice didn't mask his dislike of her.

"I came to get you, Mr. Grateful."

"Where's RachelAnne?"

"I have no idea." Not a lie. "Maybe she's out indulging in some payback." Total lie. RachelAnne would toe the line and remain a faithful wife until the papers freeing her were signed and filed—and probably for six months or six years after—but it wouldn't hurt to make him sweat.

He got up and swayed. "If you're here to take me home, do it."

"Hold your horses." She went to the counter. "Rodney called me. Do I have to sign any papers or anything to take Barney Gumble over there home?" Now there was a show that ran long enough even she'd seen it.

"You mean Rudawski? Carpenter said you were coming. Then he hightailed it out of here."

Marti didn't recognize the officer on desk duty, but she knew who Marti was.

"Just get him out of here and tell RachelAnne that sooner or later, we are going to have to charge him with something. Drunk and disorderly at a minimum."

"Would that today be that day," Marti said. She hadn't seen Grandma since they left the car nor had she caught a glimpse of Eustace. Not a bad thing, since One-Eye loathed her as much as he adored her great-grandmother. They could chat and make eyes at each other for a while longer. Grandma would bungee into the backseat before Marti got too far.

"Come on, Barney." She held the door open.

"Who?" Peter said.

He had to be drunk. She couldn't believe he'd never seen *The Simpsons.* "Two things. One, don't puke in the car, and two, I'm not tucking you in."

"EUSTACE SAID Susan's name has come up, but only as one of a long list of missing persons," Grandma said from the back seat.

Marti'd half-hoped she'd land in the front, where Peter was either passed out or doing an excellent impression of a corpse. A good freeze would have done him good. Well, she would have enjoyed it.

"Long list?" she said. "How many are there?"

"More than you'd think for a small town," Grandma said.

"Why are you going so slow?" Oh, joy. Peter was awake. "If I was driving this baby, we'd fly."

"I'm looking for the turn." The only way her brother-in-law would ever get behind the wheel of the TT was over her dead body.

"The next right," Grandma said.

She found the turn. RachelAnne's house sat at the end of Paradise Sanctuary Boulevard, a cul-de-sac lined with McMansions. A cut-rate version of the Avenue, it didn't meet Marti's definition of paradise or sanctuary and was too narrow and distinctly lacking in trees to qualify as a boulevard.

Marti had only been invited to her sister's house twice, and she saw no reason to visit without an invitation. She'd gone once for T3's birthday and once for Peter's. The first occasion was fun. The second, not so much. It wasn't solely the company. The bloated house, with its faux stucco mishmash of architectural styles, and near cookie-cutter matchy-matchiness to its neighbors left her cold. As McMansions went, it was big and bottom-of-the-line.

Mom hated the Rudawski Garage Mahal. "Tacky and ostentatious," she called it. Marti agreed. She found it hard to believe RachelAnne had any part in the choice of her family abode. Her sister had done her best to make the soulless interior, with its ridiculously high ceilings and gaudy chandeliers, feel like a home. RachelAnne's best wasn't good enough. It was Peter's starter castle, a place to mark time until he could get his hands on Bickle House.

"Ha. I knew she'd come running back," Peter said.

RachelAnne's Subaru sat in the driveway. Lights shone from every window of the house.

"I wouldn't get too excited if I were you." She pulled in behind her sister's car. Peter fumbled with the door handle before she stopped the car. Good thing the door was locked.

"What's wrong with this damned thing?" He clawed at the latch and threw his weight against the door.

Marti hit unlock from the driver's side and didn't bother to hide her laughter when he fell out.

"That was beneath you," Grandma said. "Funny, but beneath you."

"Not at all. I can go much lower."

"Are you going in?"

She didn't want to, but she should. She'd either stop Rachel-Anne from killing her husband or cheer her on. She preferred the latter but would play it by ear. She got out and followed Peter as he wove up the walk. Almost, but not quite, as funny as watching him fall out of the car.

His attempts to unlock the front door were also entertaining, but she wanted to get him inside, find out how steamed her sister was, and leave. "Give me the key," she said.

"No. I can do it." He promptly dropped his keyring and sat down on the small but ornate front steps. "Where did it go?"

If he couldn't figure out he'd sat on it, she wasn't going to tell him. "Good job." She rang the doorbell.

RachelAnne threw the door open before Marti had her finger off the button. She hadn't calmed down. "What the—"

"Rodney called me." She stepped between her sister and Peter, now on his hands and knees searching for his keys. It was entirely by accident she kicked the keyring off the stoop in the process.

Her sister didn't need any more explanation. "You should have left him there."

"Trust me, I wanted to. Baby-faced Rodney has powers of persuasion. Besides, Maggie..."

"Maggie what?" RachelAnne narrowed her eyes. "Did he call her again?"

"No, no. I just was, I don't know, I didn't want her to be upset. Sounds lame now, but it made sense at the time."

"I knew you'd come running back." Peter hadn't found his keys, but he had found his attitude.

Marti stepped to the side and planted her heel on Peter's hand. That wasn't an accident.

He howled. RachelAnne grinned.

"Ooops," Marti said.

"Beneath you," Grandma said. It sounded more like praise than reprimand.

"Come in and help me," RachelAnne said.

Four fat black trash bags sat just inside the door.

"Housecleaning?" Marti said.

"The kids' stuff. Clothes. Toys. I couldn't find anything else to put it in."

"Looks just like my luggage."

"I know. Help me get it to the car."

RachelAnne grabbed two bags. Marti grabbed the other two and followed her sister out the door.

"Where do you think you're going?" Marti couldn't see her brother-in-law, but she heard his sneer.

RachelAnne turned back.

"Ignore the little weasel. Just keep walking," Marti said.

RachelAnne replied with a word Marti'd never heard come out of her sister's mouth.

Peter moved fast for a drunk. Before Marti could stop him, he lunged between them and grabbed RachelAnne by the arm.

Marti saw red. "Get your hands off of her."

"Yeah? What are you going to do? Tickle me?" He spun RachelAnne around and twisted her arm behind her back. She winced.

Marti didn't have to do anything. Grandma Bertie was on him like a shot. He went pale.

"Wh-wh-wh-at-t-t-d-d-did you d-do t-t-o m-me?" He shivered and let go of RachelAnne. His spray tan turned buttercup yellow.

Marti laughed.

"You b-b-b—"

"YOU? What did *I* do to *you?* You selfish, lying, cheating little —" RachelAnne dove at her husband. Marti grabbed her around the waist and hauled her back.

Grandma wrapped her arms around Peter's waist. She wasn't capable of hauling him anywhere, but she didn't need to. He howled. Marti shivered just watching the full-on ghost freeze. On the other hand, it couldn't happen to a more deserving fellow. The thought warmed her.

"Get her out of here," Grandma said.

Marti opened the passenger door of the TT and stuffed her sister inside.

"What are you doing?" RachelAnne tried to get out, but Marti blocked her.

"Shut up and listen to me. This isn't doing anyone any good. We are out of here."

"But—"

"What if the kids hear about it?" Lights had come on next door. One set of neighbors, maybe more, peered out their window. "This is Bicklesburg. You're a Mickkleson. The story will be all over town before the sun comes up."

For the first time since they were three and five years old, her baby sister listened to her. RachelAnne settled into the seat, and Marti slammed the door.

She started the car before she had her door shut, threw the roadster into gear, and peeled out of the driveway. The TT could move. Grandma would catch up soon.

"We left the kids' things," RachelAnne said.

"We'll get them tomorrow."

"We left my car."

"We'll get it tomorrow."

"Something was wrong with Peter."

"Something's always been wrong with Peter."

"No. He looked sick. Maybe we should call someone."

"He'll be fine." Miserable for a while, but a ghost freeze didn't leave lasting damage.

"Are you sure?"

"Do you care?"

"No. Yes. Maybe. I don't know." RachelAnne leaned her head back and groaned.

"Do you want to go back?" Marti had no intention of turning around. If she kept RachelAnne talking long enough, it wouldn't matter.

"He's fine." Grandma Bertie joined them. "I only wish I could have done some real damage."

Marti did too. It was probably better for all of them she couldn't.

RachelAnne mumbled. Marti couldn't make out what she said.

"I have an idea," Marti said.

"Whatever," her sister said.

MARTI PULLED INTO THE KWIKIMART.

"Wait here," she said and ran inside.

It didn't take long to find what she was after.

Getting the woman behind the checkout to notice her took longer. "Kwiki" was obviously someone's idea of a joke.

Marti waved. The clerk stared blankly and continued to talk on her phone.

"I heard it was one of his girlfriends. Guess that wife of his won't be so high and mighty now."

She didn't have to be talking about Peter and RachelAnne. Bicklesburg could give Peyton Place a run for its money when it came to intrigue, gossip, and scandal. If the Mickkleson and Rudawski men were anything to go by, adultery was the town's number one pastime.

The clerk noticed Marti and turned red. "I gotta go." She

stuck her phone in the pocket of her yellow polyester smock. "Did you find everything you wanted?"

"Yep." Marti matched the woman's chipper tone and paid for her purchase.

The clerk had her phone out again before Marti picked up her bag.

"Here." Marti tossed the KwikiMart bag to her sister. "Enjoy. They cost me a few years' salary."

"How much gas is in this thing?"

"About three-quarters of a tank." Marti assumed her sister meant the TT, not the three packages of DoubleStuff Oreos she just bought. "Why?"

"I don't want to go home."

"Where do you want to go?"

"Just drive."

"I can do that." Marti gunned the little sports car and headed out of town.

CHAPTER

NINE

"Wake up."

Marti groaned. Some people might consider a great-grandmother who doubled as an alarm clock a wonderful thing. Marti was not some people.

"Lazy bones! Lazy bones! Wake up wake up wake up!" Amity's squeal pierced Marti's head.

She wasn't sure how far and how long she and RachelAnne had driven just for the sake of wandering. RachelAnne didn't utter a word until they neared Henrietta's Hollow, and the word she uttered then didn't bear repeating.

Marti'd stopped at the site of Peter's future strip mall. They sat in the car, scarfed Oreos, and said bad things about Peter. The more cookies they ate, the more creative they got. "Powder-head doody-pants" was one of Marti's favorites. She hoped she'd get a chance to use it to his face.

"Getupgetupgetup. There's a new sheriff in town."

Marti had no clue what the ghost girl was going on about. She made a note to talk to Edward about his influence on Amity's vocabulary, not to mention her behavior. It was probably too late. Over a century too late.

She and her sister made one last stop before returning to Bickle House. Hoping Peter had passed out or fallen into a black hole, either would do, they snuck back to the Rudawski McTravesty and retrieved Maya, RachelAnne's cat.

"I don't trust Peter with her," RachelAnne said.

Marti didn't need any further convincing. Next to Bernard, the little black and white charmer was her favorite kitty. Of course, they were the only two cats she knew, but that didn't matter.

The rescue mission was a breeze. Peter was nowhere to be seen. He'd forgotten to set the alarm system or lock up. Maya met them at the door, and RachelAnne scooped her up. RachelAnne locked the doors and armed the alarm. The whole operation took less than five minutes. They didn't bother with the Subaru or the bags of kid stuff. They'd still be there in the morning.

"Getupgetupgetup." Amity's screech had nothing to do with Edwards's influence. It was all her own.

Back at Bickle House, Maya wandered off to explore. Marti and RachelAnne made a dent in the brandy still sitting in the family parlor as if it was waiting for them. More than a dent. They might have emptied the bottle. She couldn't remember, but she thought her pounding head was due to too many Oreos, too little sleep, and a certain obnoxious little ghost, not the alcohol. She'd had enough of all in her time to know the difference.

"Get up. Your sister needs you." Grandma's command voice was scarier than Mom's. Grandma Bertie learned hers from horror movies.

Marti was a pro at ignoring her grandmother, had used more big-sisterly support reserves than she knew she possessed the night before, and wanted to hide from the world. She pulled her blankets over her head.

"Getupgetupgetup. There's an elephant in the room."

"Make her go away," Marti said.

"If you don't get up, I'll let her get into bed with you,"

Grandma said. "Big's downstairs. Something is wrong. Very, very wrong."

That got Marti's attention. She couldn't think of any reason for the police chief to visit Bickle House at—she peeked at the clock. Six thirty a.m. She couldn't think of any good reason for him to visit at any time.

She crawled out of bed and threw her ratty terry cloth robe over her Wonder Woman tank top and red, white, and blue striped pajama pants. The robe was in worse shape than her PJs, but in Mom's house, modesty and decorum mattered. Or maybe not. The pajamas were new and bore no rips or stains. Marti still had problems avoiding the pitfalls of Mom-terrain. Odds were whichever way she went, she'd be wrong. "Diana give me strength," she said.

"Who is Diana?" Amity said.

"Your young man is with Big," Grandma said.

"He's not my young man." Grandma hadn't approved of Dmitri and Marti's teenage relationship but remained determined to manufacture one between their adult selves. Adult-ish in Marti's case. She considered brushing her hair and maybe her teeth.

"Marti and Pretty Boy sitting in a tree, K-I-S-S-I-N-G." Amity jumped on the bed, feet planted through the pillow where Marti's head had lain moments before.

"Get her away from me," Marti said.

"Come on, sweetheart." Grandma Bertie grabbed the ghost girl. "And don't you even think about going back to bed."

"I won't."

"First comes love, then comes marriage, then comes Marti with a baby carriage."

Grandma dragged the still-singing Amity through the closet door and out of the room.

"Not in this lifetime," Marti said and headed downstairs without brushing anything.

SHE FOUND her sister in the formal sitting room. Unlike the casual comfort of the family parlor, the formal room was the essence of Bickle House. A pure reflection of Margaret Alberta Dibble Mickkleson at her most majestic. Furnished in antiques that once belonged to the original Bickles, accented by a few Mickkleson pieces and fewer pieces from the Dibbles, it looked more like a museum than a private home. Felt like a museum too. It was where Mom entertained outsiders—meaning anyone not a Mickkleson.

The sitting room was designed for neither sitting nor relaxing, and its current occupants were anything but relaxed.

Dmitri stood by the window. He gave her a stiff nod and left the room without a word. Maybe she should have brushed her hair.

Big's hulking form was stuffed into a Louis XV period bergère. Marti hoped the armchair was sturdier than it looked. The carved walnut legs were about as thick as Big's pinky finger. His fidgeting and foot tapping implied he would be uncomfortable in an over-stuffed La-Z-Boy recliner. Under normal circumstances, she would have enjoyed his discomposure. If his presence in Bickle House wasn't enough, his face told her circumstances were far from normal.

"Marti. I'm glad you're here." He spoke slowly and sadly, his sympathy a far cry from the "Marti Cray-Cray" he tormented her with in high school.

She had a suspicion the sympathy wasn't for her.

She sat down next to her sister. The couch—no, settee was the proper term—was from the same period as the chair and more uncomfortable. Stiffer, with less padding, and she immediately felt as if it was trying to eject her. Compared to her sister, it was a cradle of coziness and warmth.

RachelAnne might as well have been Botoxed from head to

toe. She perched on the edge of the settee, back stiff, knees and ankles together, hands folded in her lap, the personification of Mom's childhood lectures on posture and deportment. Except, Mom always made it look elegant. RachelAnne was frozen, an ice sculpture of an Ice Queen.

"What's up?" Marti cringed. Not only were her words lame and her perky tone phony, both were inappropriate for the situation. Whatever the situation was.

Her sister didn't blink at her faux pas. The situation was indeed grave.

Big looked at RachelAnne. For a second, Marti thought he was going to reach out and hold her hand. The Ice Queen gave him a barely perceptible nod, but the frost didn't crack.

"As I've already told your sister, I've got some bad news." Big didn't take his eyes off RachelAnne's face.

He had gone to meet the state investigators at Henrietta's Hollow at the crack of dawn o'thirty. The first order of business was a search and retrieve mission for more of the remains unearthed by Peter and his excavator. The state forensic crew had come equipped for an archeological dig. They never got to use their fancy paraphernalia.

They found more remains, all right. Much fresher than the previous day's and no question whose they were.

RachelAnne wouldn't be needing the services of Philippa Berryman or any divorce lawyer. Maybe a probate lawyer.

"Was it an accident?" A still-drunk Peter might have made his way back to the site, fallen in the hole, and hit his head. Considering the condition they left him in, Marti had a hard time believing the first part of that theory, but she could hope.

"We—" The police chief looked up and closed his mouth.

"Mommy?" Maggie wandered in, dragging a blanket in one hand and rubbing her eyes with the other. "Daddy says he wants to come home now," she said.

The ice shattered. RachelAnne burst into tears.

CHAPTER

TEN

THE OPENING NOTES of Beethoven's *Moonlight Sonata* filled the room. The melody was appropriately depressing. Big pulled his phone out of his pocket. She'd never taken him for the classical music type.

"I need to take this." He went to the window where Dmitri had been and turned his back to them.

Marti was left alone with her sobbing sister and niece. She picked up Maggie and tried to cuddle her, but the little girl was having none of it.

"I want the yady." She squirmed and pushed Marti away.

"Me too," Marti whispered. If Grandma would show up, she could coach Marti. Provide her with soothing words to parrot. Tell her what to do. Anything to cut through the raw grief filling the room.

RachelAnne rocked. Tears streamed down her face. If she heard Maggie and Marti's conversation, she didn't acknowledge it.

"I see," Big said.

"The yady can send Daddy home," Maggie said.

"Oh, honey. It doesn't work that way," Marti said. How long had Maggie been listening at the door? She must have heard something. How else did the toddler make the connection between the current state of both Grandma Bertie and Peter? Unless—Marti looked wildly around the room.

"Yes," Big said.

Peter was nowhere to be seen. Thank goodness for small favors. Or big favors. A ghostly Peter Rudawski was more than she could handle at the moment or any moment in the foreseeable future.

"Got it," Big said.

"Mommy?" Maggie crawled from Marti's lap to her mother's.

RachelAnne didn't respond.

"We'll be there ASAP," Big said.

"RachelAnne?" Marti tried to take her sister's hand. RachelAnne shook her off. At least it was a response.

"Is she okay?" Big loomed over them, phone in hand.

"I think she needs a doctor," Marti said.

"We need the yady," Maggie said.

"I'm fine," RachelAnne said. "I need to make a list of things to be done." Harriet, electro-lady of the alarm system, spoke with more life than Robo-RachelAnne, but speaking at all was an improvement.

"Not right now," Big said.

"She's not fine," Marti said.

"Is your mother up?"

On cue, Mom swept into the room. No one had the right to look that well put together first thing in the morning.

"What is going on here and why is it so cold in this house? Did the furnace break down?"

"Summon her and she shall come," Marti said.

"Sorry. It's the only way I could wake her up," Grandma said.

"Can you take Maggie out of the room? And stay with the kids?" Big said.

"Not until you explain your presence in my home," Mom said.

"RachelAnne and Marti need to come with me."

"At this hour of the morning? I think not." Mom pulled her lavender and lace satin robe close, but the chill in her words wasn't due to Grandma.

"Are they under arrest?" T3 joined the party. "Can I come with you?"

"The yady should come with us."

"What are you talking about?" Marti said.

"There are people I need to call," RachelAnne said. "Things to be attended to."

Amity burst through the wall, Edwards right behind her. "The jig is up!" she said.

"Amity, ixnay on the atterchay," Edwards said.

"My daddy's gone," Maggie said.

"Where?" T3 said.

"Mine is too," Amity said. "So am I."

"If someone doesn't tell me what's going on, I'll—"

"You'll what, Mom? Call the police?" RachelAnne channeled Marti, which worried Marti a whole lot more than robo-sister had.

"Ixnay ityay." Edwards tried to grab his charge. Amity danced out of his reach.

"Checked out, croaked, crossed over," she sang. "Departed, defunct, done in."

"Oh, this is not good," Grandma said.

Maya emerged from behind the drapes, headed straight for Mom, and twined herself around Mom's legs.

"Where did *that* come from?"

"Miao."

"Maya!" T3 and Maggie dove for the cat. T3 came up with her. Maggie howled.

Everyone, living and not, human and feline, jabbered at the same time.

"Hail, hail, the gang's all here." Marti's head felt as if it would explode.

"Everyone shut up!" Big's roar drowned them all out.

Even Amity listened.

The room fell silent.

Almost silent.

"Young man. Explain yourself." Queen Margaret took charge.

Big ignored her. "RachelAnne. Would you like to see a doctor?"

"No."

"Marti?"

"Maybe." She'd give her right arm for a sedative. Little Miss Ghost Whisperer never had problems like this. "No." She shook her head.

"Then take your mother out of the room and explain what has happened. Do not leave the premises. The children and I will wait here with RachelAnne until you return. You have three minutes." Big left no question who was in charge.

Mom said nothing. Her mouth hung open. She blinked. No one spoke to Queen Margaret like that.

"After which, you and RachelAnne will accompany me to the station," Big continued.

"RachelAnne." His voice softened. "Your mother can stay with the kids."

"Should I call Dmitri?" Mom said.

"Why?" Marti said.

"Maybe a lawyer," Big said.

"A *lawyer?*" Marti said.

"I'm a lawyer," RachelAnne said.

"Two and a half minutes," Big said. "And counting."

THE RIDE to the station was uneventful. RachelAnne returned to silent and frozen mode. Marti didn't attempt conversation. She didn't think her sister had ever ridden in the back of a police car.

She couldn't say the same for herself, but on her previous rides, she knew why she was there. Not knowing made this ride far worse.

RachelAnne had quit crying, but her face was red and her eyes swollen. Marti tried to stop feeling bad for herself and think about her sister. She couldn't summon up any sympathy for Peter.

Grandma sat up front with Big. She stayed quiet too.

Rodney met them as soon as they pulled into the station.

"Officer Carpenter will escort you inside," Big said. "Mrs. Rudawski will come with me."

"Why so formal?" Big never called her sister or his baby-faced cohort by anything other than their first names.

"This does not bode well," Grandma said. "I'll go find Eustace."

Inside, Big went off with RachelAnne. Rodney ushered Marti down a long hall and into a small room at the back of the station and indicated she should take a seat.

"Would you like a cup of coffee?" he said.

"I'd kill for one."

Baby-face flinched. Marti regretted her choice of words.

"I'll be right back," he said.

Marti waited for him to return. And waited. And waited. Maybe he'd forgotten about her. Maybe everyone had forgotten her. Maybe she should go find the coffee pot. Or Grandma. Where was Grandma? Having so much fun with old One-Eye she'd forgotten about her great-granddaughter?

The last time Marti was anywhere past the station's front desk, she'd been in Big's office. At the time, she thought the depressing room could double as a torture chamber. The same decorator had worked their magic on the room she was in. The same depressing gray paint covered the cinderblock walls. The same brown paper covered the small window. The fluorescent light overhead had the same flicker. The uncomfortable metal folding chair she sat in was identical to the one she'd parked her butt on when she sat across from Big at his desk. The desk was missing, as were the file cabinets that lined the walls of Big's office. This room was smaller, barely large enough to hold its furnishings, a small table and four metal folding chairs. If Big joined her, it would be a tight squeeze.

No clock. Big's office had a clock on the wall. The walls here were bare. She'd left her phone at home. What time was it?

"Eustace says he always knew you'd come to a bad end." Grandma perched on the end of the table.

"No need to sound so cheerful about it. I don't suppose you brought coffee?" Marti kept her voice low. There were no observation windows, not even a mirror on the wall, but that didn't mean there weren't hidden microphones.

"Don't be ridiculous. Why'd they put you in a cell? Rachel-Anne is in a much nicer room. Big's talking to her."

"You didn't think to stay and listen? And this isn't a cell."

"You need to speak up. When Big questions you, he won't be able to hear you. He might resort to rubber hoses."

If Grandma was cracking jokes to cheer her up, she was doing a lousy job of it. Marti doubted Big ever beat a suspect. Eustace, maybe. Big, never. And old One-Eye was way beyond doing her any harm.

"I do know why you're both here if you want to hear it." Grandma preened. "That Eustace is charming."

Or hidden cameras. Marti regretted never taking up ventriloquism. "You talk. I'll listen." She tried not to move her lips as she spoke.

"What was that?" Grandma said.

Marti frowned. If anyone was watching, a frown was perfectly reasonable under the circumstances.

"Oh. I get it. You're worried someone is spying on you. Eustace says they are pretty behind the times technology-wise around here. Although I don't know how he would know."

Marti folded her arms on the table and put her head down.

"Are you going to take a nap or listen to me? You and Rachel-Anne could be in big trouble. If I didn't know where you were last night, I'd be ready to lock you both up."

Marti sat up. Grandma talked.

Peter had been beaten and dumped in the hole he'd dug himself.

"Appropriate," Marti said.

"Shut up and listen. This is serious," Grandma said.

The neighbors on Paradise Sanctuary Boulevard reported an argument.

"An 'all out screaming brawl' they called it."

"That's ludicrous. You were there," Marti said.

"I know, but they didn't see me. However, they did see Rachel-Anne and 'her weird sister.'" Grandma enclosed the last words in air quotes.

"So what? It's still RachelAnne's house." Marti wasn't worried. The neighbors watched them leave. Peter was still alive and kicking—or shivering—when they left.

"It gets better. Or worse," Grandma said. "They found blood inside the house. They think that's where Peter was killed."

"He was alive when we left him."

"The doors were locked and the security system was armed."

"We can explain that."

"They found a bloody ball-peen hammer on the front seat of RachelAnne's Subaru. They think it was the murder weapon."

"I can't explain that," Marti said.

The door opened.

"Explain what?"

Marti was right. Big barely fit through the door, let alone in the room.

"I don't suppose you're bringing me coffee," she said. "Rodney promised."

"You suppose right," the chief said.

~

"TELL me once more exactly what happened when you last saw Peter. And this time, leave out the smart aleck editorial comments." Big's patience hadn't just worn thin, it had frayed and unraveled.

"Not sure I can do that. The editorial comment bit, that is. I can tell you about seeing Peter as many times as you want. It's not going to change." Marti's patience was gone. She hadn't had much to start with, and despite Grandma's admonitions to "be nice," the interview went downhill fast.

"You know you're not doing yourself any favors with this attitude, don't you?"

A knock at the door saved her from answering.

"Yes?" Big's irritation wasn't limited to her.

Rodney opened the door. A woman Marti didn't know squeezed past him and into the tiny room.

Wait. She didn't know her, but she had seen her. The woman from Peter's groundbreaking party. Harold from the bank's buddy.

"Philippa." Big might as well have said "Tarantula."

"William."

It took Marti a beat to figure out who the woman was talking to. The last time she heard Big called by his full name was their high school graduation, and she hadn't been paying all that much attention then.

"Have you charged my client with anything?"

"Just chatting."

"I'd like a word with her. Alone."

"Marti? Is this woman your attorney?"

"If she says so." Going with the flow seemed like the best plan.

"Make it quick." Big left the room and slammed the door behind him.

"Philippa Berryman." The woman stuck her hand out.

Marti took it and shook. "I thought you were a divorce lawyer."

"Your mother doesn't have any criminal lawyers on speed dial."

"She has you on speed dial?"

"It was a joke. I'll have to do for now. What did you tell our illustrious chief of police?"

There was no love lost between Big and the lawyer. Dmitri told her Big had been married and divorced, but she was under the impression it was years ago. And if what she'd heard about Philippa Berryman was true, he wasn't worth enough, cash-wise, for her to bother with.

"I was honest." She hadn't told him everything, but neither he nor Philippa needed to know that. They'd hardly believe Grandma's role in the proceedings anyway.

The door opened again.

"You can leave now." Rodney's news was better than the coffee he never brought her.

"Really?" Marti said.

"I'm that good," Philippa said.

Marti hoped the woman was as good at her job as she thought she was, because she sure wasn't likable.

Rodney led them up the long hallway. He may have had a baby face, but his back was intimidating.

"I had a high school teacher named Berryman." Marti wasn't good at small talk but gave it a shot. Anything to break the tension.

"My father. He had a long and distinguished career as a history teacher."

'Long' was believable. Marti remembered him as a full-of-himself extra-old guy, but the old-guy part could have been her teenage perception of age. If 'distinguished' was defined as being a total jerk to students—other than to his selected pets, all of whom were star jocks and pretty girls—it was believable too. As a history teacher, he was awful.

Philippa's phone rang and rescued Marti from her attempt at small talk.

RachelAnne waited at the front of the station. She wasn't alone. Oliver stood at the counter next to a man in a well-cut dark suit. Without the Ray-Bans, it was hard to be sure, but Marti thought he was one of the Men in Black from Peter's circus.

"It's like old home week around here," she said.

Oliver and his sidekick turned.

"Marti Cray-Cray!" Oliver said.

"Uh-huh," Philippa said into her phone.

"I heard you got bailed out. Back again?" Marti was in no mood to make nice.

"I know things," Oliver said. "Important things. Things you don't know." He scratched his nose.

Marti assumed he was high. His eyes were glassy. Despite the stifling heat in the room, his worn olive green parka was pulled up to his ears. He inspected the back of his hand and picked at a scab.

"I'm sure you do," she said.

Oliver nodded. Or maybe he was falling asleep on his feet. He lost interest in her and examined a loose thread on the sleeve of his parka.

"I need to go. Call my secretary and give her the details." Philippa detached her phone from her ear.

"Philippa." The Man in Black nodded.

"Terrance."

"You two know each other?" Marti said. Philippa wore a dark suit. She probably had Ray-Bans in her attaché. Maybe aliens were involved. Maybe the two of them would pull sparkly silver tubes from their pockets and make everyone forget the last twenty-four hours.

"Terrance Appleby *is* a defense attorney, among other things. You two may end up getting acquainted."

Maybe the two Attorneys in Black had already done the

flashy-flashy thing and the current situation was their idea of replacement memories. Depressing thought.

"Can we just leave?" RachelAnne swayed.

"Do we need to do anything else here?" Marti wanted to get RachelAnne home before she keeled over.

"I'll take care of it," Philippa said. "Take your sister and go."

"Um, how are we getting home? It's a long walk. I'm willing, but RachelAnne doesn't look up to it."

"Your chauffeur awaits." Her phone buzzed. She checked the screen, answered with a crisp "Make it quick," and waved Marti away.

Philippa Berryman overestimated the Mickkleson family. Not their net worth. Their penchant for ostentatious display. They hadn't employed a chauffeur since Marti and RachelAnne were toddlers. When her late father had planned to imbibe a little too much to get behind the wheel of a car, he pulled a member of the ACS team for a driver. Usually Dmitri.

"I want to go home," RachelAnne said. Marti hoped she meant Bickle House. They weren't going anywhere near Paradise Sanctuary Boulevard or the McMonstrosity.

She took her sister by the arm and led her away. Maybe Richie had come after them. She could hope.

No such luck. Dmitri leaned against the Lexus.

"Your young man has the cutest dimples," Grandma said.

He needed to smile to produce dimples.

"Ladies, your chariot awaits," he said, not a dimple in sight.

CHAPTER

ELEVEN

DMITRI GENTLY HELPED RachelAnne into the passenger-side back seat. He stopped short of buckling her seatbelt, but Marti expected him to pat her on the head and kiss her on the forehead.

He didn't. He turned to Marti. "You can sit behind me."

He should have known better. She opened the front door and said, "I'll just sit up here with you."

No argument. He kept his expression blank. Dmitri's body language was as terse as his speech.

"I'll just sit back here with RachelAnne," Grandma said.

"Buckle up," Dmitri said.

No solicitous tucking in for her. He left her to fend for herself and got in behind the wheel.

She was beginning to think she'd somehow managed to piss him off. Without knowing it. Without seeing him. While he was off on vacation in parts unknown.

"Stop at my office on the way," she said.

The look he gave her wasn't blank. It had Marti Cray-Cray written all over it. "I don't think you need to go in to work today."

"I'm not. I need to feed Bernard." She'd expected to go into the office first thing in the morning and hadn't left extra kibblets.

According to the clock in the Lexus's dash, it was past noon. Bernard expected canned food in the morning. Not only that, the bottom of his dish was probably visible. He would be starving. Wasting away to nothing. Delirious with hunger. On the verge of death and ready to tell her about it. Loudly.

"Make it quick," Dmitri said.

"Am I allowed to stop and scoop the litter box?"

The step from terse to silent was small. Dmitri took it. He didn't say another word until they pulled up in front of the office.

"I'll pop over and see if Janice has heard anything," Grandma said.

"Do what you need to do and get back here," Dmitri said.

Marti slammed the car door. Mr. Blue Eyes wasn't the only one who could do taciturn.

Bernard didn't disappoint her. As soon as she stuck her key in the lock, the howling started. She hoped it was the start. If he'd been carrying on all morning, the other tenants of the building would complain. To her. They were all justifiably frightened of her mother.

Inside, the cat leaned against her just long enough to cover the lower legs of her jeans with orange hair then launched himself to the arm of a chair. He clawed the expensive but tasteful uphol-stery, leaped to the back of the couch, and did the same.

"Stop that!" The cat was living up to her mother's worst expectations—a state Marti was more than familiar with. If he'd done any lasting damage, there'd be hell to pay. "You'll lose your happy home!"

Bernard howled.

"You're late," the Girl said.

"Not my faul—" The Girl. The Girl had spoken. Instead of cowering in the corner, she stood in the center of the room, her hands on her hips.

She wore her usual bell-bottom jeans, but her gauzy blouse was different. Brighter. Perkier. Marti didn't know how an ethereal bit of fabric could be perky, but it was. Maybe it was the bright yellow sunflowers adorning the hem and sleeves. The embroidery looked hand-stitched.

"Hello," Marti said.

The Girl didn't vanish. Her attire wasn't all that had changed. Her long hair hung in two loose braids tied with red ribbons. Marti got her first good look at the Girl's face, which would have been lovely if not for her scowl. Ghost Girl was as pissed off as Bernard the Starving Cat.

One thing hadn't changed. Her wrists were encased in brightly colored plastic bangles. Odds were it wasn't Susan Silliphant whom Peter dug up.

"That man..." Whatever else the Girl had to say was drowned out by Bernard. If "that man" was Peter, no wonder she was ticked off.

"Let me take care of the cat," Marti said. "Don't go away."

The Girl went away.

"Crap."

Bernard clawed the couch.

"All right!" She went to her office, where Bernard's dishes sat in the corner.

The Girl sat behind the desk in Marti's chair. Her scowl remained. It had deepened and been joined with an air of defiance. Groovy Girl had her groove back. Or she'd found it. Since Marti didn't know her when she was alive, she couldn't tell which.

Once Bernard buried his nose in his all-natural chicken and tuna paté with extra gravy, Marti introduced herself.

"I'm Lilith," the Girl said. "My friends called me Lili. You may call me Lilith."

Okay then. "Did your parents give you that name or did you give it to yourself?" Marti hadn't attended church in decades, and her childhood Sunday School lessons never mentioned Lilith. But Marti knew she was reputedly Adam's first wife, expelled from the garden for refusing to be subservient to her husband. That and other stories about Lilith made the name popular for self-selection at the dawning of the age of Aquarius and free love. Marti didn't disapprove.

The outer door to the office opened.

"Marti! I told you to make it quick."

Dmitri was finally speaking to her. Or yelling at her. It was a start. She joined him in the front room. Lilith followed. Bernard stuck with his food.

"Oh, he's lovely," Lilith said. "Is he yours?"

"Janice says the gossip machine is fired up and running, but nothing you wouldn't expect." Grandma Bertie joined them. "Although there is already a betting pool on whether you, Rachel-Anne, or Winter Adams did Peter in."

"I haven't scooped the litter box yet," Marti said.

"Who's Peter?" Lilith said.

"Oh, so you're talking now," Grandma said.

"Where is it? I'll do it," Dmitri said.

Marti pointed at the door to the office storage closet. She'd had a discreet cat door installed, over her mother's objections. "Follow your nose," she said.

"Your name doesn't happen to be Susan, does it?" Grandma said.

"No," Lilith said. She didn't address Grandma Bertie with the same snot-ball attitude she'd shown Marti.

Dmitri opened the closet door.

"How about Charlotte?" Grandma said.

Lilith squealed and vanished.

"Wait! Come back!" Marti said.

Dmitri stopped and turned. "Why?"

Crapola. The morning had taken its toll. Her years of practice ignoring the chatter of the dead in the presence of the living had deserted her. In front of Dmitri. She couldn't tell if the look he gave her was distrust, disapproval, or dislike, but it clearly wasn't disinterest.

"Um, I'll do that. You need to get back to RachelAnne. Why did you leave her alone? What made you think *that* was a good idea?" Maybe she could distract him from her slip-up with indignation. Righteous indignation. He *shouldn't* have left her sister alone.

He wasn't distracted. "What's in here?"

"Office supplies. Bernard's little boys' room. Which I'll take care of." She pushed past him and pulled the litter scoop and a plastic baggy from a shelf. "You get back to my sister."

"I'll help."

The two of them barely fit inside the deep but narrow closet. Marti knelt and dealt with the litter box. Dmitri was so close all she could see were his knees.

"What's he looking for?" Grandma said.

"You think I have a murder weapon stashed in here?" Marti said.

"Don't be ridiculous," Dmitri said.

"Seriously, they already found *that,*" Grandma said.

The closet was crowded. Hot. The smell of the litter—both used and unused—turned Marti's stomach. Her head swam. Did Grandma or Big tell her about the hammer in RachelAnne's car? Maybe both? Or did she imagine it? *Better not mention it.* "All done." She tried to stand.

Her legs didn't work. "I'm stuck," she said.

Dmitri backed off, extended a hand, and helped her up. "Are you okay?"

She thought she saw a flicker of concern. A glimpse of the old Dmitri. Pre-vacation Dmitri. The Dmitri she thought was her friend.

He let go of her hand and returned to Dmitri the Stony-Faced Professional.

"Whatever did you do to piss him off?" Grandma said.

"I don't know," Marti said.

She made a quick check of the two-room office under the

guise of locking up. Other than Grandma, an impatient Dmitri, and herself, the only other occupant was Bernard. He lounged on the couch performing a post-breakfast butt wash.

"She's gone back into hiding, I think," Grandma said.

"Let's go," Dmitri said.

"I still can't believe you left my sister alone," Marti said. She set the alarm, and they left.

"I think I know who she is. It'll break Janice's heart," Grandma said.

The Lexus sat on the street right where Dmitri left it. Rachel-Anne, white as a sheet, slumped in the backseat. Lilith-Charlotte the Hippy Ghost Girl and Mrs. Heedly's possible broken heart were the least of Marti's worries.

ON THE DRIVE HOME, even Grandma Bertie had nothing to say. Things were indeed bad.

Marti expected them to get worse even before they went through the door of Bickle House. The last time the Mickklesons were connected to scandal, not to mention murder, the press descended in droves. A committee of vultures. She'd resisted running any of them down when she had the chance. It was too much to hope that Dmitri would show less self-restraint than she had.

The closer they got to the Avenue, the tenser she got. Her stomach did flip-flops. Her jaw muscles tied themselves into knots.

For nothing. The Avenue was empty. Dmitri turned onto the alley behind the houses.

Empty.

"Where are—" She didn't need to finish.

"Big hasn't released Peter's name or any details yet," Dmitri said. "They'll show up."

"Goody. Something to look forward to."

Dmitri grunted. Marti wondered how Dmitri managed to know so much about police business. The apparent bromance between him and the chief might explain Dmitri telling Big things. It didn't explain information flowing in the other direction. Or it shouldn't.

Someday, she'd ask him. She snuck a look at him. His profile was pure classic Roman sculpture. By that, she didn't mean the eye-candy factor, although Dmitri did possess that. In abundance. No, he looked carved from marble. Cold, hard stone. Maybe she wouldn't ask.

The lack of clamoring reporters did nothing to relieve her tension. The ache in her jaw spread to her temples. Her stomach did flips, somersaults, and tucks. Maybe a few handstands and springs. Tumbling for tummies. She was glad she hadn't eaten breakfast.

Coffee would still be a fine thing.

Dmitri parked the Lexus next to a discreet and classy black Cadillac sedan.

"We've got company," she said. "Maybe Mom dug up a criminal attorney instead of a divorce lawyer."

A howl came from the backseat. It wasn't Grandma. Rachel-Anne sobbed.

"Was that necessary?" Grandma said.

"Really, Marti?" Now Dmitri was channeling her mother. His voice dripped with pure Margaret Mickkleson-level disapproval.

She wasn't sure if they were reacting to her mention of lawyers or her poor choice of words. In retrospect, "dug up" probably wasn't the way to go.

To be fair, the last time she'd seen her sister cry this much she was four years old and Marti had filled her bed with plastic spiders.

Dmitri made her realize one thing. The pounding in her head

and the Olympic-caliber floor gymnastics going on in her midsection had nothing to do with fear of the press.

What awaited her inside the house was far worse than pushy reporters.

Mom needed to be told her daughters, both the good one and the bad, were very possibly murder suspects.

"I'd give anything for a bag of plastic spiders right now," Marti said.

"Sometimes I wonder about you," Dmitri said.

"Only sometimes?" She might be dense, but she could tell the difference between banter and disgust. Dmitri's tone and expression both suggested the latter.

Dmitri helped RachelAnne out of the backseat. He was as solicitous of her sister as he'd been earlier. Despite the situation, Marti felt a pang of envy.

"This has to stop," she said.

"What?" Dmitri said.

Marti didn't know if she meant Dmitri's entirely appropriate under the circumstances fawning over RachelAnne, her own entirely inappropriate in any circumstances jealousy, or both. She did know she hadn't meant to speak the words out loud.

Surprisingly, Grandma Bertie hadn't weighed in on the situation. The old ghost was gone. With any luck, she'd gone on a recon mission and would fill Marti in on the current Mom-mood. Or, she'd chickened out and gone off somewhere to play pinochle with Edwards. It could be a long game since neither could pick up or deal the cards.

"I'll take it from here." Marti took her sister's arm and pointed them both toward the back door.

"Are you sure?" Dmitri asked.

"Yes." Marti assumed the concern in his voice was for her sister, not for her. "Come on, Rach. One step at a time."

"I can do this." RachelAnne shook her off and moved forward unassisted. "And don't call me Rach."

Her sister's hair might have been a mess, her wrinkled clothes the same ones she'd worn the night before, her make-up nonexistent, and her face blotchy and tear-streaked, but her voice told Marti all she needed to know. RachelAnne had reconnected with her inner Mickkleson. Queen Margaret's heiress apparent was back and in charge.

For the moment.

Marti followed her sister.

"Marti?"

Dmitri said her name so softly, she wasn't entirely sure she hadn't imagined it. She stopped but didn't turn around.

"Be careful."

He sounded concerned, but she couldn't help but take his words as a warning.

"DID YOU BRING YOUR KEYS?" RachelAnne said.

"I never thought of them." Big hustled them off to the station so fast she barely had time to get dressed.

Marti wished she could do the eyebrow thing her sister and mother did so well. It was more eloquent than words. Rachel-Anne's eyebrows plainly said that although *she* had plenty of reason not to be thinking clearly, *Marti* should have done better.

Marti banged on the back door and waited.

And waited.

"Maybe she didn't hear." She banged again.

Mom didn't show up. "Maybe she's forgotten how to answer the door. Or that there's no help today to do it for her," Marti said.

"Don't be ridiculous." RachelAnne tapped politely on the door.

Back door, open. Back door, open. Electro-Harriet greeted them, unruffled as ever.

"It's about time." Mom's greeting was as terse as Harriet's was soothing. "Big called and said he sent you home some time ago."

"We had to stop and feed Bernard," Marti said.

Mom's eyebrows were even more fluent in the language of contempt than RachelAnne's. She'd had more practice.

Back door, open. Back door, open.

Marti and her sister stepped into the kitchen. Mom shut the door, and Harriet went back to sleep or whatever she did when not called into duty.

With Mom was a middle-aged man in an expensive-looking and well-tailored black suit. Another Man in Black. Marti didn't recognize him.

"Where are the kids?" RachelAnne said.

"Who is he?" Marti said at the same time.

Mom addressed RachelAnne first. To be fair, T3 and Maggie were more important than Marti's curiosity.

"Georgia agreed to come in to help today although it's not her week. We are discussing her taking over full-time. She's taken them to Silly Sam's or some such place. I thought it better they be out of the house for a while."

"Good plan," Marti said, although she wasn't so sure. She could have used a kid-hug or two, and she assumed RachelAnne was in more need than she was.

She hoped Georgia full-time worked out better than Winter part-time. At least Georgia wouldn't be messing around with the Mickkleson men. There weren't any left to mess around with.

The woman was a saint if she'd taken the kids to Silly Sam's. Marti's niece and nephew had her wrapped around their little fingers, and they couldn't get her into the den of bad food, arcade games, and animatronic squirrels. The hordes of sticky, noisy, sugar-hyped children were bad enough. Sam the Squirrel freaked her out.

The Man in Black hadn't moved. He silently clutched his briefcase.

After the reaction to her earlier mention of lawyers, Marti decided to take the cautious route. "I don't believe we've met." She was getting good at channeling her mother, and it paid off. Mom went into high-etiquette mode, far preferable to Marti-disapproval mode.

"Gerald, this is my oldest daughter, Marcile."

Marcile. Whoever he was, this wasn't a social visit.

"Marcile, Gerald Stoneyman. The Stoneymans have taken care of the Mickklesons for generations."

Taken care of? He didn't look like a nanny.

"I've heard a lot about you. I'm sorry we had to meet under such sad circumstances, an occupational hazard I'm afraid." His voice was as oily as his slicked-back hair. He stuck his hand out. Marti took it. His hand was warm and his grip firm. A handshake her late father would have approved of.

"We've been making arrangements," Mom said.

"Arrange—oh." Marti'd never been good at arithmetic, but she finally put two and two together. "Um...don't you need a body for that? I mean, there is a body, but there's also a murder investigation."

"Don't be ridiculous." Mom didn't bother with the eyebrows. Her voice said it all. "Mickklesons don't do viewings. There will be a short period for the public to pay their respects to Rachel-Anne, followed by a private memorial service and light refreshments here at the house. As we've always done."

Marti missed her father's funeral since she didn't know he'd died until he reentered her life a month later. Great-grandma Bertie went at the age of ninety-two in a freak canoeing accident the day before Marti was born. She was too young when her grandparents died to remember them, let alone their being laid to rest. Since they'd never haunted her, she assumed they were at rest. She had no idea what the Mickklesons had "always done."

The last funeral she attended was Mrs. Heedly's, and she'd only gone to that one out of spite.

"Does RachelAnne get a say in this?"

"It's fine," her sister said. "Did you choose a date?"

"As soon as I can book the caterer," Mom said.

Marti wondered how she could be related to the two women. She and they were from different planets.

"Call me once you decide." Gerald Stoneyman sidled toward the door. "Marcile, it's been a pleasure. RachelAnne, my deepest condolences. Mrs. Mickkleson, please call me with any concerns or questions. Now, I need to be getting back." The funeral director stopped just short of a courtly bow and made a gracious exit. Or an expeditious exit.

Marti wished she could go with him.

"I want to hear exactly what you two were up to last night," Mom said.

"So, Mom," Marti said. "Philippa Berryman? Have you found us a real lawyer yet? Rumor has it we might need one."

CHAPTER

TWELVE

TELLING the kids their father wasn't coming back was as bad as Marti thought it would be. Worse.

When Georgia brought the kids home, she offered to stay and make dinner. Marti was ready to take her up on the offer, but Mom graciously thanked her and sent her on her way. They ended up with peanut butter sandwiches, most of which went into the trash. No one had an appetite.

After their non-dinner, Marti, RachelAnne, Mom, Grandma Bertie, and the kids gathered in the parlor. Maya joined them. Mom didn't comment. Edward had promised to keep Amity busy in the farthest corner of the house. The bratty little ghost was the last thing Marti needed at the moment.

While the kids were gone, RachelAnne had showered, dressed, done her hair, and applied makeup. Other than her swollen red eyes and nose, which no amount of concealer could hide, she was as immaculate as ever. Her posture had returned to normal. Marti suspected it was armor.

The kids sat cross-legged on the floor and didn't make a peep. Entirely unlike them. They knew something was wrong. Kids always do. If they didn't, the dark and silent television would have given it away. They didn't even ask about the prancing ponies.

RachelAnne relayed the news to her children in simple and appropriate terms, leaving out details. She remained calm and projected strength and reassurance. Marti was in awe.

T3 went stiff. Marti waited for tears, but they didn't happen. She reached for him. "T3—"

"Thaddeus." He moved just out of her reach. "I'm the man of the family now."

Marti held her breath and fought off her own tears. Mom wasn't so successful. She choked, and a waterfall ran down her cheeks. RachelAnne held out her arms. T3 ran to her but stopped short of hurling himself into her embrace. He veered off and took his place at her side, looking as much like a miniature version of Gerald Stoneyman as a seven-year-old could.

"Aunt Marti?" Maggie tugged at her sleeve. "Daddy says he wants to go home now."

Marti lifted her niece into her lap. "Oh, honey. I wish that could happen, but it can't." One little lie to soften the truth.

"He says the yady can help."

Marti couldn't help herself. She looked at her great-grandmother. "What?"

"I haven't seen him," Grandma Bertie said.

Maya meowed.

"When did he tell you that?" Marti turned her attention back to Maggie.

"I couldn't do anything if I had," Grandma said. "And if I could, I wouldn't."

"This morning." Maggie stuck her thumb in her mouth.

"On the phone?" Not possible, but Marti had to ask.

"Well, maybe for the kids I would," Grandma said.

T3 finally broke. Tears ran down his cheeks. He leaned against his mother. It was hard to tell whether he was looking for support or trying to provide it.

"In my room," Maggie said.

Marti's heart fell. Peter as a ghost was worse than the idea of Peter dead. That thought probably made her a bad person, but having dealt with spirits as long as she could remember, experience told her it was true.

"I haven't seen him. Of course, that doesn't mean he hasn't seen me," Grandma said.

Maya meowed again.

Marti groaned. This was too much to deal with, especially with an audience of the living.

Mom stopped crying. She pinched her lips and laser-focused her attention on Marti and Maggie. Or maybe on Maya, who'd decided to use Marti's legs as a scratching post. She winced and pushed the little cat away.

How much had her mother heard? Maggie had barely spoken above a whisper, and Marti answered in kind. Mom couldn't hear Grandma Bertie. But Mom had that "I know everything and I want an explanation" expression Marti remembered so well from her childhood.

Or maybe Marti was projecting, and it was just her mother's return to standard demeanor. Whichever, the best way to handle it was to pretend she hadn't noticed and keep going, one of her favorite survival strategies.

Mom apparently decided to take the same tack. "RachelAnne? Would you like me to take the children upstairs and put them to bed?"

"I'll do it myself." RachelAnne got up and held her hand out to Maggie.

Marti gave her niece one last hug and whispered, "It'll be all right." It wouldn't, but it was the only thing she had.

RachelAnne led her children away. Maya followed.

Left alone with her mother, Marti braced herself for a confrontation. Not just over her exchange with Maggie. A lot had happened over the last twenty-four hours, and Marti was sure her mother thought she hadn't heard all of it, which was true.

She didn't have to wait long.

"So. Marcile—"

Big Ben pealed. Someone was at the front door. Marti wanted to be grateful for the interruption, but it scared her. The only person she might be happy to see was Dmitri, and that was iffy. Besides, he always used the back door. She grabbed the remote. Both she and Mom knew better than to answer any door before finding out who was on the other side.

The television sprang to life. Marti clicked on the security feed. "Did you find a defense lawyer or is it still Philippa? Family time looks like it's over."

"He wouldn't arrest RachelAnne in front of her children. Not tonight. I won't permit it," Mom said.

Big reached out, and Big Ben tolled again.

MARTI USHERED Big into the formal sitting room. For once, she understood and agreed with her mother's hierarchy for Bickle House visitors. No way would Mom let the police chief arrest her daughters in the warm comfort of the family parlor.

"Have a seat," she said.

Big surveyed the antique furniture. "I'll stand," he said.

Probably a wise decision, considering his earlier experience stuffing his enormous form into one of the small and fragile-looking chairs. Or it could be a power play. If he was going to arrest anyone, better to do it while towering over them.

"Why are you here?" Marti had no patience left for small talk. Did cops make small talk with suspects? It didn't matter. The direct approach was the best approach.

"I need to talk to RachelAnne." Big shifted his mass from foot to foot.

"She's unavailable right now. I'll have to do." Was his fidgeting a good sign or a bad sign? He could simply be nervous about arresting a Mighty Mighty Mickkleson or two. It would be a first for Bicklesburg. The Judge died before his misdeeds were public. She and her sister were innocent, but she was still a teensy-weensy bit envious of her father's timely exit.

"No offense," Big said, "but—"

No offense was a sure sign he was about to be offensive. She was in no mood.

"Listen up, big guy. Over the past—what, forty-eight hours?—my sister found out her husband was cheating with the babysitter, left him, was attacked by him, found out he was dead—murdered—and got hauled into your crummy police station and interrogated by you and your goons. To top it all off, she had to tell her children their father isn't ever coming home. He may not have been much of a father—he certainly wasn't much of a husband—but he was their daddy. She's with the kids now and you're not going near her. If you want to talk to or arrest or beat out a confession or whatever tonight, it's going to have to be me. And I'm not going anywhere without a good explanation. And a lawyer." Marti ran out of breath. She reloaded to continue.

"I'm so proud." A round of applause accompanied Grandma Bertie's praise.

Ghosts can't clap, not audibly.

"Well done," Mom said.

Marti hadn't noticed their arrival. She was too busy channeling her mother for—she'd lost count of how many times in the past two days.

"Sometimes, I forget you're a Mickkleson. Then you remind me," Big said. It wasn't a compliment.

This had to stop. She was turning into someone she didn't recognize.

"Ferguson," Grandma said. "She gets it from my side of the family."

"I didn't interrogate your sister. And I'm not here to arrest either one of you," Big said.

"Then tell me just exactly why you are here." Marti was on a roll. No sense in wasting the steam she had left.

Big stared. His towering bulk deflated. "Mickklesons." He made it sound like a swear.

"I heard that." Mom sounded like Grandma Bertie.

"Fergusons," Grandma said.

"I must have fallen down the rabbit hole." Maybe later she could pry the key to the good liquor cabinet out of her sister. Or not. This conversation was already making her head spin.

"You and me both," Big said. Apparently, he got that literary reference. "Why don't you take a seat and I'll explain. Mrs. Mickkleson, can you give us the room?"

"No." Mom plopped herself into the Louis XV bergère Big had occupied that morning. She fit the chair better than he had, but the plop rather than her usual graceful descent disturbed Marti. How deep was this rabbit hole?

"I'll sit if you sit," Marti said. She wasn't giving up the higher ground. Or as close to higher as she could get next to Big. But, as long as he wasn't arresting anybody, she'd give him one concession. Two concessions. "I'll take the chair. You get the couch." Not much of a concession, since the couch was more uncomfortable than the chairs, but it wouldn't take a shoehorn and a winch to get him out.

She stood in front of the twin to her mother's chair. Big stood in front of the settee. She wasn't about to lower her butt until he did. "I can stand here all night," she said.

"I give up." Big carefully lowered himself onto the seat.

Marti'd never noticed—she spent as little time in the awful room as possible—but the couch was lower to the ground than the chairs. Big looked like he was at the child's table at a party. She and her mother, the adults in the room, looked down at him.

So this is what a power play felt like. Nobody expects the Mick-kleson inquisition.

"First, if I was going to arrest you, do you really think I'd come alone?" Big had a little spunk left.

Marti didn't answer. Neither did Mom. Grandma snickered, but Marti was the only one who heard.

"I only came to update your sister on where we are in the investigation. And explain why we're not arresting you both. Yet."

"Begin," Marti said. She'd have to call in an exorcist if Mom's voice kept coming out of her mouth.

BIG BEGAN with all the reasons he should arrest them. All the reasons making her and RachelAnne the infamous "persons of interest." Marti tried not to interrupt.

"Motive galore. He was cheating on RachelAnne. He tried to assault her."

"How do you know about that?" So much for not interrupting. His buddy Dmitri might have told him about Peter's visit to Bickle House, but as far as she knew, only she and RachelAnne knew about Peter's attempted assault on her sister. Grandma and Peter knew, but they weren't talking. Not to Big.

"I didn't know about it." Mom no longer sounded like Grandma Bertie. Full-strength Margaret Mickkleson was back. Her tone said she'd have hired a hitman herself if she'd known.

"Probably the only reason Big's not arresting her," Grandma said.

"I'll get to that," Big said. "Then there's the ever-popular divorce and money motive. If Peter died while they were married, RachelAnne would get everything rather than half."

"Half?" Mom said. "She'd have had everything by the time I was through with him."

Marti didn't need to interrupt. She'd sit back and let Mom do it for her.

"He wouldn't have had a pot to piss in." Now Grandma sounded like Edwards. Marti thought longingly of the liquor cabinet.

"I have no doubt," Big said. "However, when Peter was drinking in the Starlite Lounge last night, he was bragging about his connections and a lawyer from the city. He said if RachelAnne insisted on divorce, by the time he was finished, RachelAnne would have nothing, not even the kids, and he might end up with Bickle House. Philippa Berryman was a lightweight, and he was calling in a heavyweight champ."

"How would we know about that?" Big freely sharing so much information was unnerving, but Marti was game. "And how did he know about Philippa?"

"No idea, other than this is Bicklesburg," Big said.

"Let's forget about motive," Marti said. "I admit, everybody but the kids had motives. Is there any real evidence my sister and I are Bicklesburg's answers to the Menendez brothers?"

"The probable murder weapon was found in RachelAnne's vehicle—"

"Do you seriously think my daughters are that stupid?"

"Mrs. Mickkleson. If you keep interrupting, we'll never get to why I'm not arresting them. Yet."

The corner of Big's mouth twitched. He was enjoying the opportunity to tell Margaret Mickkleson to shut up, even if he didn't use those exact words. Marti empathized.

"Why don't we just skip the reasons for hanging us and get to the reasons for not hanging us? Yet." There couldn't be much more than ample motive and one little ball-peen hammer against them.

Big calmly laid out the case against arresting them, which was better than listening to him list the reasons he should arrest them.

"First." Big held up one finger. "The lab reports aren't all back yet, but the hammer shows...signs...of being used on Peter. However, it had been wiped clean of fingerprints. And no, Mrs. Mickkleson. I may think a lot of things about your daughters, but stupid isn't one of them."

Mom replied with an elegant "humph." She was the only person Marti knew who could manage that combination.

"Second, you put on quite a show. RachelAnne's neighbors saw the exchange between the two of you and Peter—"

"We're calling it an 'exchange'? It was assault."

"If you'll let me finish, these are supposed to be the reasons I'm not taking you in. Yet."

There was that "yet" again. Was he keeping his options open or doing it to needle her?

"They confirm Peter was alive when you peeled out of there like a bat out of hell with RachelAnne in the car."

A wave of love for the residents of Paradise Sanctuary Boulevard washed over Marti. Well, maybe a light sprinkle of fondness.

"Third, the cashier at the KwikiMart confirms your stop there. She can't confirm RachelAnne was out in the car, and she was vague about the time, but she called Dawn when you left. Dawn confirmed the time."

"Dawn Pernelli? *Dawn?*" If Dawn Pernelli had provided her with an alibi, the world truly was off its axis. Or pod-people had invaded Bicklesburg. Or something.

Big ignored her.

"Fourth, the neighbors say Peter had more visitors. They thought you were back for an encore and were disappointed when this batch was quiet. When there weren't any more fireworks, they went to bed."

"So they missed the main show," Marti said.

"You can't even count on nosey neighbors," Grandma said.

"I didn't say that," Big said. "But they didn't report anything else out of the ordinary. And that's it. That's why you get to sleep in your own bed. For tonight, anyway."

"You've only used four fingers. Can't you come up with something else? Like you know my sister and I couldn't possibly be murderers?"

"I find it hard to picture RachelAnne as a killer," Big said. "I have some questions to follow up on your statement this morning. How long were you and RachelAnne at Henrietta's Hollow?"

"Um, long enough to finish three bags of Oreos?" Marti had no idea how long they stayed.

"You can't do better than that?"

She shook her head in the negative.

"What time did you get home?"

Marti didn't know that either. "Honestly, we came in, saw the Rémy, and after that, everything's pretty much a blur until you showed up the next morning. I'm not sure how I got up to bed."

"There was crawling involved," Grandma said. "It was like old times. Sadly."

"Is there anything else you can remember or might have left out of what you told me previously?"

Marti bristled. "I told you everyth...wait. Winter Adams."

"Winter? How does that poor girl fit into this? Other than—"

"Don't call her 'that poor girl.' After Baby Face, I mean Rodney, called, I went to get Peter." If she'd gone with her instinct and left him at the police station, they wouldn't be in this position. "Someone followed me from the time I pulled off the Avenue. They pulled in beside me at the station. It was Winter. As soon as she saw me, she took off. How did she know Peter was there? I only knew because I answered RachelAnne's phone."

"Hmmm." Big pulled a small spiral notepad out of his pocket and wrote in it. The chief was old-school.

It dawned on Marti that her mother had been uncharacteristically quiet. Right on cue, a loud snore rattled the room. Mom had fallen asleep in her chair.

"She must be more comfortable in that thing than I was," Big said.

"You didn't see or hear that, and I think we're done for the night," Marti said. Her mother would be humiliated at Big seeing her splayed in the chair snoring. Marti wasn't above filing it away and using it at some future point, but it was no business of Big's.

She showed him out.

"You know," he said. "You've been back five months, and so far we've had more murders than this town's seen in ten years. Combine that with the ghost thing, and are you sure you're not a character from a horror movie?"

"Good night, Big." She shut the door. He had a point, but she wasn't going to give it to him.

MOM WAS AWAKE. "Why is it so cold in here?" She hugged herself and shivered

Grandma put on her best *I don't know what you're talking about and if I did, I'm innocent* face.

Marti wasn't buying it, but there was nothing she could say in front of Mom. "It's been a long day. I think we both need some rest. I'm going to bed."

Mom agreed, and they both went upstairs.

CHAPTER

THIRTEEN

EVEN AFTER FIVE MONTHS, Marti wasn't used to being back in her childhood bedroom. It still looked the way she left it when she ran away, other than a few slight upgrades. Her goth girl posters hung in frames rather than being stuck to the wall with blue putty. The books on her shelf were arranged by spine height and color—which made her shudder—and her collection of dancing skeletons was lined up precisely on her desk.

The only change she'd made was to put her beloved quilt on the bed, hidden under the new black bedspread that had taken up residence while she was gone. Marti'd had the quilt as long as she could remember, and it was well-worn. Mom had tried to get rid of it numerous times before Marti left, but she always rescued it. It was the only non-clothes thing she took when she left. She'd carted it from town to town, from crappy apartment to crappy apartment.

Other than the hidden quilt, the room was the Museum of Marti, and it creeped her out.

"You know, you could do something about making this room your own," Grandma said. "You've been here long enough."

"First, it is me. Young me, but still me. Second, that would imply I'm staying."

"Ha. You're settling in well. The job at the Foundation. As close as I've ever seen to getting along with your mother. You and RachelAnne are becoming, dare I say it, friends."

"Have you seen the size of that trust fund The Judge left? I just want the big bucks." Not true. Well, not entirely true. She did want the money, but she found herself sort of maybe actually caring about her family. Just a little bit. After a decade of cutting them out of her life, the feeling was disconcerting.

"What about your young man?"

"For the umpteenth time, he's not my young man." Dmitri avoiding her was probably for the best. Sooner or later, Rachel-Anne would recover from Peter—both Live-Peter and Dead-Peter —and return to her old ways. Mom, well who knew what Mom would do? Marti and her mother and sister would return to their normal relationship, the one in which Marti was a constant source of disappointment for all involved. As long as the current peace lasted another month, and she and RachelAnne didn't end up in jail, she could leave and everyone could live happily ever after.

She might come back to visit Maggie and T3.

"Come on. You've adopted a cat," Grandma said.

"Bernard can come with me. Us." Right on cue, there was a scratching at the door. Marti opened it, and in sauntered Maya. "Not you. You have to stay here."

Maya jumped on the bed, blinked, and stared expectantly at Marti.

"Are you going to your office tomorrow?"

"The office. It's not 'mine.'" Best to start cutting ties now. "And we'll see. I should go check on Bernard. Why?"

Maya stretched and flexed her claws. Maybe she didn't like talk of another cat. Marti sat down next to her.

"I'm pretty sure I know who Ghost Girl and the skeleton in Peter's hole is," Grandma said.

"Way ahead of you on that one. They're one and the same."

"Yes, but do you know who—"

"Lilith. Charlotte. Mrs. Heedly's mysterious little sister," Marti said. "I figured it out a long time ago."

"Were you planning on mentioning it?"

"Well, I have had a few other things on my mind. Besides, I wanted to be sure. You get to tell your buddy." She'd dealt with a wailing Mrs. Heedly once and wasn't about to do it again. "We found her sister. I'm out of it."

"I'd hardly let you do it, Ms. Sensitivity. I do have a question. If Charlotte—"

"She prefers to be called Lilith."

"If Charlotte was buried in Henrietta's Hollow, why's she haunting your office? Explain that, Ms. Smarty Pants."

A good question, but Marti wasn't going to give the old ghost the satisfaction of admitting it. "I'm more worried about how Peter ended up in that hole with her, being the sensitive smarty pants I obviously am."

"Miau."

"You want scritches?" Marti waggled her fingers at the little cat. Out shot a paw, claws bared.

"Ouch!"

"Guess she doesn't," Grandma said.

"She drew blood!"

"Don't be a baby. It's barely a drop. That cat's trying to tell you something."

"I don't speak cat." Marti yawned. Maya licked the offending paw.

"Neither do I."

"You know, instead of hanging around here keeping me awake, why aren't you in Maggie's room keeping an eye out for Peter or what's left of him?" Ghosts didn't sleep, but if Marti didn't get some shut-eye soon, she would keel over.

"Good plan." Grandma floated away through the door.

Maya jumped to the floor and followed. Unlike Grandma, she was stopped by the closed door. She sat in front of it and glared. Her whole attitude said, "Peon. Get off of that bed and do the thing. Now."

"I may not speak cat, but are you sure you're not related to my mother?" Marti opened the door, and Maya strolled away.

BREAKFAST, such as it was, was a subdued affair. The kids played with their sugary cereal. They didn't make their usual mess, but they didn't eat either. RachelAnne wrapped her hands around her coffee cup so hard her knuckles turned white. The cold toast in front of her was nearly as disgusting as the kids' cereal congealing in their bowls.

Marti concentrated on getting her first cup of coffee down so she could move on to her second. Nothing unusual there.

Mom must have gotten up at the crack of dawn o'thirty. Impeccably dressed, coiffed, and made up, she had no right looking as chipper as she did. "What are your plans for today?" she said.

RachelAnne shrugged.

"Are we going to school?" T3 lifted a spoonful of coagulated Chocolate Cinnamon Oaty Puffs, examined it, and dumped it back in his bowl. Wise move.

"Not today," RachelAnne said.

"What about Daddy?" Maggie slid out of her seat and leaned against her mother. RachelAnne answered with a hug, but that was it.

"He never showed up while I was standing guard," Grandma said.

As long as Grandma hadn't snuck off for a game of pinochle with Edwards, Dead-Peter hadn't visited his daughter. She probably hadn't. She'd been guarding her great-great-granddaughter, and Marti knew from experience Great Grandma Bertie turned into a pit bull where granddaughters were concerned. Maybe Peter had moved on to that great used car lot in the hereafter. Marti could only hope.

"Marti?" Mom spread blackberry jam on a perfect triangle of toast.

"I should go check on Bernard." She drained her mug and got up to get a refill.

"If you'd hired an assistant, they could have taken care of that."

Mom's familiar disapproval, a sign of Mickkleson normalcy, was a comfort. Except…"Oh, crap."

"Language," Mom said. "The children are present."

"Daddy says worse," Maggie said.

"Your Aunt Marti does too," Grandma said.

Marti pulled out her phone and checked her office email. She'd offered each of her would-be assistants' interview times on Thursday. Either she'd know right away whom she would hire, would let them know on Friday, and could mark 'hire assistant" off her to-do list, or she'd have the weekend to recover, make up her mind, or both. It was Thursday, and they'd all accepted.

"Crappity-crap-crap-crap. I'm supposed to interview four applicants this afternoon." She had no idea how to conduct a job interview. She didn't know what she could legally say or ask, something she needed to be sure of before talking to Dawn Pernelli. She'd planned on hitting the internet for research, but that plan had gone out the window over the past couple of days. "Maybe, in light of the circumstances I can call them and reschedule."

"Nonsense," Mom said. "Mickklesons carry on. Have you arranged for background checks?"

"Um, of course." It hadn't dawned on her.

"Talk to Dmitri," RachelAnne said. "You can use the same firm he uses for ACS hires."

All of the employees of the Avenue's private security—all

three of them—were Bicklesburg-born and -bred. Their backgrounds were common knowledge, and the only one with a hint of disrepute was Dmitri, but okay. Marti thanked her sister.

"Before you go to the office, you need to talk to your sister."

"About what? Oh." RachelAnne needed to be told about Big's visit. Since Mom slept through half of it, Marti was on deck.

"Come, children. Ponies."

The kids followed Mom out of the kitchen. They lacked their usual exuberance. Much to Marti's relief, Grandma went with them. She didn't need the old ghost supplying editorial comments while she updated RachelAnne.

Marti filled her sister in on everything Big said the night before. She kept her own editorial comments to a minimum. Just the facts, ma'am. Just the facts.

"So, we're not going to be arrested," RachelAnne said.

"Yet. He made that very clear, but no. It sounds like they have other avenues of inquiry, as they say."

"You know, I could have killed him." Her sister attempted to pick up her coffee. Her hand shook so badly that she set the mug back on the counter.

"No, you couldn't. You were with me. I would have noticed if you committed murder. In this case, I might have cheered you on, but your greatest crime was hogging the Oreos."

"No. I mean if I'd had the hammer and you hadn't dragged me away, I *could* have killed him. I wanted to."

"Oh. Well. Me too, but if I killed the jerk, I wouldn't stash the murder weapon in your car. Unless you'd really pissed me off somehow, and you haven't done that lately. Not for a week or two."

RachelAnne's lips quivered. Marti hoped she wasn't going to cry. Nope. A full-blown smile lit up her sister's face.

"If you had a car of your own, I would have stashed the hammer there. Then I could keep control of your trust fund."

"Are you serious?"

"No." RachelAnne's smile evaporated. "I need to go into the office today too."

"I think you are currently exempt from that 'Mickklesons carry on' thing."

"I need to talk to Benjamin. Peter took care of all of our finances. Other than what's in my personal checking account, I have no idea where I stand. Financially. The kids and I can't stay here forever, and we're not going back to that house."

"You need to do that today?"

"Yes, I need to know."

"Intruder alert! Intruder alert!" Amity did her best imitation of Electro-Harriet the Alarm Lady.

Edwards was right behind her. "Peter's been spotted in the attic."

"He's a dirtbag," Amity said.

"Excuse me." Marti raced from the room. She'd come up with an explanation later. This was her chance to get answers. If Peter could—or would—tell her who killed him, she could point Big in the right direction and get rid of that "yet."

By the time she made it to the fourth floor, she was not only out of breath, the only ghosts to be seen were Amity and Edwards. Without three flights of stairs to deal with, they'd beaten her to the attic.

"He's skedaddled," Edwards said.

BERNARD GREETED HER WITH A YOWL.

"He was fine until you got here," Charlotte-Lilith said.

"He's a drama queen." The cat flopped on the floor at Marti's feet, obviously weak, starving, and near death. "You can't even see the bottom of your food bowl." She'd left him enough dry food and water to survive a week, although she would never leave him alone that long.

He yowled again.

"You're more trouble than you're worth." She refilled the dry food and opened a can of the good stuff.

"He did save your life." Charlotte-Lilith lounged on the sofa and examined her nails.

"You speak cat?" Grandma didn't, but that didn't mean other ghosts couldn't. The girl might have been some sort of cat whisperer when she was alive.

"Nah. Your grandma told me. Where is the old bat anyway?"

Grandma Bertie'd headed straight for the Green, intent on telling Janice Heedly they'd found her sister, although the news wasn't exactly good. Marti suggested they wait until they were one hundred percent sure, but Grandma disagreed. It wasn't like Mrs. Heedly would have a heart attack if they were wrong. That ship sailed years ago.

"Charlotte—"

"Lilith."

"Fine. Lilith. Do you—or did you—happen to have a sister named Janice?" If the skeleton in Peter's hole belonged to Ghost Girl, she died long before Janice Monahan became Janice Heedly.

Lilith's eyes widened. She paled and wavered and was gone. So much for her new attitude. One mention of Janice Heedly, and she was out of there. Marti took it as confirmation of their relationship. Mrs. Heedly had the same effect on her. Marti just didn't have the same means for a quick exit.

"So Bernard, it's just you and me."

Bernard cleaned his whiskers, turned his back to her, and struck a cat-yoga pose.

A spiritless morning was a luxury Marti didn't often have, and she had work to do. She opened her laptop and typed "how to interview an administrative assistant" into the search bar.

"Fake it till you make it," she said.

Bernard cleaned his butt.

"I DON'T KNOW how you can eat that stuff." Grandma Bertie arrived at the office as Marti finished the peanut butter and dill pickle sandwich she'd brought for lunch. "Where's Charlotte?"

"Peanut butter goes with everything. Lilith. She goes by Lilith now. How did Mrs. Heedly take the news? Better than Lilith, I hope? She evaporated at the mention of her sister." Come to think about it, Mrs. Heedly evaporating might not be such a bad thing. Except Grandma would miss her. And hang out all day in the office annoying Marti. Not good.

"It's hard to tell with her. You have peanut butter on your nose. What time's your first interview?"

Marti checked her watch. "Crap. Fifteen minutes." She'd lost track of time, but her morning research had her halfway prepared for what was to come. She hoped.

"The peanut butter lends a nice professional air to your image," Grandma said.

Marti spent the next ten minutes washing her face, reapplying make-up, and doing everything she could to turn herself into her best imitation of a Mickkleson Woman. She had a long way to go to hit Mom or RachelAnne's level, but she didn't have peanut butter on her nose.

She left the powder room to find a petite silver-haired woman in a navy blue power suit waiting in the front room.

Sandra Booth was right on time for her interview.

CHAPTER

FOURTEEN

MARTI CONSULTED the list of questions she'd printed from a website. "Why do you think you're well-suited for a position as an administrative assistant, and for a job at The Mickkleson Foundation in particular?"

The tiny woman sitting across from her was a surprise. Her resumé gave no solid indication of her age, nor should it have. Marti guessed somewhere between late sixties and early seventies, much older than she expected for an applicant for an administrative assistant.

She forgot about Sandra Booth's age once they started talking. Marti liked her.

Sandra—she'd already asked Marti to call her by her first name—rattled off the list of qualifications from her application, the ones that made Marti decide to interview her in the first place. She had extensive experience at nonprofits, something the other applicants lacked.

Marti watched more than she listened. She could swear they'd met before, but that wasn't possible according to what Sandra told her during the getting-to-know-you phase of the interview. She spent most of her life in another state. Miles away and no place Marti had ever visited. Sandra'd only recently moved to Bicklesburg.

"Wonderful," Marti said. Sandra had stopped talking and watched Marti expectantly. She'd missed most of Sandra's answer. Time to fake it. "Just out of curiosity, what brought you to Bicklesburg?"

"When my husband passed, I wanted a fresh start—but not too fresh. I spent some time here when I was young, so I knew a little about the town and thought I'd get reacquainted."

Marti wanted to ask how young, but that was probably beyond the scope of acceptable, and Sandra didn't offer the information. The chances of them having met were slim. Marti wound up the interview, thanked Sandra, and showed her to the door.

"I'll get back to you as soon as interviews are complete and I've made my decision." The woman was well qualified. Whatever made her so familiar made Marti like her more. Sandra Booth was by far the leading candidate for the job. Marti fought the urge to offer her the job on the spot. With three more candidates, best not to. Two more, since chances of her hiring Dawn fell in the slim to none category. Why had she thought interviewing her was a good idea?

They shook hands, and Sandra left.

"I liked her," Grandma said. She'd promised to stay quiet while Marti was interviewing and, so far, had kept her promise.

"Did she look familiar to you? I could swear I know her from somewhere."

"Mrs. Partridge." Grandma didn't hesitate before replying.

"Of course!"

Mrs. Partridge was the Mickklesons' housekeeper when Marti and RachelAnne were growing up. She not only kept Bickle House running like a well-oiled machine, she picked up the girls from school, ran them to the many activities they were enrolled in whether they liked it or not, bandaged scraped knees, fed them homemade cookies, and applied hugs as needed. She was the only living adult who always made Marti feel loved no matter what. Even Grandma adored her.

If Mrs. Partridge had worn a power suit instead of an apron, Sandra would be her double. A definite point in Sandra Booth's favor.

~

FAUSTYN ANGUISH LOOKED FAMILIAR TOO, but Marti knew why. Based on his name, Marti half expected Lurch from the Addams family. The dapper gentleman sitting on the other side of her desk was about as far away from Lurch as he could be. If Burgess Meredith, in his later years, and Leslie Jordan had gotten together and had an offspring, that son would be the man before her.

Faustyn looked to be in his mid-to-late forties and managed to convey the gravitas of Meredith while sparkling with the charm and wit Jordan was famous for. He would certainly brighten up the office. Marti would enjoy working with him.

She consulted her list of questions and his resumé. He had extensive experience, but none of it with nonprofits. Something about him made her confident enough to go a little off-script. "Why do you think you're well-suited for a position in a nonprofit organization and for a job at The Mickkleson Foundation in particular?"

"Although my experience was with law firms, the technical skills should be about the same, and frankly, I excel at those. Microsoft Office bows to my every command."

Marti wondered if the puns were intentional. She bet they were and suppressed her smile, which was hard to do with Grandma laughing. Marti made a note to send her to check on Mrs. Heedly before the next interview. Grandma Bertie's good behavior had its limits.

"If there's anything I've learned from years of working with attorneys, it's organization, time management, and discretion.

Because of the variety of law firms I've worked for, I'm comfortable dealing with a wide range of clientele."

So far, skills-wise, he'd said nothing to set him apart from or above Sandra Booth.

"As for the Mickkleson Foundation in particular, on a purely practical level, it'll reduce my daily commute from over an hour each way to about twenty minutes."

He lived in Edgecastle, rather than Bicklesburg. Edgecastle wasn't on the edge of anything, nor did it possess a castle. It was in the county, which was good for a local foundation. It was mostly out of range of the Bicklesburg gossip network, also good. Marti wondered if she was legally allowed to factor that into her decision. If she didn't tell anyone, who would know?

"Having been born and bred in this county, I'm entranced by the opportunity to help give something back. And frankly, considering some of my former employers, being part of the Mickkleson Foundation and your stated mission is a chance to balance my karmic scales while I still have the chance."

His resumé showed three years at Clark, Broom, & Grubb, LPA—the most infamous ambulance chasers in the state. Their billboards and ads were everywhere and promised no matter what your issues, they'd make someone pay.

Marti checked the time. As much as she enjoyed talking to Faustyn Anguish, she needed to wrap things up or she wouldn't get the fifteen-minute break she'd allotted herself between interviews.

"Finally, do you have any questions for me?"

"Just one. May I see that?" He tilted his head toward the coffee station.

"Of course."

His eyes lit up.

He trembled as they stood at the counter. "Is that a De'Longhi—"

"Yes."

"Ooooo. Have you named her yet?"

"Not yet." It wasn't a bad idea. "Would you like to try it?"

He backed away. "Not yet. I'll save that for when I come back."

He was pretty confident, but the awe in his voice marked him as a fellow coffee aficionado. Or addict. Either one was a point in his favor.

She thanked him and ushered him through the outer room of the office with the same promise she made Sandra Booth. Good thing she hadn't offered Sandra the job on the spot. The decision was going to be tougher than she thought.

The main door flew open. A whirlwind blew in and barreled straight into Faustyn. Marti caught him before he hit the floor, barely avoiding going down herself.

The cyclone bounced back and dropped something. It hit the floor with a hollow thump. A briefcase. From the way it bounced, it was likely empty.

"I'm sorry. Am I late? I didn't want to be late. Did I hurt you? I know first aid. Maybe you should sit down. I don't have a first aid kit with me but I bet I can find you a glass of water. Is there a kitchen here or should I run down to the pizza place? What time is it? I don't want to be late..." The young woman ran down.

The very young woman. Almost a girl.

Marti wondered if she'd looked that young when she graduated high school. She wondered if she ever looked that young.

"That's one way to take out the competition." Faustyn righted himself and straightened his jacket. "But probably not the best. I'm fine. Are you okay?"

"I'm good, but —"

"Ah, the resilience of youth." Faustyn smoothly cut her off before she could rev up again. People skills indeed.

"Emmy Penny, I presume?" Marti said. Her next interview was early. She wasn't going to get her break.

Emmy Penny's interview didn't take long. Once they got started, the girl's answers to Marti's questions were concise and to the point. She'd probably spent her time since being offered the interview practicing and rehearsing, which wasn't a bad thing. She might have used the same list of questions from the web Marti was using.

Despite their rough start, Marti liked the young woman, but she was woefully inexperienced. Since Marti's prior job experience was in the fast food industry, one of them needed to know what they were doing. She finished her list of questions and again went off script.

"In this job, you will find yourself dealing with a wide array of people. My mother, for instance. Have you ever met Margaret Mickkleson?"

Emmy blanched. "No ma'am, but maybe she's not as bad as they say? I mean, they say a lot of things about you too, and you're not as…" She clapped her hand over her mouth and went from ashen to lobster in an instant.

"She's adorable," Grandma said. "I like her."

Marti couldn't help herself. She burst out laughing.

Emmy looked like she was about to cry.

"No—don't worry about it," Marti said. "I know what they say. Trust me, I've heard it all. But, out in the working world, you're going to need to install a filter between your head and your mouth. Again, trust me. I've been there." She'd lost plenty of minimum wage service jobs due to her lack of filter, one of the reasons she spent most of her fast food career sweating over hot grills rather than dealing with customers.

"I'm so sorry," Emmy said. "I blew it, didn't I?"

"So eager to please. Like a puppy. Also, you know she's honest." Grandma said.

Marti didn't want to tell her she'd blown it the moment she

flew through the door. Grandma wasn't the only one who liked the girl. She had an idea. She'd have to run it by the board—and Mom—but she was the director and this was as good a time as any to direct.

"Listen, this job requires experience you don't have. I have a feeling that someday, you'll be the perfect candidate, but not yet."

Emmy deflated.

"However..." Marti said. Emmy sat up straight. "...it's possible once we get up and running, we'll require additional help. Sort of an internship. Paid, of course. If that happens—and I emphasize 'if'—I encourage you to apply. In the meantime, keep applying and interviewing for jobs. Sooner or later, whether it's here or somewhere else, I am sure you'll find the perfect position."

"Listen to you, sounding all professional and grown-up and supportive," Grandma said.

Emmy left, happy and encouraged. The whole interview had taken less than fifteen minutes. Marti would get her break after all. Double time. She needed it.

"Isn't Dawn Pernelli next?" Grandma said.

"Don't you need to go check on Mrs. Heedly?"

"Oh, I wouldn't miss this for the world."

"I really should keep a bottle of booze in this place." Marti settled for another cup of coffee and a raid on her office Oreo stash.

To say Dawn Pernelli Gunderson hadn't changed since high school would be a lie, but only if you were talking about looks. Every time Marti saw her, she wondered if Dawn possessed a mirror, and if so, did she use it? Maybe she needed glasses.

She was as slim as ever and still sported her cheerleader figure. However, too much sun exposure had turned the dewy complexion of youth into wrinkly leather. She was as crispy brown in March as she'd been at the end of the summer. Bicklesburg hadn't had enough sun in the last five months to account for her tan. She wasn't orange enough for a spray-on. It had to be tanning beds. Marti shuddered. Good thing she was happy with her pale-as-a-vampire complexion. Her claustrophobia wasn't bad enough to affect her on a daily basis, but the thought of being shut into one of those ultraviolet coffins was the stuff of nightmares.

"So, Dawn. You're looking healthy."

Grandma didn't say anything. Marti'd bought her silence with a promise she'd go talk to Mrs. Heedly "later." Marti hadn't specified how late that later would be. She was planning on at least a year or two.

"Why, thank you." Dawn preened. She wouldn't recognize a backhanded compliment if it hit her in the face.

Dawn had put in extra effort dressing for her interview. Her slacks and sweater fit business-casual mode more than office-job-interview mode but were far more appropriate than her usual tight T-shirts and second-skin jeans. Although the powder settling into the crows' feet around her eyes didn't do her any favors, she'd toned down her makeup by about eighty percent. Maybe this wasn't a joke and Marti's arch-nemesis really wanted the job.

As Marti ran through her list of questions, it was apparent she wasn't going to get it.

For the most part, Dawn managed to avoid any solid answers. At the same time, she offered too much information. She was on a quest to upgrade her life. She'd left Bob Gunderson. She was taking night classes, which she assured Marti would make up for her current lack of office skills.

Grandma yawned. "This is boring. I'm disappointed in both of you. I'm going to go see Janice."

Marti wasn't sorry to see her go.

"I want a position where I'll meet a better class of men—I mean people." Dawn didn't blush at her slip.

Marti didn't know Dawn's husband. Dmitri'd told her Bob moved to town during her absence and married Dawn shortly after. All she knew was he drove a tow truck for Rudawski Motors and was probably the one who hauled her now-dead Taurus to its final resting place.

Rudawski. Dawn hadn't mentioned Peter or expressed her condolences. Neither had the other interviewees, but neither Sandra nor Faustyn were lifelong Bicklesburg residents, and Emmy was young. Failure to mention Peter's passing—without bringing up the circumstances—in the most sympathetic of tones, real or faked, was a serious breach of Bicklesburg etiquette. Too serious for even Dawn's lack of social skills.

"One last question," Marti said. "Why do you want to work for the Mickkleson Foundation in particular?"

Dawn stared. Marti could see the gears grinding in her head. She could hear them. They needed oil. Dawn's leathery face tightened. Her crows' feet quivered.

"Money," she said. "Mickkleson money."

Marti was a good poker player, but she couldn't hide her shock at Dawn's honesty. Not simply because of her answer. "Honesty" and "Dawn" were two words that didn't go together.

"Look," Dawn said. "We both know I'm not going to get this job. I never was. I was surprised you offered me an interview, but I decided to go with it. On the off-chance I got the job, I could have taken my time with this. Since that's not going to happen, it'll have to be now."

"Taken care of what?" Marti was far more comfortable with the return of Brazen-Dawn than she was with Let's-Have-a-Heart-to-Heart-Dawn spilling details about her personal life. She'd known Brazen-Dawn since Kindergarten.

"You Mickklesons owe Winter money. A lot of money. Peter promised her. If I was working here, I could have made sure she got it one way or another."

Scratch Brazen-Dawn. This was Off-the-Rails-Dawn.

"Peter? He wasn't a Mickkleson. He was a Rudawski, and anything he promised your tramp of a niece is no business of ours."

"He was married to your sister. That makes him a Mickkleson. My niece made a better Mrs. Rudawski than RachelAnne ever did. Peter told her so. And he would have made it official if that Berryman woman hadn't come along."

"Berryman woman?" The only one Marti could think of was RachelAnne's would-be divorce lawyer. "Philippa Berryman?"

"Yeah. You know. The lawyer. Her dad was our creepy history teacher."

Something didn't make sense with the Peter-Winter-Philippa connection, but little over the past few days did make sense. Marti would think about it later. Dealing with Brazen-Nutsy-Cuckoo-Dawn was her immediate priority.

"Whatever happened to him?" Marti redirected the conversation. Dawn still lived in her high school glory days and loved talking about anything vaguely related to them.

"Ha. He's at the Blissful Meadows Care Center. From what I hear, he's bedridden and at death's door. Serves him right."

The viciousness of Dawn's words shocked her. Back in the day, Old Man Berryman made no bones about having favorites. Star jocks, cheerleaders, pretty girls, all were invited to hang out in his office during their off-periods, spend time with him after school, and afforded every privilege a teacher could award. Dawn was a cheerleader. Part of Berryman's in-crowd. Marti belonged to his other club, the students he regularly humiliated in class. Although Peter was ten years ahead of her in school and a mid-level jock, she had the impression he belonged to the same club.

"He probably enjoys it," Dawn continued. "He gets nurses giving him sponge baths to make up for not getting to play touchy-feely with cheerleaders."

Whoa. Marti was unaware of any of this in school, but it didn't surprise her now. A vague memory stirred.

"Didn't you fail—"

"Yeah. I failed American History as a junior and had to take it again. He didn't like anyone telling him no. I passed with flying colors as a senior. He also didn't like people threatening to tell the world what a dirty old man he was. Now he gets to lay in his own waste, and Philippa is the only one who visits him. She shows up a couple of times a week. His darling daughter never wanted to hear a word against him."

"How do you know all this? Not the old stuff, the stuff about him now?" Marti didn't know much about nursing homes in general, but she did know Blissful Meadows was top-of-the-line and expensive. Most of the residents weren't from Bicklesburg or Battlesborough County. Its reputation was such that people from the city brought their elderly or infirm family members there. Locals couldn't afford it. Of Mr. Berryman's problems, dirty sheets were unlikely to be one of them.

"Oh. One of my cousins works at Blissful Meadows."

Of course they did. Too bad the Pernelli clan hated anything Mickkleson. If Marti could tap into that resource, nothing that happened in Bicklesburg would get by her. With a resource like that, she might take Grandma Bertie's suggestion and hang out a shingle as a private investigator. For the living, not the dead.

"What's wrong with her?" Lilith was back, all signs of her Mrs. Heedly-induced trauma gone. She bent and extended a finger toward Dawn's wrinkled cheek.

"Ah..." Marti didn't know if Lilith knew about her one power to affect the living.

"What?" Dawn said.

"Don't do that, dear." Grandma Bertie was back, and her timing was excellent.

Lilith gave Grandma a withering look. "I didn't die yesterday, you know."

As far as Marti knew, there was no such thing as an Orientation for Spirits class, so Lilith must have spent some of her afterlife around people. Maybe she learned about ghost freeze by trial and error. Had she been in the office since her death? Since her bones were—or had been—buried in Henrietta's Hollow, why the office? Time to wind things up with Dawn and have a heart-to-heart with Ghost Girl.

"Look at the time." Marti stood.

"On what?" Dawn exaggeratedly checked the office walls. There wasn't a clock in sight.

"I need to prepare for my next interview," Marti lied.

"I'll show myself out," Dawn said.

"I don't like her," Lilith said. "Are you sure you don't want me to give her a great big hug?"

"If I've resisted all these years, you can too," Grandma said.

"Just a little squeeze?" Lilith said.

"No need." Marti escorted Dawn to the door. Not out of courtesy. For Dawn's protection.

"I'm sure I'll see you around." Marti saw no point in promising to get back to her. Both of them knew Dawn wasn't getting the job. "Bicklesburg's small."

"Don't forget Winter. She earned every penny coming to her. Peter promised her a cut. And she knows things. Things I'm sure you and your high and mighty family would rather keep quiet." Dawn flounced out the door.

FIFTEEN

"WHAT DID SHE MEAN BY THAT?" Grandma said.

Marti shut and locked the door. She was done dealing with people for the day, and there was no need to risk Dawn hearing her talk to herself—meaning the ghosts—while she waited for the elevator.

"Well?" Grandma said.

"I'll fill you in later. The conversation got better after you left."

"Of course it did."

"How was..." Marti hesitated. Across the room, Lilith squatted, engaged in a staring contest with Bernard. "...your buddy?"

"Do you mean my sis...my sis...Janice?" Lilith turned her attention to Marti. Bernard won the stare-down and celebrated with a regal stretch. "How is she?"

"Well, first of all, dead like you," Grandma said.

Marti wouldn't have been so blunt, but it didn't faze Lilith, who shrugged and said, "I figured as much since you two are best friends and all."

"Second, pleased to have an answer about your whereabouts

even if she's not happy about the answer. She's been worrying about you for decades."

"It's not my fault," Lilith said.

"Whose fault is it?" Grandma Bertie was in interrogation mode. Lilith pouted.

"Well?" Grandma said.

"I don't know," Lilith whispered.

Marti felt sorry for her. Lilith wouldn't be the first spirit Marti met who couldn't remember their death—some didn't realize they were dead—and Lilith was so young. "Maybe you can wander over to the Green and visit your sis—Janice." If Lilith wouldn't use the word "sister," Marti wouldn't either.

"I can't leave this office. I've tried. These two rooms are it."

Grandma Bertie's haunting range was tied to Marti's location, and she was the most mobile ghost Marti'd ever met. Other than The Judge. Her father had managed to hunt her down far from Bicklesburg after his death, then stuck to her like glue until he moved on. Maybe her personal ghosts were special. Most were tied to a place. Sometimes the place made sense, like Edwards and Amity at Bickle House. Sometimes it didn't, like Mrs. Heedly in the Green. Marti had no idea why Mrs. Heedly ended up in the park. She assumed the old bat just liked it there.

If Lilith was confined to the small office, her afterlife had to be boring. It was unlikely she chose to spend eternity there, so there must be a reason.

"You don't expect me to help you move on or anything," Marti said. "I don't do that."

"You did it for your father," Grandma said.

"That was an accident. And The Judge did it himself."

"I don't want to go anywhere," Lilith said. "I like it here. I do now, anyway. You all are much more fun than the last guy."

The last guy was Nathaniel Worthington, CPA, a crony of The Judge. Marti'd met the accountant. He was indeed boring. When he retired and closed up shop, Mom took the space for the Foundation. He sent Marti a note saying he hoped they'd fix the thermostat. In all his years there, and there were plenty, the place was prone to temperature drops. Winter or summer, both he and his secretary suffered from sudden chills. More than chills. Downright freezes. Maintenance tried but never found a cause.

Lilith had found a way to keep herself entertained.

"But why here?" Marti said.

Just like at the first mention of her sister, Lilith wavered and vanished.

Marti made a note to find out who occupied the office before Nathaniel Worthington.

"I'm beat. Let's get out of here," she said.

Bernard yowled.

"I'm not forgetting you." Marti filled his kibble bowl with enough dry food to last a week and did the same for his water. She planned to be back in the morning, but the way things were going, better safe than sorry.

"Don't forget the litter box." Grandma held her nose. A total passive-aggressive act. Ghosts had no sense of smell.

"Has Mrs. Heedly ever mentioned Philippa Berryman?"

"No. I don't recall her mentioning any Berrymans. Should she have?"

"Maybe. I don't know." Marti got the Dawn-Winter connection. Pernellis stuck together. Dawn had implied she wasn't above blackmail back in high school or now. But where did Philippa Berryman fit in? She hadn't come into RachelAnne's life until after her sister found out about Winter and Peter.

"Are you going to fill me in on Dawn and Winter?" Grandma said.

"On the way home."

Marti pulled the litter box out of the storage closet. Grandma was right. She did a complete change rather than just a scoop.

Peter. Winter. She dumped the nasty litter into a bag.

Philippa. As a Mickkleson—and the particular Mickkleson formerly known as Marti Cray-Cray—she wasn't fully privy to the Bicklesburg tittle-tattle network, but she knew who was.

"On the way home." she said, "Before we stop to visit Dmitri."

~

MARTI PULLED up next to the ACS office.

"Now, be nice," Grandma said. "You've been sort of rude to him lately."

"Me! I'm not the one who—"

"Who's that?"

Someone was leaving the security building. Someone not in an ACS uniform. Someone in a green parka.

"Oliver," Marti said. "What's he doing here?" Not to mention, how did he get there? No other cars were parked near the office. Oliver had a way cool Camaro back in high school, but he lost it after The Judge's shenanigans. She didn't know if he drove anymore. She'd only seen him on foot. The Avenue was a long way from town. Walkable, but a long walk.

"That coat looks new," Grandma said.

It did. Maybe someone took pity on him. Maybe the same someone who bailed him out and hired Terrance Appleby to get him out of whatever trouble he was in.

Oliver wandered out of sight. Toward the main road, not down the Avenue. However he'd gotten there, he'd have a long walk back to town.

"Are you going to just sit there? Your young man awaits."

"He's not my young man."

Grandma was out of the TT and headed to the building. She didn't bother with the door and passed through the front wall.

Marti went to the glass door, knocked once, and tried to open it. Locked. Inside, Dmitri had his phone to his ear. He looked up, waved, and turned his back to her. Did he think she could lipread? More important, why did he care?

He stuck the phone in his pocket and let her in. "Is something wrong?"

"Why does something have to be wrong? Can't I stop to say 'hi' for old times' sake?"

"I told you to be nice," Grandma said.

Marti hadn't meant to sound so defensive. It just came out.

"Uh-huh," Dmitri said.

"He's not buying it," Grandma said.

"Nothing's wrong," Marti said, "but I do have a couple of things to talk to you about."

"Have a seat."

He didn't sigh, but Marti felt like a toddler being addressed by a long-suffering adult.

"I'll make this quick so you don't need to put up with me too long." She didn't know what caused the rift, but two could play this game. "I wouldn't want to waste your valuable time." She stopped short of adding *even though my mother pays your salary*.

"Do you even know how to be nice?" Grandma said.

"That's not what I...I'm just busy. Things on my mind."

Was that contrition in his voice?

"I wanted to thank you for the other night. When Peter showed up looking for RachelAnne. Before—you know. I don't know what would have happened if you weren't there."

"Hey. I helped," Grandma said.

"You're welcome, but it's my job," Dmitri said.

"You weren't in uniform. You were off-duty," Marti said.

"No such thing as off-duty for the boss. You said a couple of things. What's the other?"

"I've been interviewing potential administrative assistants for the Foundation. RachelAnne said to ask you about the company you use for background checks. I need more than the company name. I have no clue how background checks work."

"I'll text you the name of the company and their details," he said.

So he still had her number. He just hadn't used it in months.

Dmitri explained the process. The potential employee would have to supply some info to the investigating company and be fingerprinted. It would take about five business days for the report to come back.

"There is a charge, but there are two ways to handle it. You can open a company account for the Foundation or use the ACS account and have it billed directly or have the job candidate pay up front and reimburse them later, contingent on them passing the check and accepting the job."

On neutral ground, the man of few words was downright talkative. Marti no longer felt like a toddler.

"Which method do you use?"

"My last hire was Richie. He'd already passed the unofficial Bicklesburg-from-birth background check. Since there was little danger of him not passing the official check, we paid for it upfront. If I was hiring someone from out of town, I'd go the reimbursement route. Where's your candidate from?"

"There's two in the lead. One just moved here, and the other's from Edgecastle."

"No Bicklesburgians?"

"I interviewed two. One was a youngster without enough experience. The other was Dawn."

"There's those dimples," Grandma said.

"You interviewed *Dawn*? To be *your assistant*?" Dmitri's smile broadened and expanded until it lit up his face and eyes. His shoulders shook with restrained laughter.

"I've missed that smile," Marti blurted before she could stop herself. Her cheeks warmed. Emmy Penny wasn't the only one who needed to work on her filter. At least she hadn't mentioned the dimples.

"Was there anything else?" Dimples-Dmitri turned into All-Business-Dmitri.

"Um, yeah. I do have one or two teeny-tiny questions."

"Make them quick."

"What do you know about Philippa Berryman?"

"Battlesborough County's answer to celebrity divorce lawyers, although she dabbles in a few other areas as needed. That creep Berryman's daughter. Went to fancy colleges. Likes money. That's about it."

Nothing Marti didn't already know.

"Why?" Dmitri said.

"Dawn seems to think the Mickklesons owe Winter money. Peter promised it to her. Why did Peter promise Winter money?"

"You don't think she was with him because of his innate charm, do you?"

"Good point," Marti and Grandma said in unison.

"Dawn also said Winter expected to become the next Mrs. Rudawski and would have if Philippa hadn't shown up."

"Didn't your mother call Philippa in when RachelleAnne left Peter?"

"Exactly," Marti said. "How could she work for RachelAnne if she was working for Peter? Besides, I still find it hard to believe Peter was willing to divorce the Mickkleson family unless it was for someone with more money and social standing. He was a climber if there ever was one."

"That would not be Winter Adams," Dmitri said.

"You don't think Philippa, how shall I put this, replaced Winter in Peter's affections, do you? If RachelAnne and Winter are any indication, she was a little old for him."

Dmitri laughed.

"You two are getting along well," Grandma said.

Marti's chest tightened. Her cheeks burned again.

Dmitri either didn't notice or chose to ignore Marti's blush. "From Peter's standpoint, Philippa might have been a step up, but

I doubt she'd have anything to do with him. From what I know of her, a used-car salesman, even one with aspirations, would be beneath her. Last I heard, she was seeing some guy from the city. I have a question for you."

"He's going to ask you out," Grandma said. "Say yes."

"How did RachelAnne find out about Peter and Winter?"

"You mean the Bicklesburg newswire doesn't have that already?"

"Not unless she really walked in on the two of them. That story includes lots of leather, chains, a whip, and a few other juicy tidbits."

"Ask him who was whipping who," Grandma said.

"Whom," Marti said.

"Don't be pedantic," Grandma said.

"What?" Dmitri looked confused.

"I'm trying to remember," Marti said. "I know she told me. There was wine involved. In the telling, not the finding out." RachelAnne did tell her. The night Peter was killed. With all that had happened since, Marti hadn't thought about it.

"She'd received a couple of anonymous letters but more or less ignored them." RachelAnne claimed she ignored them, but Marti knew they'd bothered her more than she let on. "The last letter was different. RachelAnne didn't say how, but it pushed her over the edge. She checked Peter's phone and laptop and found the evidence, including sexts and photos." Marti hadn't questioned her sister about the sexts and photos. Some things, she didn't want to know.

"Letters?" Dmitri said. "Not emails or texts. Real, physical, old-fashioned letters?"

"Yeah. Stamps and all. RachelAnne said they were too well written to come from Winter, but considering the situation, that might have been justified cattiness." Or they might have been written by a well-educated divorce lawyer.

"Does she still have them?"

"I don't know. Do you want me to find out?" Maybe Winter and Philippa were in on it together. Maybe they found out about each other and decided to do Peter in. Like that Carrie Underwood song, "Two Black Cadillacs." Except nobody was calling Peter a "good man."

"Get that look off your face," Dmitri said.

"What look?"

"I've seen that look before. I don't want you to find the letters. I want you to stay out of it. Let Big deal with Peter, his girlfriends, and his death. There is absolutely no reason for you to get involved. You know what happened the last time."

"He does care," Grandma said.

"It all worked out for the best," Marti said. She could see Winter doing in her cheating lover, but Philippa Berryman didn't seem like the type to land herself in the middle of a country song.

"Barely. Promise me you'll stay out of it."

"I might consider it if you'll answer one more question."

"That depends on the question."

"Are you ever going to tell me where you disappeared to for months?"

"Wrong question," Grandma said.

"Sooner or later."

"Told you," Grandma said.

He'd answered the question she asked. She hated it when Grandma Bertie was right. "Is that sooner, like over beers tonight or later, like a deathbed confession?"

"Not the first. I have plans tonight. And I hope it's not the latter."

"Where were you?" She wanted to ask what those plans were but knew better.

"You said one question, and I answered it."

"Hi, Dmitri." Richie stopped when he saw Marti. He backed to the door. "Do you want me to come back later? I can hang out outside for a while."

"Oh, look. Time for shift change," Dmitri said. "No need. Marti's just leaving."

He walked her to her car. "I'm not kidding. Go home. Play with the kids. Console your sister. Fight with your mother. Stay out of this. Leave Peter to the professionals."

"Mom and I don't fight as much nowadays. By the way, what was Oliver doing here?"

"You're out of questions. Promise me you'll stay out of it."

"Sure." She crossed her fingers behind her back.

"If this was a movie, he'd kiss you now," Grandma said.

He shook his head. "I still can't believe you interviewed Dawn."

"It seemed like a good idea at the time. And look what we learned about Winter and Philippa Berryman." They'd learned something. Marti wasn't sure what.

"You're like a dog with a bone. I'm serious. Let it go."

Marti got in the TT and slammed the door.

"I wish he hadn't done that," Grandma said.

"What? Called me a dog?"

"Ordering you not to do something is the best way I know to get you to do it."

CHAPTER

SIXTEEN

RACHELANNE AND MOM sat across from each other at the kitchen island. Neither looked up when Electro-Harriet announced Marti's arrival. The kids were nowhere in sight.

"This doesn't look good," Grandma said.

It didn't. RachelAnne again clutched a glass of red wine. From the look of the bottle in front of her, it wasn't her first.

"Déjà vu all over again," Grandma said.

Mom radiated fury. The last time Marti saw her this angry, she'd discovered teenage Marti sneaking a boy into her room. He escaped before Mom got a good look at him. As far as Marti knew, she never figured out it was Dmitri.

"What now?" Marti said.

"And hello to you too." RachelAnne twirled her wine glass, examined it, drained it, and reached for the bottle.

"Sit down," Mom said. "Family meeting."

Panic hit Marti. In her youth, too many family meetings resulted in her being shipped off to The Birches. She'd been on her best behavior, such as it was, for months. Maybe it was RachelAnne. An intervention over all that red wine. Marti didn't think, considering the circumstances, that her sister's consumption had hit intervention level. Yet. RachelAnne wasn't anywhere near the drinking levels of Marti's fairly recent past. Not that that was anything to brag about.

"I'm broke," RachelAnne said.

"Is that all?" Relief replaced panic.

The scowls her sister and mother turned on her were enough to send her to join Grandma Bertie, The Judge, and a whole passel of other dead ancestors.

"I didn't mean...I was afraid..." She needed to work on that filter.

"Steady," Grandma said. "Don't dig yourself in deeper."

Marti took a deep breath. "Look. You're a Mickkleson. We're Mickklesons. How bad can it be? Mom can help. In a month—less than a month—I can help. Unless you decide not to hand over my inheritance, in which case—hey! You have money again. You have a support system, and I don't mean just in the financial sense."

"Good save," Grandma said.

Marti meant every word.

"Sit down," RachelAnne said.

Mom got out two more wine glasses. The bottle was empty. She reached under the counter, retrieved another from the rack, and filled the glasses.

RachelAnne talked. She wasn't just broke. Peter left her deeply in debt. The McMansion was mortgaged to the hilt. The car lot—the one Peter's father left him—was so far in the red it was a wonder it was still in business. Peter left a trail of credit card debt and personal loans a mile and a half long. Maybe two and a half.

The Henrietta's Hollow project was financed by investors from the city.

"Scary investors," RachelAnne said. "Benjamin suggested the leg-breaking kind."

Marti reached for her untouched wine and stopped. "Wait. I thought the Bicklesburg was financing Peter's strip mall."

"High-end shopping center," RachelAnne said.

Marti hoped the sarcasm in her sister's voice was a good sign. "Ashley sent Harold Binks to represent the bank at the ground-breaking."

Mom harrumphed. "That was out of deference to the Micklesons' long association with the bank. It was an insult to Peter. If the Bicklesburg was financing Peter's foolishness, Ashley or someone higher up would have gone. You have a lot to learn about hierarchy in the Bicklesburg business world. I may need to take a more hands-on approach at the Foundation."

Marti shuddered.

"That man was in the attic, the sitting room, the dining room, and the bedrooms today," Amity said. "I followed him *everywhere*."

"The subject was also spotted in the parlor watching television with the kids, but he made a break for it as soon as I showed up," Edwards said.

"Now isn't the time," Grandma said.

Peter. Why was he at Bickle House? True, he'd coveted the family home beyond reason and planned on one day becoming Lord of the Manor, but the evidence pointed to him being killed on Paradise Sanctuary Boulevard. He was certainly dumped in Henrietta's Hollow. What kept him here? His family? The one he'd not been all that concerned about when he was alive? Unless. Oh, no.

Maggie.

Other than Amity and Edwards, Maggie was the only one who'd seen him. He'd spoken to her.

Grandma Bertie following Marti around for her entire life was bad enough, especially during her teenage years. And Grandma had Marti's best interests at heart. If Maggie had to grow up with her father haunting her, it didn't bear thinking about.

"Marti!" Mom called her back to the conversation. "Are you listening?"

"Um. Yes. No. Maybe?" What had she missed?

"You're in charge of dinner," RachelAnne said.

She probably missed more than that, but "dinner" gave her an idea. "Then it's pizza. The kids and I will run into town and get it."

"They can deliver. You've been drinking," Mom said.

"Nope, I never touched it."

"I'll take care of that." RachelAnne swapped her empty glass for Marti's full one.

Maybe an intervention was in order.

"If I run into town, I can get ice cream too." The ice cream parlor was next door to the pizza place, and they didn't deliver.

"The kids have been shut up in the house all day. It'll do them good to get out. Get Cookies 'N' Crunch. For the ice cream. Not the pizza," RachelAnne said.

Marti phoned in the pizza order, one extra large with everything but anchovies and one extra small with pineapple. Margaret Mickkleson's taste was exquisite in everything but pizza.

"Kids! Grab your coats! We're going on an adventure!" Marti yelled.

"Do not bellow," Mom said. "Go to them and speak like a civilized human being."

"So says the person who eats pineapple on pizza," Grandma said.

Marti didn't need to go after the kids. Maggie and T3 flew into the room like felons released after a ten-year stretch.

"Everyone to the car," Marti said.

If Peter joined them, she'd have one answer. She might need to watch a few more episodes of *Ghost Whisperer* and see if she could pick up a few tricks of the trade.

∼

"WHAT ARE YOU DOING, AUNT MARTI?" T3 said.

"I told you he isn't there," Grandma said.

There'd been no sign of Peter on the drive to town. Marti spent more time checking the rearview mirror than the road in front of her. Grandma moved around, making sure he wasn't hiding in the back of the giant SUV. Marti wasn't taking her word for it. She finished examining the third row of seating and opened the back hatch.

"The yady said 'not here'," Maggie said.

"The llllady is your Aunt Marti." T3 spoke in perfect imitation of his mother. "When did she say that?"

Grandma sat cross-legged in the cargo area. "Told you so," she said.

The good news was Peter was probably not tethered to Maggie. Unless he had an extremely long leash, he would have shown up long before she parked on the Green. The bad news was that meant he'd taken up residence in Bickle House, which burned Marti's butt. He hadn't managed to move in while alive, and she'd be darned if she would let him achieve his holy grail in death. There was some *Ghost Whisper* in her future.

She slammed the hatch shut. "So kids, where first? Sicilian Heaven or The Scoop?" She overdid the perky. It sounded fake, even to her.

"What's wrong with you?" T3 said.

"I'm hungry. Which first, pizza or ice cream?"

T3 decreed pizza first, because "if we get stuck in a traffic jam on the way home, we can reheat the pizza but we can't refreeze the ice cream."

"Bright boy," Grandma said.

Marti agreed, although a traffic jam was unlikely. Bicklesburg rolled up both its sidewalks and roadways early.

The pizza and ice cream parlors were on the ground floor of the building three doors down from the Mickkleson Foundation building. The *Bicklesburg Gazette* occupied the upper stories, which explained the name of the ice cream parlor. It didn't explain the pizza parlor's name. Sicilian Heaven was owned by Sterling Cromwell. His grandmother Biddy was, along with Mom, one of Bicklesburg's last two living and active members of the DAR.

Sterling wasn't behind the counter.

"Name?"

"I thought you worked at So-nutt-ee Donuts?" On her return to Bicklesburg, Marti stopped to fortify herself with donuts before facing her family. Pimples Pernelli was the first person she'd spoken to, and by now, he knew who she was.

"I'm moving up in the world. Name?" He stared over her shoulder.

"Mickkleson."

"I'm sorry, I didn't catch that." His eyes darted from side to side.

"Mickkleson," she said louder.

"Come again?" He twitched to his left and looked behind her.

"Mickkleson." She didn't raise her voice. Whatever game he was playing, she wasn't.

"Was that Mickkleson?" he shouted.

Something clattered behind her. She spun around in time to see Winter Adams and Harold Binks run out the door.

"Interesting," Grandma said.

"That'll be $23.42." Pimples set two pizza boxes on the counter.

Marti handed him a twenty and a ten. His hands shook so bad he dropped her change.

"Keep it," Marti said. "It's your tip."

Pernelli or not, Pimples had the grace to blush.

EMMY PENNY WAS behind the counter at The Scoop. She acted genuinely happy to see Marti and introduced herself to the kids. Bicklesburg really needed to provide more job opportunities for its young people. Marti put it on her list of things for the Foundation to look into.

The ice cream transaction went off without a hitch, other than their inability to make up their minds between The Scoop's forty-six flavors. They ended up with not only a pint of Rachel-Anne's Cookies 'N' Crunch, but pints of Mint Chocolate Chip, Rocky Road, Bubblegum Sorbet, Rainbow Delight, and something called Superhero Supersmash. T3 was adamant on the need for the last.

Emmy deserved a bigger tip than Pimples, and she got it.

"I hope you urchins are happy," Marti said as they left. "That was a few decades worth of my annual salary."

"Does that mean you're staying?" T3 said.

"Pyeeze stay," Maggie said.

Marti never told the kids her stay was temporary. RachelAnne asked her not to. If she asked that of Marti, she would have asked the same of Mom. Peter might have mentioned it to them before his unexpected demise—it had to be before if T3 knew—but she doubted it. As far as her brother-in-law'd been concerned, she was a nuisance and beneath his notice unless he was trying to sell her a car or get something out of her.

"Little pitchers," Grandma said.

How many other adult conversations had the kids overheard?

BY THE TIME they got home, Mom and RachelAnne had set the table in the dining room. The family dining room, not the formal dining room, but the plates were china, not paper.

"We need to start behaving like a civilized family," Mom said.

"Standards have been lax around here. Under the circumstances, I've let things slide. No more."

"Ugh," Grandma said. "I'm going to go find Edwards and Amity. See if they've made any more Peter sightings."

Mom's pronouncement was a sign of Mickkleson-normal. Not so much what she decreed. If anyone had told Teen-Marti—or even Last-Week-Marti—she'd find solace in her mother's demands for decorum, she would have laughed herself silly. Yet there they were, sitting in uncomfortable chairs eating take-out off fine china, and she felt more at ease than she had in days. It had the same effect on her sister. RachelAnne had switched from red wine to sparkling water and ate more than Marti'd seen her eat since her world fell apart. Excepting the Oreos, of course. Those didn't count.

"I suppose I'd better clean up," RachelAnne said.

"Marti will do it. You go spend time with your children."

"Hey. I made dinner!"

"And you did a lovely job of driving into town and picking up food," Mom said. "RachelAnne, take the kids and find a movie for us all to watch. Make sure they're not sticky before they touch anything." Maggie wore as much of her ice cream as she'd eaten.

"Marti?"

Marti was surprised at her sister bothering to consult her, but Mom's tone left no room for argument. She shrugged. "Pick out a good movie."

RachelAnne and the kids left in a flurry. Marti started stacking dishes. The china needed to be washed by hand. Clean-up could take a while.

"Sit down," Mom said.

Uh-oh. She should have seen this coming. She blamed the ice cream. Bubblegum Sorbet was a powerful soporific.

"While you were gone, RachelAnne and I finalized arrangements for Peter's services."

Was that all?

"Did RachelAnne have any input?"

Her mother's full-strength Margaret Alberta Dibble Mickkleson glare reduced Marti to a terrified twelve-year-old. Her filter had failed her again. On the other hand, things were steadily heading back to normal. "Tell me about them. Has Big released the body?"

"No. We don't need it. There will be no viewing. No visitation. The service will be private. Burial will be at a later date, once we decide where to put him."

"How private?" If it was just family, Marti wouldn't have to figure out what to wear. Thanks to a shopping trip with Rachel-Anne, she had a little black dress, unworn, but she hardly wanted to waste it on Peter. Besides, it wasn't appropriate for a funeral.

"You don't need to attend unless you want to. I'm not." Mom wasn't above giving her late son-in-law one last diss.

"Won't that cause talk?" Marti didn't care. Mom was the one who wanted a return to "standards."

"We've survived worse. We survived your father's idiocy. Do you see any reporters outside? Peter's not national news. Even in death, he can't hold a candle to The Judge." Mom's voice held a hint of pride. Despite The Judge's misdeeds, she had loved her errant husband.

"Works for me," Marti said. "Since I've got you here..." It was as good a time as any to ask Mom about the previous tenants of the Foundation offices. She needed a reason. *I've been talking to the office ghost* wouldn't cut it.

"Yes? Are you going to finish that sentence?"

"I've been doing some research for a history of the Foundation." Bad improvisation, but it might work. "Do you know what was in the office before the accountant?"

"I don't know what that has to do with the Foundation, but the Worthingtons were there as long as I can remember."

"I was thinking of continuity, involvement with the town, stuff like that," Marti said. "If you don't know, are there records I can check?"

"I do remember your grandfather Mickkleson mentioning something. Some sort of men's club, I think."

"Men's club? Like strippers? Or like the Tams?" The Tams were a supposedly secret club made up of the county's wealthiest and most influential men. "Men" being the operative word. The Judge had died after returning home, drunk, from one of their monthly meetings.

"Hardly like the Tams. Not that exclusive. As for strippers, I wouldn't know. There was some sort of scandal, though. They got evicted. I believe it was a relief when Nathaniel's father took over the lease. Nathaniel later joined him in the practice. Much better tenants."

"What kind of scandal?"

"The kind the men didn't talk about in front of ladies in those days. Your grandfather never said, or not in my presence. I don't believe I ever discussed it with your father."

"You never heard anything? This is Bicklesburg."

"It was before my time and not the sort of topic my friends and I discussed."

Mom's crowd wasn't above gossip, but they were fascinated with each other, not the unwashed masses.

"Oh. That history teacher was somehow involved with the club. Philip Berryman. Philippa's father. He was a founder or an officer or something that passed for important. He must have been quite young at the time. Your grandfather never liked him and your father despised him, but they never said why."

Marti tried to pump her mother for more, but Mom either didn't remember anything else or wasn't willing to share it with Marti.

"Don't you think it's time you clean up this mess? I'm going to go check on our movie. Who knows what they've chosen. Join us when you've finished." Mom left.

Whatever the kids picked, Nana-Mom would approve it. She wouldn't be so forgiving if Marti left a crumb of pepperoni on the dining room table. She concentrated on cleaning up and not chipping the china.

The men's club and Philip Berryman would have to wait. Grandma could find out if Mrs. Heedly knew anything. Marti would ask Lilith. Tonight, she was going to enjoy the movie, whatever it was.

CHAPTER

SEVENTEEN

MORNINGS HAD FALLEN INTO A ROUTINE. Marti was always the last one up, and that morning, she was later than usual.

Amity and Edwards woke her up with their latest report on Peter and his whereabouts. They were enjoying their roles as Peter trackers. After over a century of hanging around Bickle House, it was the most excitement they'd had in years.

The attic was Peter's favorite spot, if the number of sightings meant anything. Grandma said he tried to pop into Maggie's room but took off when he found her standing guard.

Hunting for Peter was like playing Whack-a-Mole. With the size of Bickle House, he always had somewhere to run. Or re-materialize. Or whatever you called what ghosts do.

"Everybody out," Grandma said. "Marti needs to drag herself out of that bed and get moving."

Amity and Edwards left, chattering about their plans for enhanced Peter stalking.

"Hurry up. You're running late." Grandma Bertie left for who knew where.

Who knew where, as long as it was within her designated Marti-perimeter. Amity and Edwards, and it looked like Peter too, could wander at will, as long as they did it within the confines of Bickle House.

If Lilith was confined to the office, where did she go when she fled? She wasn't crossing over. According to Grandma, once a spirit crossed over, they weren't supposed to come back. Marti'd only seen one ghost cross over and return. It took a lot out of them. On their second coming, they were deader than dead. Lilith, despite her comings and goings, was growing stronger by the day. Part of that could be chalked up to the discovery of her long-buried bones, but that didn't explain how she could vanish and come back brighter—and more confident than ever.

"You have five minutes. Maggie and T3 are talking about forming a search party." Grandma was back.

"Where does Lilith go when she evaporates?"

"I never thought about it," Grandma said. "The supply closet? The powder room?"

"We need to find out."

"Right now, you had better get yourself out of bed and downstairs before the search party arrives. Maggie and T3 have finished their cereal, and they're sticky with it."

Oh, yes. The new morning routine. Marti needed to join her family in the kitchen. More than that, she needed coffee.

"I'm going to go help Edwards and Amity. Peter's here someplace," Grandma said.

"Good luck with that." Marti threw the blankets back and crawled out of bed.

SHE HEADED DOWNSTAIRS in her pajamas and robe. Mom would have something to say, but Marti needed coffee before thinking about propping herself upright in the shower and making clothing choices for the day. She expected both her sister and mother to be dressed and ready for the cover of a fashion magazine, but she'd given up trying to keep up with either one of them, let alone both.

It was a wise decision. As soon as she walked into the kitchen, she was slammed with an assault hug. Maggie and T3 nearly knocked her off her feet.

"Not dressed yet?" Mom said.

"Good thing." Marti picked pieces of neon-colored cereal donuts off her robe. "I'd only have to change."

"Nana's taking us shopping!" T3 said.

"They need some things and the house is still sealed," RachelAnne said.

"What is seeyed?" Maggie said.

"Sealllled," RachelAnne said. "And it means you get to spend the day with Nana."

"Aunt Marti should come with us!" T3 bounced up and down. The sugary cereal was working its wonders.

"Yes!" Maggie threw her arms around Marti's legs and buried her face in Marti's robe. When she surfaced, her milk mustache was gone.

"Stop shouting, and that's not a bad idea," Mom said.

Marti had, much to her surprise, come to enjoy shopping outings with RachelAnne. Not as much as RachelAnne, but shopping for new clothes to replace Marti's old wardrobe of thrift shop jeans and sweatshirts with absurd sayings was one of their first bonding experiences. Marti had to admit, it worked out well. RachelAnne knew where to find the good stuff at good prices—the latter had surprised Marti—and didn't try to force her own style on her.

Shopping with Mom was a different story. The stuff of Marti's nightmares. Their one outing together since Marti's return was one too many.

"Ahhh." Marti put on a sad face. "I'd love to, but I need to take care of a few things at the office before the weekend. Friday's still a working day, you know."

"If you'd hire that assistant, they could take care of the day-to-day business," Mom said.

"As a matter of fact, hiring my new assistant is number one on today's to-do list," Marti said.

"You've found someone? Already?"

Already? After acting like she was taking six months for a simple task, now it was *already?* Marti took a deep breath.

"Yep." Two someones. She'd have to make up her mind between Sandra Booth and Faustyn Anguish fast.

"You set up background checks?"

"Got it covered. If you want me to be the director—*interim* director—of the Foundation, you're going to have to leave me alone and let me direct."

"I left your sister alone and look where that got her."

"Mom. Please. Not in front of the kids." RachelAnne refilled her coffee cup and poured one for Marti. Marti wanted to tell her sister under some circumstances, red wine for breakfast would be considered appropriate. She refrained and gratefully accepted the steaming mug of magic elixir.

"Come, my pretties. Let's get ready for our outing." Margaret Alberta Dibble Mickkleson, disgruntled Queen of Everything, was replaced by Nana-Margaret, with a dash of Margaret Hamilton thrown in.

The transformation was, as always, disconcerting.

"What's the one thing, other than boring old clothes, you each want most? Don't touch me with those sticky hands. And get that cat out from underneath my feet."

Maya meowed and twined around Mom's ankles. Despite a bad case of Grandparent Syndrome and a chance to spoil her grandchildren, Mom was in a mood. Marti swore the cat knew just what she was doing.

"Anything?" T3 said.

"Well, almost anything." Mom led the kids away.

"I'm glad she has some limits," Marti said. "Aren't you going with them?"

"We all, including the kids, agreed I need a break, and I do," RachelAnne said. "Have you really set things up for the background checks?"

"I stopped to talk to Dmitri last night. He explained how it works and said he'd text me the info, but I haven't heard from him yet. I don't think." She checked her phone. "Nope."

"You'll hear soon. He called me. I told him to set up access for you on the ACS-Mickkleson account."

Marti's spark of resentment at Dmitri checking up on her with her sister was quickly wiped out by another thought. As head of the Albion Court Residents' Council, Rachel-Anne was Dmitri's boss. The Judge's place on the council wasn't the only thing she'd taken over since his death. RachelAnne now oversaw most of the Mickkleson family business and investments. Mom only handled the things she was interested in, like the Foundation. She said she'd earned that right.

RachelAnne was a lawyer. RachelAnne was not stupid.

"RachelAnne, um..." How could she ask without antagonizing her sister, or worse, sending her into tears and red wine territory again? "I was wondering..."

"Spit it out."

"How did Peter pull off his financial hanky-panky? I mean, for you to co-sign something, wouldn't you need to, well, actually sign something?"

"You're not going to lecture me, are you? Mom's already done that to death."

"No. I'm genuinely curious. Pulling it off was one thing. Pulling it off behind your back takes it to a whole 'nother level."

"First, when I was young and stupid-in-love, Peter convinced me to let him handle all of the family finances. After all, he was already running a business. I was a young, sheltered bride, and Mom was busy setting me up as heiress apparent in all her charities and committees. Peter thought I should concentrate on that side of things."

Marti tried to hide her reaction, but if the look on Rachel-Anne's face was any indication, she was unsuccessful.

"I know, I know. I was an idiot. Or naïve. Whatever. As time went on, I tried to get involved, but then I started law school and with the kids and Mom's committees and The Judge dying—he always had a reason to put me off. And I was just so tired. I didn't want to fight about it."

"You didn't actually co-sign those loans, did you?"

"Ha. No. I stopped being stupid-in-love a long time ago. If he'd tried anything like that, I would have pushed back. Things hadn't been right between us for some time. Winter was just the final straw."

Marti suspected trouble in paradise since she first met Peter, but RachelAnne hadn't let on.

"Who did sign them? Wouldn't they have to show I.D. or something? Don't these things need to be notarized?" Marti'd never applied for a loan herself. If she'd wanted to, until recently, she didn't have the credit rating or the means to pay it back. She still wasn't sure she had the first.

"It's still early, but Benjamin made some calls. Big made some calls. Ashley Fysh made some calls. Sometimes, being a Mickkleson has its advantages."

"And?"

"Nothing was done in town or in county. No place where anyone knows me. In the city. A few counties over. Places where they know the Mickkleson name, but not me personally. Peter had a woman with him, and she had identification saying she was RachelAnne Mickkleson Rudawski."

"Was Peter bright enough to pull all of this off? He never struck me as a criminal mastermind." Or a mastermind of anything, for that matter.

"There was a lawyer involved in some of it. Whoever they are, they were good at covering their tracks, but we'll find out. It can't be anyone local. They would have known Peter's phony Mrs. Rudawski wasn't me. Unless they were in on it."

Peter's phony Mrs. Rudawski. What had Dawn said? Peter told Winter she made a better Mrs. Rudawski than RachelAnne.

"Excuse me, I need to make a call." Marti grabbed her coffee and left.

ALONE IN THE PARLOR, not a ghost in sight, she punched in the police station number. Not exactly "punched in." It said something about her life that she had the cops on speed dial, but she didn't want to think about what. At least it was the general number and not the emergency number.

"Bicklesburg Police. How may I help you?"

Marti didn't recognize the polite voice on the other end. "This is Marti Mickkleson. I need to talk to Big."

"I'll see if he's available." The words may have been polite, but the temperature dropped by a good fifteen degrees.

Marti waited. And waited. And waited. The canned on-hold music got on her nerves. They'd forgotten her. Or lost her. Or were ignoring her. Or maybe Big had solved Peter's murder and was preparing for a press conference, which would basically be him and MaryEllen Pernelli. She could always hang up and call again.

"Hello? Are you still there?" The question sounded like an accusation, and the speaker wasn't Big.

"Yes. I'm waiting to speak to Big."

"Chief Fysh isn't available at the moment. If you'll leave a message, he'll get back to you when he has time. If it's important."

And here she'd thought she and Big were developing some

sort of amicable relationship. "It is important, and I'd like to speak to him now, please."

"That's not possible, but if you'd like to leave a mess—"

Marti hung up. She bristled. Big might have been busy, but since his biggest busy at the moment involved Peter's death and the bones in Henrietta's Hollow, two things she was connected with, you'd think he'd speak to her. It was more probable he was avoiding her.

Her phone dinged. Dmitri'd texted her the company website and account number she needed for the background check. *You can set everything up online.*

Her phone dinged again. *Your temporary password is 5TAYout-O4iT! Be sure to change it. It expires tonight.*

Everybody's a comedian.

She brought up Dmitri's number in her contacts and hit "Call."

"I take it you got my text."

"Yeah. Ha ha. Very funny. Big won't take my call."

"And you expect me to do what?"

"Be quiet and listen." She told him what RachelAnne told her about the other Mrs. Rudawski and what Dawn said about Winter and waited for him to make the same connection she had.

"That's interesting. Again, what do you expect me to do about it?"

Was he dense or just being irritating? Not even nine o'clock yet, and her patience was at an end.

"You told me to let it go, so I am. I'm turning it over to the bro-network. You can tell Big. He can investigate it or not, but I have the feeling Winter had a few dress rehearsals as Mrs. Peter Rudawski."

"I told you to stay—"

Marti hit "End." She should have called on the landline. Slamming down a receiver would be so much more satisfying. Mom wasn't the only one in a mood. However, hers was justified.

She was sure Dmitri would relay the info to Big, whether either of them gave her credit for it or not. Now, if she could figure out a way to let Big know she knew the identity of the skeleton in Peter's hole. *I met her. She hangs out in my office* would hardly make him take her seriously.

5TAYoutO4iT!

Who did Dmitri think he was dealing with?

CHAPTER

EIGHTEEN

"HAVE you made up your mind yet?" Grandma said.

Marti stared at the two resumés lying on the desk. Would she rather spend time with Mrs. Partridge or the late, great Leslie Jordan? Metaphorically on the latter. The actor himself wasn't haunting her.

Both Sandra Booth and Faustyn Anguish impressed her with their interviews. They had roughly equivalent experience. True, Sandra's was with nonprofits, but Faustyn's experience in law offices could come in handy. If the last few months were any indication, especially where Mickklesons were involved.

Lawyers were popping up everywhere lately. Philippa Berryman. Terrance Appleby. Benjamin Bowman.

Peter's mysterious lawyer.

Faustyn Anguish wasn't a lawyer, but he'd spent years around them, and those who ran offices usually knew more about what the bosses did than the bosses themselves. He might not have ever met RachelAnne, but he was from Edgecastle. Since the *Gazette* was the only local paper in the county, he must have seen her picture at some point. Winter could never be mistaken for RachelAnne even if the only reference was a smudged and blurry newspaper photo. Not that the *Gazette* would ever print a bad photo of a Mickkleson, unless it was Marti. Faustyn had implied his current, and maybe past, employers weren't paragons of virtue. He mentioned balancing his karmic scales. How much did he have to make up for?

She was stretching things. Maybe she should stay out of it. Like that was going to happen.

"Well?" Grandma asked.

"I was going to flip a coin, but I'm going with Mrs. Partridge."

"Sandra Booth? I'm sure she'll be a good choice." Grandma sounded disappointed. She liked people who made her laugh.

Marti opened her laptop, went to HireAdvantage.com, and signed into the Mickkleson/ACS account with her temporary password. When prompted for a new password, a few snotty replies to Dmitri ran through her mind. Most were not safe for work. He'd never see them anyway. She went with the super-secure password suggested by her Mac. HireAdvantage.com sent her a confirmation email, she clicked a link, and she was in.

She set up Sandra's background check and, in an act of minor defiance, billed it directly to the account with a "Mickkleson Foundation" notation. Not what Dmitri recommended, but she couldn't imagine Mrs. Partridge not passing. She was about to click "Send Invitation to Candidate" when it dawned on her that maybe she should call Sandra and officially offer her the job first.

It wasn't Marti's day for phone luck. Sandra's phone went directly to voicemail. She left a message offering Sandra the job, contingent on passing a background check, and warned her to be on the lookout for an email from HireAdvantage. The company would collect some information from her and set up a local appointment to collect her fingerprints.

Hoping she'd accept, Marti clicked "Send Invitation" on the HireAdvantage website and closed her laptop.

Now all she had to do was call Faustyn and break the news he wasn't going to get to play with the De'Longhi. She'd had enough of phones for the day. Breaking Faustyn's heart would have to wait until Monday.

❧

"NOW, WHAT TO DO ABOUT YOU."

Lilith sprawled atop the conference table. At least it was getting used for something.

"Oh, how do you solve a problem like Lil-i-ith?" Ghost Girl sang.

Marti cringed at the insertion of the extra syllable. "You're into musicals?"

"That one was big when I was a kid. You couldn't get away from it." She played with her bracelets. "How about this one? What do you do with a drunken Lil-ith?"

"Nice voice, but you're not drunk," Grandma said.

Lilith blew her a raspberry.

Grandma was right. Since ghosts didn't eat or drink, Lilith wasn't drunk. She had continued to gain both presence and atti-tude—with a few notable exceptions—since the discovery of her bones. Marti wondered if Lilith knew the connection. "What do you know about Henrietta's Hollow?"

"Way hay and up she rises, early in the morning." Lilith's voice held a slight quaver. The sea shanty sounded like a lament.

"Is that an answer?"

"Maybe," Grandma said.

Lilith said nothing.

"Do you know anything about a men's club here before the accountants?" Marti said.

"I don't remember." Lilith was still present, but her attitude was fading.

"How about Philip Berryman? Was he a member?"

Lilith was gone.

"How does she do that?" Marti said. "She just disappears. The rest of you walk, stalk, or waft away through walls."

"She does too," Grandma says. "She's just fast. Really fast. Like when you leave me behind and I bungee back to you. It might look like I appear out of nowhere, but I promise, I pass through everything in between. It's not always pleasant, you know."

"And she can't leave the office."

"Ghost hunt!" Grandma said.

Lilith wasn't in the front room unless she was hiding under—or in—the furniture.

"You take the storage closet. I'll take the water closet," Grandma said.

It was amazing how many euphemisms Americans had for "that room that holds the toilet," but Marti agreed.

She carefully searched the shelves, checking in and behind boxes too small to hold a living human. She'd have to ask Grandma if the dead could shrink themselves. The subject had never come up. She made it to the back of the long narrow closet.

"Not there!" Grandma emerged from the wall.

Marti put one finger over her lips and pointed to the floor. Two sets of toes, encased in cork platform sandals, stuck out where the back wall met the floor.

Marti knocked on the wall. The toes didn't move. The wall sounded hollow. It should be a wall from the building's original construction. A century or more of plastering shouldn't sound like drywall.

"I wonder if I've got a floor plan somewhere." She wasn't sure, but it was possible the closet wasn't as deep as the powder-room-bathroom-water closet.

"Don't be ridiculous." Grandma dove into the wall, and out popped Lilith.

Marti jumped back just in time to avoid a freeze. "What's in there?"

Lilith took the direct route out of the storage closet, and there was no avoiding a freeze.

"Sorry," Grandma said.

"I-I n-n-need-d-d-d a ha-m-m-m-m-er."

"It's not like I can get you one."

She hadn't seen any tools in her search of the closet and didn't know where else they would be. There had to be something around to use.

She ran to her office and grabbed an oversized Millefiori glass paperweight from the bookshelves. She didn't know if it was an antique or a reproduction, but it was heavy enough to anchor a stack of papers in a hurricane. When Mom added it to the decor, Marti's first thought was it would make a good murder weapon.

"This'll work." She still shivered, but her teeth had stopped chattering.

"I'm sorry." Lilith blocked the door.

"Out of my way. I've got a wall to murder." She was going to feel silly if she didn't find anything, but why would anyone build a false wall in a closet if they didn't have something to hide?

"Before I make a total fool of myself, did you see anything in there? It's not just pipes or something?" Marti hefted the paperweight.

"There's a metal lock box on the floor. Nothing fancy. The kind that's been around for years and you can buy anywhere," Grandma said.

"Here goes nothing." Marti swung the paperweight, hit the wall with all her might, and fell forward. If the hidden cubby was any deeper, she would have done a face-plant. As it was, only her dignity was dented, which was better than she could say for the fake wall.

"That was overkill," Grandma said.

"Not drywall, then." Whoever built the false wall wasn't concerned with quality construction. Whatever they used wasn't cardboard, but it wasn't much stronger. Marti ripped the remainder away with her hands.

On the floor, just as Grandma said, sat a small green metal box.

Marti retrieved it. "Locked. Maybe Nathaniel Worthington kept a secret stash of cash."

"Right," Grandma said. "Where he could easily get to it any time he wanted."

"Are you going to open it?" Lilith joined them.

The closet was getting crowded. It wasn't big enough for three people, even if two of them had long ago shed their corporeal bodies. Marti had no intention of getting another freeze, even if just an elbow.

"Everybody out. We'll see if we can open it, but not here."

In her office, Marti put the box on her desk. The three of them stared at it.

"Maybe you can pry the lock off with a screwdriver. It doesn't look all that strong," Grandma said.

"No tools, remember?" Marti said. "Wait." She ran back to the storage closet and retrieved the heavy paperweight.

One good whack and the lock fell off.

"Ready?"

They took a collective deep breath. Or Marti did. The two who didn't breathe pretended to. She opened the box.

All it contained was two photos. The first was a group of five men. They looked to be anywhere from mid-twenties to mid-fifties in age. Their clothing placed them in the late nineteen-sixties or early seventies. Lilith's era.

"Do either of you recognize any of them?" Marti said.

Lilith shook her head. She was a bit more transparent, but still with them.

"We can take it to the Green and show Janice. 'We' meaning you," Grandma said.

Marti examined the second photograph. Two of the men stood on either side of a teenager. Not Lilith, but she looked to be the same age. One of the men had his arm around her shoulder. She looked familiar, but Marti couldn't place her. There was a lot of that going around lately.

"Marley. I remember." Lilith flickered and faded.

"Is she crossing over?" Marti'd met ghosts who crossed over once they realized they were dead, but Lilith had known she was dead for a long time.

"I don't know," Grandma said.

"No. I don't want to go. I want to tell you." Lilith was transparent and shaky but back.

"And we want you to, dear," Grandma said. "Let's get comfy and have a talk." She led Lilith to the front room.

The ghost girl looked so miserable, Marti would have made her tea and fed her Oreos if she could.

"WHO'S MARLEY?" Marti asked.

"She is—was—my best friend," Lilith said.

"The two men in the picture?"

"Mr. Berryman and Mr. Harrigan."

"Who's Mr. Harrigan? Does he have a first name?" Marti knew who Berryman was. She'd never heard of the other.

"He was a teacher too. Math. I think his name was David."

Lilith was on the verge of a ghostly meltdown. Marti worried about losing her before she finished her story.

"Stop interrogating her," Grandma said. "Let her talk."

Marti shut up, and Lilith talked.

When Lilith and Marley were high school seniors, Marley became involved with Berryman. She ended up pregnant.

"That slime," Marti said.

Everyone knew the baby was Berryman's, but he didn't admit it. He spread the word Marley was "easy." She was a tramp. The baby could be anybody's. Marley was sent away. When the baby was born, they took it away from her. They never let her hold it. They never told her whether it was a boy or a girl.

"When she came home, she wasn't the same," Lilith said.

Marti steamed but kept her mouth shut and let Lilith continue.

"She was so sad. My parents and Janice told me to stay away from her or I'd get a reputation too, but she was my *friend* and I knew Mr. Berryman was a liar. Marley thought she loved him, and he wouldn't have anything to do with her."

Lilith grew more and more worried about her friend. The Berrymans adopted a baby, and Marley got worse. She was drinking and probably using drugs.

Marti realized why the girl in the photo looked familiar. She was a young Philippa Berryman.

Marley quit talking to Lilith, and they'd always shared everything. There was a student teacher Lilith trusted. A young woman. Susan Silliphant. Lilith went to her and told her everything, including that Marley and Mr. Berryman had used the men's clubhouse for their secret rendezvous. Lilith and Marley went to a party there once. There'd been a couple of other women, but Lilith and Marley were the youngest. Lilith left early.

"I didn't want to hang out with a bunch of touchy-feely old guys. Marley stayed. I never went back."

"Smart girl," Grandma said.

"Miss Silliphant tried to talk to Janice, but she didn't want to hear it."

"Some friend you've got there, Grandma." Marti added one more thing to her list of reasons to dislike her former teacher.

"Attitudes were different back then," Grandma said.

"That doesn't make it right."

"No, it doesn't. Go on, Lilith."

Susan Silliphant decided to confront Berryman and his cronies. Lilith went with her, but Miss Silliphant made her wait in the car. Miss Silliphant went up to the clubhouse. Lilith waited over an hour. Worried, she went to find the teacher.

"Mr. Berryman was talking about Henrietta's Hollow. Burying something there. Miss Silliphant was on the floor. She didn't look like she was breathing. Mr. Berryman told me that was what happened to little girls who told lies. He said, 'We can always dig a hole for two.'"

"Did you tell anyone?" Marti knew she'd told Janice Heedly, for all the good that did.

"Not right away. The next day Marley killed herself. She did it here, but they found her in Henrietta's Hollow. Everyone said it was a drug overdose."

"How do you know it wasn't?"

"She sent me a letter. I got it after they found her. She told me where she was going and why. She apologized for not being a better friend."

Ghosts didn't have tears, but Marti did and her face was wet.

"I went to Janice. I told her about Miss Silliphant and Marley. She didn't believe me until I showed her the letter. She told me to destroy it. Marley's parents had had enough heartbreak and suicide was worse than an overdose. When I refused, she grabbed the letter and ripped it up."

No wonder Mrs. Heedly was such a miserable old witch by the time Marti met her. All of those secrets would turn a saint into a shrew, and it didn't sound like Janice Heedly was a saint to start with. Marti couldn't dredge up any sympathy for her.

"I was so angry. I didn't know what to do. I got a bottle of cheap wine and went to the gazebo. The lights were on up here. My friend was dead. As far as I was concerned, those men killed her, just like they had Miss Silliphant. And they were up here enjoying themselves. I was drunk, but I knew what I had to do. I came up here to confront them."

Lilith's presence had grown stronger as she talked, but she wavered and flickered again. Marti was afraid of what was coming. Grandma moved to the couch and put her arm around the girl.

"I don't know what I said, but I know I was loud. Mr. Berryman hit me. The next thing I knew, I was here and couldn't leave."

NINETEEN

MARTI STARED at the photo of the five men. The only two Lilith identified were Berryman and Harrigan. The others she either didn't know or didn't remember. Marti hadn't pressed her. The poor girl had remembered more than enough for one day.

The oldest man looked like a Pernelli, which meant he probably was. That was no help. Even if she could figure out which Pernelli, if he was still alive, and if she could find him, no Pernelli was going to talk to her.

Another might have been the younger version of Peter's father or grandfather. Marti only met him once, back when she and Dmitri were teenagers. Dmitri was saving for a car, and the two of them liked to roam the car lot and dream. She remembered the then-owner as a good-natured old guy. She might have to revise that opinion. He was long gone, and as far as she knew, not haunting any place. He wouldn't be any help.

She had no clue who the fifth man was. She could show the photo to Mrs. Heedly, but that was a last resort. She was too angry with Janice Heedly to be near her.

Someone still among the living had to know what happened in the office all those years ago. Lilith's remains needed to be officially identified and her killer brought to justice. Marti needed someone to back Lilith's story. It all happened before she was born, and as much as she'd like to, there was no way for her to introduce Big to Lilith. She needed someone alive.

She knew where to find Philip Berryman, but if what Dawn said was true, it would be hard to get any sense out of him. Besides, why would he admit to murder after getting away with it all these years?

She Googled "David Harrigan." There were a lot of them. She added "Bicklesburg Area High School" to her search. A David P. Harrigan had indeed taught math there. He'd left the year after Lilith's death. She added a time frame to the search, including three years before and after his departure from Bicklesburg. Bingo.

Unfortunately, what she found was an obituary. He'd moved across the country and taught for two more years before dying "suddenly at home." No help there.

That left Philip Berryman. Dawn said his daughter was the only one who visited him. She'd also said he was at death's door. There was no time to waste.

"Come on, Grandma."

"Where are we going?"

"Blissful Meadows."

"Mr. Berryman doesn't get many visitors." A white-haired aide led Marti down a long hallway. 'Volunteer' was emblazoned across the back of her blue T-shirt. "His daughter visits regularly —so devoted, that one. How do you know him?"

Marti fished for an answer. She'd signed a visitor log to get in and signed it with her real name. She was too well known—or infamous—locally to do anything else. A Mickkleson using a false name would raise flags. She couldn't claim Berryman was a dear old uncle she hadn't seen in years. He'd once been her teacher, but if the aide knew anything about his history with students, both the ones he didn't like and the ones he liked too much, that wouldn't wash.

"I'm working on a brief background piece for the Mickkleson Foundation, including our headquarters. His name is on a lease from years ago, but it doesn't say what he used the space for." Always best to stick some truth into little white lies.

The aide beamed. "Local history is so important! So much gets lost when those who know leave us. I don't know how much help he'll be, but on his good days, he's still pretty sharp. On other days, well..." She lowered her voice. "Dementia." She opened the door to the last room on the hall. "Here we are."

If Blissful Meadows encouraged residents to decorate their rooms with their belongings from home, Mr. Berryman hadn't brought much. In one corner was an overstuffed recliner, its brown leather cracked with age and use. The only other chair in the room looked like standard hospital issue. He had brought photographs. Every available surface and a good part of the walls were covered with photos. All, Marti assumed, of Philippa through the years.

Mr. Berryman's eyes were closed. His chest rose and fell in a deep rhythm.

Marti picked up a framed photo from his bedside stand. The young Philip Berryman sat on one side of a girl who looked to be about five. A woman she didn't know sat on the other.

"His daughter and his late wife," the aide said. "He's always saying how much his daughter looks like her mother, but I don't see it. Ms. Berryman says her father's friends used to tell her the same thing when she was young. I think she's convinced herself it's true. Do you know her?"

"We've met a couple of times." Philippa bore no resemblance to either of the adults in the photo, but Marti had no problem believing she looked exactly like her mother. She couldn't find any physical likeness to her father, but maybe he was responsible for her personality. "I'll just sit and wait a while and see if he wakes up."

The aide helped her move the non-reclining chair to the bedside and showed her the call button. "Just buzz if you need anything."

As soon as they were alone, Marti poked the old man. "Hey. You. Wake up."

"Nice," Grandma said.

"I don't care," Marti said.

His eyelids fluttered. "Marley?"

"No. Wake up. Open your eyes."

"Charlotte? No, you're too old. Susan?"

"Wrong on both counts."

"Who are these men?" She stuck the photo of the five men in front of his face.

"Haven't you heard the one about catching more flies with honey?" Grandma said.

"I don't care." It didn't matter anymore if Philip Berryman heard her talking to ghosts.

His eyes cleared. The Mr. Berryman she remembered was back. The cruel one.

"Where did you get that?" he said.

"Who are they?"

"Little girls need to mind their own business."

"That one's David Harrigan. That one's you. Who are the others?" She just needed to locate one—one still among the living. Maybe he'd back up Lilith's story. If he had a conscience.

"Go away. Leave me alone." He closed his eyes and pulled his blanket up to his chin.

She was losing him. "Did you kill Charlotte Monahan?"

"I want my daughter. You're not Philippa."

"Did you kill Charlotte? She says you did. You know we found her bones. It's just a matter of time before we find out who put them there."

"Help! Nurse!" His voice was weak. He reached for the call button.

Marti grabbed it and held it just out of his reach. The photo fluttered to the floor. "Tell me and I'll leave."

"What's going on here?" Philippa barreled into the room.

"Marley! Help me! This woman's crazy!"

Marti backed away. Philippa rushed to her father's side. Marti kept backing.

"It's Philippa, Daddy." She took his hand. "Ms. Mickkleson, what exactly are you doing here and why is my father so upset?"

Marti reached the door and fled.

Grandma stayed behind.

SHE'D BLOWN THAT ONE. Other than confirming, for herself, who Philippa's mother was, all she'd accomplished was upsetting a dying man and his daughter. She didn't care about the first. He deserved it. The latter was a lawyer and could be trouble.

She turned on the radio in the TT and waited for her designated eavesdropper. Unless Philip Berryman had faked his confusion, she didn't expect Grandma to have much to report. It didn't hurt to try. He might say something useful to Philippa.

A knock on the car window made Marti jump. A nicely dressed woman peered in, looking concerned. Marti lowered the window.

"Are you all right? It's...you've been sitting here awhile."

It hadn't been that long. Marti made a sad face. "These visits are hard. Seeing your loved ones deteriorate." She'd had some experience with that, so it wasn't all an act. She faked a sob. Too bad she couldn't summon tears on command.

"It can be traumatic. Here." The woman handed her a card. "If you want to talk, I have some time now."

Blissful Meadows' resident social worker. She hadn't given any sign she knew Marti, and Marti didn't recognize her or her name. Out of towner. Sometimes, luck was on her side.

"No, I need to get home. People waiting, you know." Marti started the TT. She could leave. Grandma would be along soon enough.

"Well, anytime. Just give me a call."

"Philippa wasn't pleased with your visit, and she let her father and the staff know," Grandma said.

"Thanks. Gotta go." Marti put the window up, backed out, and left the social worker behind. She didn't speak to Grandma until they were well on the road.

"What did you find out?"

"Not much. As soon as you left, Philippa asked what he told you. He babbled about Marley and Susan. She kept asking, and he kept not answering. Or, he answered, but it didn't have anything to do with her questions or your visit. He was confused. Didn't know who she was at first. He called her Marley more than once. Philippa didn't seem to know why. Every time he did it, she asked him who Marley is. He didn't answer that question either."

Marti took that as one more confirmation that Marley was indeed Philippa's mother. Interesting that Philippa didn't know.

"The old SOB did have one moment of lucidity, just before I left."

Marti waited. "Are you going to tell me?" Grandma Bertie's sense of drama got on her nerves.

"You left your photos behind."

Marti groaned. She'd used her phone to take pictures of both photos as backups, but a photo of a photo wouldn't count as evidence if things got that far. She still had the picture of Berryman, Harrigan, and Marley. Or did she? Grandma said "photos."

She checked her bag. No photos. She must have pulled out both together. Which meant she dropped them together.

"Philippa found them. She asked her father about them, and he said, clear as a bell, 'Philippa. You've got your own mess to clean up. Stay out of mine.'"

"He must know something. What's Philippa's mess? Does it involve Peter?"

"That's all he said. He closed his eyes and pretended to sleep. Philippa wasn't happy."

Finding out what he knew about Philippa would be a challenge, if not impossible. And Marti still had questions about his "mess." Nice way to refer to murder.

"Why would he wall up those photos in the storage closet? If he didn't want anyone to find them, why didn't he just destroy them?" Marti said.

"How would I know? Maybe he couldn't bear to destroy them. Some kind of memento or something. He obviously likes photos."

"Did the men's club break up after they were evicted?"

"Again, how would I know?"

"If they didn't, where did they go?"

"You know who might be able to answer these questions? Janice. That's who. Janice might be able to answer these questions."

The last person, dead or alive, Marti wanted to talk to was Janice Heedly. "Okay, but I'm staying in the car and you'd better keep her away from me." Marti headed to the Green.

"The mood you're in, nobody needs to be near you." Grandma was out of the car before Marti parked.

She hoped the two old ghosts weren't going to indulge in any long heart-to-hearts. If she sat and stewed for too long over Mrs. Heedly's failure to help her sister or Susan Silliphant, who knew what she might do.

She needn't have worried. Grandma was back in no time.

"Janice didn't know for sure, but she heard rumors they moved to Philip Berryman's hunting cabin. It's not far outside of town."

One thing about a mostly rural place like Battlesborough County, you didn't have to go far to leave the bright lights and big city of downtown Bickleburg and end up in a wooded wonderland. With the strip malls and chain stores springing up on the fringes of the village proper, what were once isolated hunting cabins were now within walking distance of the expanded town.

"Did she tell you where it was?"

"No. I don't know if she knows."

"You didn't ask?"

"I was distracted by bigger news."

This time, Marti out-waited Grandma. If the news was big enough, she'd spill eventually.

"You are no fun." Grandma sighed dramatically.

Marti waited for her to continue.

"Gossip in the Green today is Winter Adams has been arrested."

"What? For Peter's murder?"

"That's the story."

Marti started the car and pulled out.

"Home's the other way," Grandma said.

"We're going to the police station. I'm talking to Big. You're talking to Eustace."

CHAPTER

TWENTY

MARTI MARCHED TO THE COUNTER. Baby Face Rodney was on duty. Time to channel her mother again.

"I'm here to see Big."

"I'll see if he's available." He didn't sound cowed by her at all. Maybe Baby Face was growing up.

"Tell him I'm not leaving until I see him." If she wasn't careful, she'd end up stuck in Queen Margaret mode.

"I hope you realize how lucky you are to have me. I'm always welcome here." Grandma left to find Eustace.

Rodney walked away and picked up a phone. The conversation was short.

"I'll take you back," he said.

Too easy. Big either had something to tell her or it was a trap.

Big's office hadn't been redecorated since her last visit, months ago. Same utilitarian desk painted in the same ugly green. The same file cabinets lined the walls, making the cramped room feel smaller. Unlike the ones in her office, Big's were metal and probably stuffed to the hilt. The cinderblock walls were painted the same depressing gray, and brown paper still covered the single window. The paper looked clean and fresh. That was an upgrade.

She was sure the metal folding chair she sat in was the same one she'd sat in five months ago.

"I'm sure this isn't what you're used to, now that you're an executive and all."

He was mocking her.

"The interrogation room you had me in a couple of days ago was fancier than your office. What's that all about?"

"It wasn't an interrogation room. What did you want to see me about?"

Which should she bring up first—Winter or Lilith?

"I hear Winter Adams has been arrested for Peter's murder." Winter was the safer bet. Big knew the Bicklesburg grapevine as well as anyone.

"Where did you hear that?"

"It's all over town."

"Of course it is." Big heaved his shoulders. "She hasn't been arrested, only brought in for questioning. She's not a suspect in Peter's murder."

"Why not?"

"She has an alibi. She was with Harold Binks. They were seen in Sicilian Heaven. She says he's been giving her financial advice."

"Financial advice?"

"That's their story and they're sticking to it."

"Who's backing up her alibi? The Pernelli kid behind the counter? How credible is he?"

"The Pernelli kid, Sterling Cromwell, and half a dozen other patrons. It was a popular night for pizza. Her alibi's stronger than yours."

Marti wondered if that was a threat. "So why's she here?"

"We've found some evidence she was involved with Peter's financial, um, dealings. She's been identified as posing as Rachel-Anne for various transactions. I expect to charge her with identity fraud and forgery. State investigators are interested in talking to her too."

"So, what you're saying here is the tip I gave Dmitri paid off?"

Big's face colored. "That's all I can tell you right now and more than I should have. Anything else?"

He wasn't going to admit to her help. Too bad. He was about to get more of it. "Any word on who Peter dug up at Henrietta's Hollow?"

"We have an idea when the bones were buried from artifacts found at the scene. We know the body was female and young, but we don't know who she was."

Artifacts. The bracelets. They were her first clue too, but she knew more than Big.

"What are you doing to find out who?" She was surprised he was answering her questions but did her best not to show it.

"I've got people looking at missing person reports from the time. There were a surprising number of them, but most were hippy-dippy kids running off to have fun. Most came home, sooner or later. We're sending a sample for DNA analysis, but that'll take a while. Maybe we can find a match through one of those online genealogy places."

That could take a long time, and Marti didn't want to wait. Lilith deserved better. "Have you looked at Charlotte Monahan?"

Big leaned forward. "Where did you come up with that name?"

"Let's just say a little ghostie told me."

"She was one of the runaways."

"Did she ever come back?" Little did he know the answer to that one.

"No. I think we're done here." Big stood.

She wasn't going to get anything else out of him. She stood too. "I can see myself out. I've been here often enough."

"Marti."

She stopped at the door.

"Have you seen or talked to Dmitri recently?"

"Not since this morning when I told him to tell you about

Winter. Why?"

"Just wondering. And Marti, stay out of this. Leave the investigating to the professionals."

He sounded like Dmitri. "Do your job and I might." There was that Margaret Mickkleson voice again.

GRANDMA WAITED IN THE CAR. "Eustace kept trying to get frisky. I wasn't in the mood," she said.

It had never dawned on Marti what might happen if Grandma Bertie was in the mood. It didn't bear thinking about. She tried to scour the image from her mind. "Did you find out anything before leaving him in the lurch?"

"Of course. What do you take me for? An amateur?"

"Of course not," Marti said soothingly. Grandma liked to think of herself as the Mata Hari of ghosts. If Marti irritated her, it might take hours to get her to talk.

"Don't use that tone of voice on me. Eustace was full of news. Winter hasn't been arrested—yet. Just hauled in for questioning and not for Peter's murder."

"I know all that. Big was exceptionally talkative."

"Humph. Did he tell you Terrance Appleby showed up claiming to be her lawyer?"

"He wasn't that talkative."

"It gets better. Winter emphatically denied it. She wouldn't let him in the room while they questioned her and refused to go with him when he tried to spring her. Said she was safer in jail."

"Okay. That is interesting." Was Appleby Peter's mysterious lawyer? Philippa said he was a defense attorney, "among other things." What were those other things?

"Oh, it gets even better. I got the impression it wasn't so much Appleby she was afraid of. It was his friends, especially— and I quote—'that witch Philippa.'"

∼

FRIDAY EVENING at Bickle House was quiet, the quietest evening since the arrival of RachelAnne and the kids.

Mom, T3, and Maggie were all worn out from their shopping trip. They'd gone to a big mall in the city. Mom bought the kids whole new wardrobes. Kid-friendly wardrobes, not the kind she'd dressed both Marti and RachelAnne in before they were old enough to fight back. Grandparent Syndrome in action.

T3's "anything you want" was a superhero play set with lights, sounds, and about a hundred pieces. According to the box, fully assembled it would be about three feet deep by four feet wide.

"Where are we going to put that?" Marti asked.

"I thought we'd turn one of the unused bedrooms into a playroom," Mom said. "Or maybe the ballroom on the second floor. We seldom use it."

It hadn't been used in Marti's lifetime.

"Who is this woman and what did she do with my granddaughter?" Grandma Bertie said.

The only thing Maggie wanted was a book. She showed Marti a beautifully illustrated version of *There Was an Old Lady Who Swallowed a Fly*.

"She yooks yike the yady," Maggie said.

"Lllllooks lllllike the lllllady, Maggie. Lllllady," RachelAnne said.

"She doesn't look like me at all," Grandma said. "Much too old."

"She does look a bit like your Aunt Marti," RachelAnne said.

Marti didn't react. Mom stared at her, her lips pinched and her eyes hard.

She knows. RachelAnne might have her head in the sand, but Mom knew exactly who Maggie's yady was and what it meant. There was a long conversation in Marti's future, but not now. She had enough to deal with, as did everyone else. "What's for dinner? I'm starving. Do you want me to cook?"

"No," Mom and RachelAnne said in unison.

"We've had enough spaghetti and pizza for one week," Rachel-Anne said. "Also, Georgia came by this afternoon. She left us dinner. All we need to do is set the table and serve."

"Marti can help. As for the rest of us, isn't it time for ponies?" Mom grabbed the remote.

"As soon as I change," Marti said.

RachelAnne headed for the kitchen. Mom turned on the television, and Marti went up to her room.

Edwards and Amity were waiting with their nightly Peter account. He'd shown up in all the usual places, but they had one new development to report.

"He's afraid of us!" Amity said.

They'd found him in RachelAnne's room—Marti didn't like the idea of *that*—and backed him into a corner.

"We held out our arms and wiggled our fingers and went 'woooohoooo' and he just kept backing up." Amity giggled.

"Like a lily-livered skitterbrook," Edwards said.

That was one Marti'd never heard, but she got the meaning.

Once they had him cornered, he fled through the wall. They chased him from room to room woooohooooing until Amity got bored.

Marti added it to her list of useful tidbits. She didn't know how she'd use it, but it felt important. Her head was so stuffed with useful tidbits it felt like it would explode.

"I want to keep him," Amity said. "I had fun. You never play with me anymore."

"Right now, I need to change my clothes and get downstairs before someone comes looking for me."

Edwards grabbed his charge and fled. His sense of propriety kept him away when there was any chance of Marti shedding her clothes, thank goodness.

~

AFTER DINNER, everyone—except Peter—settled in for a movie. A kids' movie, one Marti'd never heard of or seen. It failed to keep her attention. Her eyelids felt like lead. She struggled to stay awake. Edwards and Amity were the only ones enjoying the on-screen antics. Mom and RachelAnne both snored in their respective corners of the couch. The kids, stretched out on the floor in their new pajamas, were asleep. Maya, curled up next to Mom, catnapped.

Marti considered joining them. She'd had a long day. Her anger had burned out and left her drained. Lilith and the Berrymans and Winter and Peter would have to wait until tomorrow. She closed her eyes and gave in.

Her phone went off and woke her with a jolt.

"What was that?" RachelAnne mumbled.

"Nothing."

The caller ID said "ACS." Maybe it was Dmitri. She made a break for it before the ringing phone woke everyone.

It wasn't Dmitri. It was Richie, and for a change, he didn't sound frightened of her.

"Do you know where Dmitri is?" he said.

"Why? What's wrong?" Any leftover drowsiness from her snooze vanished.

"He's missing. No one knows where he is. Big's looking for him. That Terrance Appleby's looking for him. Even Oliver's looking for him."

"I talked to him this morning, but that was it." She checked her watch. "His shift only ended four hours ago. Why's everyone in such a tizzy?"

"He's been gone more than four hours."

In the early afternoon, Dmitri called Richie to cover for him. He said he'd be back within an hour, and Richie could come in for his shift two hours later than usual to make up for it.

"He was not happy when he left. You know. The kind of not happy where he gets real quiet. And scary."

Marti knew.

"He never came back or called. He's not upstairs and he's not answering his phone," Richie said.

If Dmitri was pulling another disappearing act, she was the last person he'd tell. Still, it was out of character for him to flake out on work. Adult-Dmitri was one of the most responsible people she knew.

"Maybe he's got a hot date?"

"That's why I called you."

Marti snorted. Poor misguided young man. "If I hear from him, I'll let you know."

She hung up and called Dmitri. He didn't answer. Of course, that could be because he knew it was her. Caller ID was both a blessing and a curse.

She headed back to the parlor. The television was off, and everyone other than Maya was gone. Marti was wide awake. Hyper-awake. If she went to bed, she'd toss and turn for hours.

"It's just you and me, Miss Maya." She picked up the remote. "What'll we watch?"

Maya meowed.

"I don't speak cat, so I guess it's up to me."

Both *America's Most Mysterious Missing Persons* and *Ghost Whisperer* were too real to her. What she needed was something with no relation to Marti-world. Something that qualified as pure fantasy. She found a rom-com and settled in.

"So, Maya. Where do you think Dmitri's hiding?"

Maya blinked. If she knew anything, she wasn't telling.

Maybe he'd finally given in to Dawn's continual advances and was on a hot date. That would be worth keeping secret.

More important, why were Big, Terrance Appleby, and Oliver looking for him?

CHAPTER

TWENTY-ONE

"WHOSE IDEA WAS THIS, ANYWAY?" Marti, along with RachelAnne and the kids, had spent most of Saturday cleaning the unused ballroom. Compared to movie ballrooms, it was small but more than big enough.

Marti sat cross-legged on the floor, T3's new play set spread out in front of her, ready to assemble. Much to her relief, it only had eighty-eight pieces, not a hundred, and eighty of those were action figures and accessories.

The remaining eight needed to be put together, and whoever wrote the directions had a twisted sense of humor. RachelAnne took one look, tossed them to Marti, grabbed Maggie, and fled.

She read the first line for the fourth time. "Take the gobbledy-gook amplifithingy thunderbolt housing and insert tabs A-X into recepticalaries 142-148." Maybe not exactly what it said, but it might as well have for all the sense it made to her.

Edwards and Amity joined them.

"We have a visitor," Edwards announced.

Marti frantically checked the room, searching for Peter.

"Not him," Amity said. "The fish-man is here."

"The Hulk is in the house," Edwards clarified.

Why was Big there? And on a Saturday afternoon. Didn't he ever take a day off? Maybe it was a social call. Fat chance.

"I don't suppose we could take a break and finish this later?" Marti said.

"All done," T3 said.

Deluxe Superhero Play Set Model 2743 towered over her in all its fully assembled glory. The three-by-four measurement was when it was closed. Open, it wasn't as deep, but its wingspan was double. Good thing they went for the ballroom rather than a spare bedroom.

"How did you do that?"

"I looked at the pictures. It wasn't hard."

Marti reminded herself how much she loved the little hooligan. The smart little hooligan. "That deserves a cookie. More than one. Let's go down and reward ourselves."

"Three cookies?"

"At least." She could find out why Big was there. T3 could sugar up.

"Okay."

On the way to the kitchen, Marti peeked inside the formal sitting room. Empty. Had she missed Big?

Nope. In the kitchen, he sat across from RachelAnne at the island counter, steaming mugs of coffee in front of both of them.

"Did you get it put together?" RachelAnne said.

"T3 did." Marti reached into the cookie jar and pulled out a handful of cookies. Not Oreos, but they'd do. "Where are Mom and Maggie?"

"In the parlor. Mom's reading *There Was an Old Lady* to Maggie for the umpteenth time."

Marti gave the cookies to T3. "Take these and share with Maggie. Nana too, if she insists."

"It's too late for cookies. You'll spoil their supper," Rachel-Anne said.

"They earned it. So did I." Marti took a cookie for herself and got out a coffee mug.

Big hadn't spoken.

She took her cookie and settled in next to RachelAnne.

"So, to what do we owe the honor of a Saturday visit?"

"When was the last time you saw Dmitri?" he said.

Dmitri was still missing. She buried her panic. "Saw? That would be, let me think. Thursday. I stopped at his office on the way home. But, like I told you, I talked to him yesterday morning."

"Nothing since?" the chief said.

"He hasn't turned up yet? He does have a track record of taking off and not telling anyone, least of all me, where he's going."

"This is different."

"How?"

"First, the last time, I knew where he was going," Big said.

"And he didn't just take off," RachelAnne said. "He asked for a leave of absence."

"Do you know where he went?" Marti asked her sister. Did everyone know but her?

RachelAnne shrugged. "I didn't ask. He needed time off, and I thought he'd earned it."

"You said 'first'. What else?" Marti said.

"His car was found last night at Henrietta's Hollow. He was nowhere to be found."

"Didn't anyone see him? What about the construction guys? The ones in the trailer-office?" The ones who discovered Peter's body.

"It's still a crime scene. Between that and the, er, unresolved finances..." Big glanced at RachelAnne. "...all work has been shut down. No one was around yesterday."

Except for Dmitri, Marti thought. What was he doing there? "Is that it?"

Big stared into his coffee cup.

"Tell me," she said.

"We've had a witness come forward. They identified Dmitri as one of Peter's visitors the night he was killed. After you and RachelAnne left. They said he was with a woman. They implied it might be you but wouldn't swear to it. Since you were with RachelAnne, we know it wasn't you. Probably."

Why would Dmitri go to RachelAnne's house that night? True, he was furious when he dragged Peter away from her the night before, but he couldn't have known about Peter's attempted assault on RachelAnne until the day after Peter's murder. If he somehow did, although he took his job protecting Mickklesons seriously, she couldn't imagine his dedication extended to murder. It didn't fit the Dmitri she knew, in the past or the present.

"Who is this supposed witness?" she said.

Big refused to tell her, but he had more news—and more questions.

"Philippa Berryman has also been reported missing. I hear you had a run-in with her at Blissful Meadows yesterday."

"Just a minor skirmish."

"What were you doing at Blissful Meadows?" RachelAnne said.

"Good question," Big said.

Thanks, RachelAnne. What good did it do to have a lawyer sister if she was going to ask Big's questions for him?

Marti gave them the same story she used on the Blissful Meadows volunteer, researching the history of the Foundation's offices. Eventually, she might have to do some research and produce a history. An edited history. The Foundation—meaning Mom—might not want it all public if it could be avoided. "I went to see Mr. Berryman, but he wasn't any help. He's not well. He was distraught and confused. Philippa showed up, and I left her with her father. What makes you think she's among the missing?"

"She didn't show up where she was expected last night and

again, not answering her phone. Everybody answers their phones at all hours these days. Especially, from what I understand, Philippa Berryman."

"Maybe there's a rabid phone thief on the loose," Marti said. "They wouldn't answer stolen phones." She knew how silly she sounded, but it was worth a shot.

"A Blissful Meadows employee said there was a strange woman in the parking lot. She described you—and not just the 'strange' part. She also wrote down the woman's license plate number. It's your mother's TT, which I understand you were driving yesterday."

"I had to take a minute. Seeing Mr. Berryman like that brought back memories. You know, when Mom..." She didn't finish the sentence. She'd let Big fill in the blank. *When Mom was ill. When Mom and I were nearly murdered.* Either worked, and neither was untrue.

"I need to get going. RachelAnne, thank you for the coffee. Marti, keep your nose out of places it doesn't belong."

"Wait," Marti said. "What about Winter?" Too late, it dawned on her she'd never told her sister about Winter and her not-quite-arrest.

"Big filled me in on that before you interrupt—joined us," RachelAnne said. "Are you sure you won't stay for dinner? I'm cooking, not Marti."

Big blushed. "I n-n-n-eed to get back to the station." He stammered, and there were no ghosts around to blame it on. "Too much going on. I'm basically living there for the duration."

"It's been nice to see you," RachelAnne said.

Marti looked from one to the other. Big wasn't the only one with red cheeks. It couldn't be. Well, they were both single, even if recently for one of them. She couldn't say much for her sister's taste, but Big was a step up from Peter.

〜

"MARTI, ARE YOU WITH US?" Mom said.

"Huh? Did I miss something?" Marti's mind had drifted throughout dinner. She couldn't stop thinking about what Big said.

Dmitri missing. His car at Henrietta's Hollow. She hoped he wasn't the latest occupant of Peter's hole. Surely Big and crew would have checked.

Philippa missing. She hadn't been AWOL for long, but from what Marti had seen, the woman was pathologically incapable of not answering her phone.

Most of all, who was Big's new witness? The last she heard, the neighbors said someone else had shown up at the McMansion that night but couldn't identify them.

"We are discussing the decor of the new playroom," Mom said. "Do you have any input?"

"Superheroes," T3 said. "And a wall we can draw on."

"He saw that in a movie and has been begging for one ever since," RachelAnne said.

"Sounds perfect," Marti said. She needed to find out who Big's witness was and exactly what they said. She could get a list of RachelAnne's neighbors on Paradise Sanctuary Boulevard and visit them.

"Purpyo," Maggie said. "I want purpyo."

"Purplllllle," RachelAnne said.

"You're too much like your aunt," Mom said.

Or she could take the shortcut. "I need to run out. I'm taking the TT."

"In the middle of dinner? Where?" Mom said.

"Errands. I'm not very hungry."

"It's your turn to clean up," RachelAnne said.

"Mommy cooked," Maggie said.

"Can I go with you?" T3 said.

"No. And leave the dishes. I'll get them when I get back. Oh, and Maggie? Purple's a good color." Marti left.

~

"THAT WAS UNEXPECTED," Grandma said. "One minute Edwards and I are discussing ways to trap Peter and the next, here I am."

Marti headed toward town. "Sorry, I didn't have time to warn you."

"I take it we're going somewhere important?"

"The station. You need to have another talk with Eustace." Marti explained what she needed. "And do not even think about getting frisky."

"No promises," Grandma said.

Instead of turning into the Municipal Services Center, Marti turned into the Episcopal church across the street.

"What are you doing?" Grandma said.

"I'm not going in. Nobody needs to know we're here. You should be able to get in far enough to find Eustace without me."

"It'll be tight. The cemetery's closer."

"I'm not in the mood." Marti had a small fan club among the residents of Oakdale Memorial Gardens. They were happy to have someone alive to talk to. A larger group despised her. Grandma said that unable to move on, many grew bitter over the years. Marti's ability to come and go as she pleased—and see and hear them—both frightened and confused them. She was perfectly capable of dealing with one or two angry spirits at a time. A horde was a different story. Oakdale Memorial Gardens was over two hundred years old. It was easily the most populated place in Bicklesburg. She didn't have the patience to deal with her fan club, let alone the stomach for the others.

"I'm sure Eustace will find me if need be," Grandma said.

"Just go, and make it quick."

Marti didn't need to wait long.

"The witness is Derek Bailey," Grandma said.

"I don't know him."

"I don't know him, but I know about him. He was big news in

Bicklesburg last month. Janice filled me in. She said the Bailey divorce was all people talked about for weeks."

Derek Bailey had taken everything and left his ex-wife with nothing. She'd accused him of hiding assets, but no matter how hard her lawyer searched, none were found. He kept the house, and as soon as the divorce was final, bought himself a shiny new sports car. Philippa was his lawyer.

"There may be only two Berrymans, but they're everywhere. Worse than Pernellis," Marti said.

"I've noticed," Grandma said. "You know, just because Philippa is missing doesn't mean she wants to be found."

"Do you think she'd run off without telling her father? She does seem to care about him."

"Do you think he understood if she did tell him?"

"There's only one way to find out."

"I'm sorry. You're on the do-not-fly list. I can't let you in to see Mr. Berryman, on orders of the family." The woman behind the desk detached her phone from her ear. Her name tag said "Kristyl." Marti was sure she was the cousin Dawn mentioned.

"Just for a minute? I think I left something in his room yesterday."

"Nope. You need to leave. If you don't, I'll call an orderly."

"Please?"

"And the police."

Definitely a Pernelli. No one else—well, hardly anyone else—would be so gleeful at the prospect of having Marti arrested.

"Pretend to leave," Grandma said. "I'll take care of this. Be ready to make a dash for it."

"If you say so." Marti slumped and shuffled toward the door.

"Don't overplay it. You're not going for an Oscar," Grandma said.

Outside, Marti lurked off to the side of the glass door and watched Grandma in action.

Kristyl's phone was stuck to her ear. Her mouth moved a mile a minute. Grandma stuck out a finger and touched her, just enough to make her shiver. She did it again. And again. Never enough for a full-on freeze, but Kristyl was definitely feeling the chill. She got up from the desk and disappeared through a door. Not the one to the resident's wing.

Marti made her break. Once she reached the hall, she slowed down and tried to act nonchalant. If she ran into anyone, she didn't want to be out of breath. If she did run into anyone, she hoped they either wouldn't know her or hadn't gotten the No Marti edict.

"She went after a sweater," Grandma said.

"Good work."

Luck was with her. She reached the end of the hallway without getting caught and opened the door to Mr. Berryman's room.

He already had a visitor.

"You have to talk."

Marti recognized her voice. Sandra Booth.

Sandra turned. "What are you doing here?"

Marti knew why she looked so familiar. She wasn't just Mrs. Partridge's twin. She looked like an older Karen Valentine.

"Susan Silliphant, I presume?"

"Oh, dear. I wish you hadn't figured that out. Now I'll have to kill you."

TWENTY-TWO

"Relax. I'm kidding."

Marti's heart thudded. It didn't sound like a joke.

"Don't be a baby," Grandma said. "I would have frozen her before she could do anything. Besides, you could take her."

"You need to go away. No one cares about you anymore," Mr. Berryman said.

"Philip here never checked the internet or watched *America's Most Mysterious Missing Persons*," Susan said.

"I...what are you doing here?" Marti stopped shaking. Almost. Susan Silliphant didn't look dangerous. Not that that meant anything. She did look like a good ghost freeze could stop her, which was reassuring.

"Define 'here.' In this room? In Bicklesburg? A philosophical observation on my place on the planet and in the circle of life? All of the above?"

"The first two."

"It's time for me to come out of hiding. I needed to take care of a few things first, and those things were in Bicklesburg. One of them's in this room."

"Don't listen to her," Mr. Berryman said. "It's all her fault.

Where's Marley? Where's Philippa? I want my daughter." He reached for the call button.

Susan held it up and waved it at him. "Oh, why don't you go to sleep, you old fool."

"What things?" Marti said.

"Sit down. We need to talk. I'm tired of running."

GRANDMA STOOD lookout in the hallway, and Susan Silliphant talked.

Her story echoed Lilith's, up to the part where she left the teenager in the car and went to confront Berryman and his cronies.

"It was stupid of me to go up there alone, but I was young and full of righteous anger—and Charlotte knew where I was going. If I didn't come back, she could tell someone."

"She did. Her sister." Marti hoped Susan wouldn't ask her how she came by her knowledge.

"I'm guessing talking to Janice Monahan did her about as much good as it did me."

"Pretty much."

Susan couldn't remember how many men were present, but three of them were teachers at the high school. She accused them of inappropriate behavior with students. They laughed at her.

"Philip here was the worst. He always was a bully."

Philip Berryman had told her no one would believe her story. She was just a mini-skirted nobody outsider. Even if someone did, those girls were asking for it.

"I told them it didn't matter. I'd go to the school board. If that didn't work, I'd find someone outside of Bicklesburg. Someone higher in the food chain. I'd keep going until someone believed me. I told them I knew who the mother of the Berrymans' new daughter was. That's the last thing I remember until I woke up on the ground in Henrietta's Hollow with a headache and David Harrigan and Philip standing over me."

"Back up. How did you know about Marley and the baby?"

"I didn't. It was a wild guess. But it looks like I was correct." Susan waved at the Berryman family photos surrounding them. "Wait. How do you know about Marley?"

Crap. Too much information. She was losing track of what she should know and what she shouldn't. "I, um, found some old photos, and..." She gestured at the same family photos. "Keep going. Henrietta's Hollow?"

Susan nodded. "Philip told David to 'take care of me' and left. I thought he was going to kill me."

"You're dead," Mr. Berryman said. "Why are you here?"

"I'm not dead, you dolt. Do I look dead?"

"Trust me. She's alive and breathing," Marti said.

"David said he was supposed to kill me." Susan's voice shook, but she continued her story. "He said he couldn't do it. Instead, he took me to the bus station in Martinsville. He gave me fifty dollars and told me to disappear. If I ever came back, Philip Berryman would do the job himself.

"The last bus had gone. I spent the night in the station, waiting for Philip to come after me. By morning, I decided to go as far as Harrigan's money would take me. The next bus to California wasn't until late in the evening. I bought a ticket, hid in a corner, and somehow fell asleep. When I woke up, the station was full of people. People talking about a body found in Henrietta's Hollow. I knew it was Charlotte."

"It wasn't," Marti said. "Charlotte came later."

"I know that now," Susan said.

"Stupid girl," Berryman said. "Philippa's smart. Not like her mother."

"In those days, California was the place for anyone who didn't want to be found. It was easy. I went to San Francisco and did the whole flowers in my hair bit. I changed my name. A lot. For a while I was Clover. Then Rainbow. Then Cloud. I settled in. I even had fun."

Marti understood. Her years in hiding hadn't been exactly fun, but they did have their highlights.

"After a few years, I'd almost convinced myself to come back and tell what I knew about Charlotte. I was in a park one day. I looked up and saw David Harrigan staring at me. I thought he'd come after me to finish what he was supposed to do. I ran and never looked back.

"The longer I was someone else, the harder it was to come forward. I met Jack. He was running from something big. Jail time big, in those days. Nothing bad, nothing violent, barely a misdemeanor now, but we did what we had to do. We became John and Sandra Booth and built a life together. We were so respectable and boring, no one ever guessed we weren't who we said we were."

"Why did you come back?" Marti got why Susan ran—she'd taken off for far less reason. Unlike Marti, Susan Silliphant hadn't run from something. She'd run for her life. "Why now?"

Jack died. He'd been her only family for most of her life. She was lonely. She wanted to reconnect with the rest of her family, but to do that with a clear conscience, she needed to face what happened in Bicklesburg.

"I started reading the *Gazette* online. I read about the development of Henrietta's Hollow. I knew I had to tell someone what happened there. I still thought the body they found was Charlotte, and I knew who killed her."

"It was an accident." Philip Berryman said. "Stupid girl. So many stupid little girls."

"That sounds like a confession," Marti said.

"What are you going to do about it?" Berryman was coherent. And vicious.

"We'll figure something out," Susan said. "I came back to Bicklesburg and saw the job opening with the Mickkleson Foundation. It was right up my alley. I took it as a sign, especially when I saw the address."

"Out of curiosity, how did you expect to pass the background check?" Marti asked.

"Ha. It wasn't my first, you know. Any background that showed up would be for the spotless Sandra Booth. Arranging things was easier back when Jack and I became the Booths."

"What did you plan to do once you were here—other than work for me?"

"I hadn't figured that out yet. But when they dug up that skeleton, I recognized Charlotte's bracelets. She wore them all the time. I found out where this creep was and came here to find out whose body was found in the Hollow all those years ago. He won't tell me."

"It was Marley. She killed herself." Marti didn't tell her Berryman had likely moved the body.

Susan snatched a pillow from the foot of the bed and turned on Berryman. "You scum. How many lives did you ruin? Tell me why I shouldn't smother you now?"

Marti grabbed the pillow and tried to wrestle it away. Susan held on with a strength powered by decades of pent-up rage.

"As much as I'd like to help you, he's not worth it," Marti said quietly. "There's already been too many deaths."

Susan let go of the pillow. "You're right. What now?"

"Are you ready to come in out of the cold? Someone needs to tell the world who Philip Berryman was. Is. And soon, before he dies on his own. Maybe not as satisfying as smothering him, but almost."

"Now?"

"Now. If you're willing to talk, I know a guy."

Susan hesitated. She picked up a loose photo off the bedstand and stared at it. Her face hardened. "Let's do it," she said.

"Let me see that." Marti took the photo. It was the one she'd dropped, the one of Berryman and his cronies. "Is there another?"

"Just this." Susan picked up the framed photo of the Berrymans.

"That's not the one." Marti checked the floor and under the bed. She scanned the walls. The picture of Marley and the two men wasn't there. She needed to get Susan to Big before the older woman changed her mind. "Let's go."

"Someone's coming." Grandma stuck her head in. "It's that Kristyl."

Marti ran into Kristyl in the hall. Literally. They collided a few steps outside Berryman's door.

"You! What are you doing here? I'm calling the cops." Kristyl pulled out her phone.

"You'd better check on Mr. Berryman first. He's been calling for you."

"There's something wrong with his call button," Susan said.

Kristyl raced into the room, and Marti and Susan sauntered away.

BABY FACE RODNEY refused to let them beyond the front desk. Big was taking a well-earned nap. He left orders only to be woken in the event of fire, blood, or major developments in any of the cases he was juggling.

"He specifically excluded you from reasons to wake him up. You were on the list of reasons *not* to wake him. You *were* the list," Rodney said.

"I can get him up," Grandma said. "He won't like it, but I can."

"You do have a way with people, don't you?" Susan shook her head at Marti. "Young man. I assure you your Chief will want to talk to me. If you don't get him now, fire and blood will be the least of your problems."

"Wow. Are you sure you won't stay when this is all over? That job's still yours if you want it." She still needed an assistant. Susan's command voice was right up there with Mom's. The thought of the two of them facing off was magnificent.

"No. I'm going home. It's well past time I let my family know I'm still alive."

"He'll be right out." Rodney was pale. Marti wondered whether it was the aftereffect of Susan or of waking Big.

"This conversation needs to be in his office. I promise he won't want it out here." Only a few people sat in the plastic chairs along the wall, but they watched the Susan and Marti show with interest. "I know the way. We'll show ourselves back."

"You can't do that!" Rodney started around the counter.

Susan gave Baby Face a she-who-must-be-obeyed look.

He crumbled. "I give up. I can't be in any more trouble than I'm already in."

"MARTI MICKKLESON, I told you to stay out of things. I swear on my mother, I've half a mind to lock you up right now. The only thing that's stopping me is your sister. RachelAnne doesn't need any more headaches."

Marti decided to attribute Big's anger to lack of sleep. He looked pretty rumpled. Still, she couldn't resist. "Everybody likes RachelAnne better." She stuck out her lower lip and did her best impersonation of a whiny five-year-old.

Big's face reddened.

"Young man," Susan said. "I think you're going to want to hear what I have to say. As for you, young lady, you need to work on your people skills."

"Excuse me, ma'am. I didn't see you." Big cocked his head and scrutinized the tiny woman. He looked like an owl. "Do I know you?"

Susan returned his stare and drew herself as tall as all five-foot-nothing of her could get.

"Susan, I'd like you to meet Chief William Fysh, Jr., head of Bicklesburg's finest. Known as "Big" to his friends. I call him that too."

"Pleased to meet you." Susan's nod was regal. Marti half expected her to extend a hand for him to kiss.

"Big, I'd like to introduce Susan Silliphant. You may have heard of her." Marti was willing to bet her next ten years' salary he had. Big Fysh's mouth opened and closed like a guppy.

He recovered. "Huh. Last I heard, you were off dancing with Elvis in Miami."

"I never had the pleasure," Susan said. "We need to talk."

"I guess we do." Big reached for two folding chairs.

"I'm not staying," Marti said.

"I'm going to need to know your part in this." He unfolded the chairs and parked them in front of his desk.

"I have no part in this." Susan's return was going to be big news. Big was about to have his brush with fame. Marti wanted no part of it. "Whatever comes next, keep me out of it."

"If you want to hear my story, you'll listen to her," Susan said.

"Are you sure you're not a Mickkleson?" Big asked.

"You're always telling me to stay out of things and leave them to the police, and that's what I'm doing." Marti headed for the door.

"Where are you going? Home, I hope," Big said.

Instead of answering him, Marti asked, "Have you heard anything from Dmitri?"

"I'm sure, wherever he is, he can take care of himself. Go home." Big's answer was far from reassuring.

"Oh, I almost forgot." Marti pulled out the photo she retrieved from Philip Berryman's room and took it to Big. "One of these men, maybe more, is a murderer. Susan can identify them for you." She knew who Lilith's murderer was, but Big could work it out for himself.

TWENTY-THREE

"Janice will be pleased, even if the answers aren't what she hoped," Grandma said. "Thank you."

Marti leaned her head against the steering wheel. Susan's story wasn't going to reflect well on Mrs. Heedly. "Remind me not to do any more favors for your friends. From now on, my policy is 'let sleeping ghosts lie.'"

"Of course, dear."

Marti didn't see Grandma's eye roll, but she heard it in her voice.

"Speaking of lie, are we really going home?" Grandma asked.

"I never said we were." She hadn't asked Philip Berryman about his daughter. Once she recognized Susan, she forgot her reason for going to Blissful Meadows in the first place. It wasn't like she could go back. Kristyl was probably guarding the gates with six large orderlies and a trebuchet.

"Grandma, did we ever one hundred percent absolutely for sure establish that one of your crew isn't hanging out at Henrietta's Hollow?"

"One of my crew? It's not like we all know each other."

"Just answer. Please."

"Since you said please, no. I didn't see anyone, but I only checked the crowd. What there was of it. Someone could have been hanging around the perimeter or in the trees. Depends on how far their range is."

"I'm an idiot," Marti said. Just because she'd never heard anything other than standard urban legends about the Hollow didn't mean there were no eternal residents. If someone was making the Hollow their afterlife home, they might have seen something. They didn't need to have been there long. She knew who put Lilith in the hole. They might know who did the same to Peter. And how Dmitri's car got there. She couldn't help but think the two were connected, and she had a good idea what—or who—connected them.

"Where are we going?"

"Henrietta's Hollow."

"I thought you were going to let sleeping ghosts lie?"

"Shut up."

THE HOLLOW WAS DARK. Really dark. Marti could swear there'd been security lights on the construction site when she and RachelAnne stopped for their Oreo feast.

"I think I'll stay in the car. You go check things out," she said.

"Like I'm going to leave you alone. Here, of all places," Grandma said.

"I don't want to sprain an ankle in a hole." It wasn't like she was afraid of the dark or anything.

"I'm not going anywhere without you. I may not be much protection, but I'm all you've got."

Marti argued. Grandma refused to budge. Marti turned on the flashlight on her phone. It was better than nothing. She wasn't afraid of the dark. She was terrified. "Let's go."

After a few unsteady steps, she pointed the light at the

ground. She wasn't kidding about spraining an ankle. The rough ground had been difficult enough to navigate in the daylight. Neither she nor Grandma needed a light to recognize the post-living anyway. She crept forward. "See anyone yet?"

"Yes. And they're not dead," Grandma said.

"Talking to ghosts? Living up to that reputation of yours?"

Marti shined the light forward. The beam reached far enough to see two people ahead but not far enough to see who they were.

"Keep moving this way. Slowly."

She didn't need to see Philippa Berryman to recognize her voice.

"Stay right there."

Nor did she need to see Dmitri to recognize his.

Marti took a few more steps, and her light illuminated the couple.

Philippa pointed something long and narrow at Dmitri. The barrel of a rifle. "Keep going, or I'll just shoot him now."

Marti kept going. She didn't know much about guns, but if what she'd gleaned from movies meant anything, Philippa had a hunting rifle aimed squarely at Dmitri's chest. Close enough she wouldn't need to be a good shot to hit him. Something about the way she held the gun told Marti she was a good shot.

"Go stand next to him," Philippa said.

"You never listen, do you?" Dmitri's hands were tied behind his back. The red rectangle around his mouth suggested duct tape at some point, but he wasn't gagged.

"Sometimes I do. Didn't there used to be security lights here?"

"She shot them out."

So Philippa was a good shot. Running wasn't an option.

"I'd tackle her, but the gun might go off," Grandma said.

"Drop the phone," Philippa said.

"What are you doing here?" Dmitri said.

"Looking for you, but this isn't where I expected to find you." Marti held her phone up. The harsh glare of the flashlight did

Philippa no favors. She looked old. Worn out. Her eyes were red-rimmed and swollen. She'd been crying. If she hadn't had a gun pointed at them, Marti might have felt sorry for her.

"Where did you think I was?" Dmitri's voice was calm. Steady. Just a simple question in an evening chat.

"I said drop the phone." Philippa pointed the rifle at Marti.

"I'll just lay it down here. Don't want to scratch up the screen or anything." Marti knelt and laid the iPhone on the ground. She took a deep breath and straightened. She half expected Philippa to shoot her as soon as she moved. "Dmitri. Long story. I'll tell you later." She matched Dmitri's tone. Just another conversation. No big deal.

"What is with you two? I'm standing here, pointing a gun at you, and you act like you just ran into each other at the grocery store."

"You know she killed Peter," Dmitri said. Same calm, steady voice. *Oh, by the way, did you see the persimmons are on sale?*

Marti's eyes adjusted to the dark. Philippa moved her aim back to Dmitri.

"You need to get her to point that rifle somewhere else," Grandma said.

"I know. I just don't know how—I mean why," Marti said. "Peter was a sniveling, lying, cheating pig, but that didn't mean he deserved to be murdered." In her fantasies, yes, but not in real life. Nobody deserves to be murdered.

"Don't say those things about him." Philippa transferred her aim back to Marti. "I mean, he was all those things, but *you* don't get to say it."

"Well, that's somewhere else but not helpful," Grandma said.

"I think she was in love with him," Dmitri said.

"Wasn't she a little old for him?"

"Don't go too far. She does have a gun," Dmitri whispered.

"What was that?" Philippa said.

"I don't get the attraction," Marti said. "RachelAnne, Winter, you. Two out of three of you are bright, professional women. Why hook up with a slimy little toad with delusions of grandeur?"

"I said, don't talk about Peter like that." Philippa pointed the rifle at Dmitri. "I was just going to shoot him and make it look like suicide."

"Not helping," Grandma said.

"Why would Dmitri kill himself? I mean, he doesn't seem suicidal. Not that that means anything, but still."

"Guilt over killing my Peter. Everybody knows he'd do anything for you Mickklesons. I'll make it look like murder-suicide. You get to be the murderer." Philippa pointed the rifle at Marti again. "People will believe anything about you."

"Don't you owe me a deathbed confession?" Marti said.

"Will you just drop it?" Dmitri said.

"I don't owe you anything."

Philippa thought the question was meant for her. Marti went with it. "If you're going to kill us anyway, tell me what the attraction to Peter was. I never saw it myself. Call it my last request." She hoped it wasn't.

"I loved him," Philippa said. "It didn't start that way."

She said when Peter decided to expand his empire beyond the used car lot, he had trouble raising capital. The car lot wasn't doing well. Even his connections to the Mickklesons weren't enough. Philippa heard and offered to help. "At that point, it was all about money," she said.

"How did you hear about his financial troubles?" Marti asked. "RachelAnne didn't know." The longer she kept Philippa talking, the longer she and Dmitri got to hang around.

"I have a connection at the bank. Harold's not good for much, but he likes to talk."

"I never heard anything about you being involved with Henrietta Square." Marti tried to sound interested. Anything to keep Philippa talking.

Philippa talked. She and Peter kept their business relationship quiet. The investors she put him in touch with liked things that way. The longer they worked together, the closer they grew. They were two of a kind. He was ambitious and intent on achieving those ambitions. "And he was so charming," she said.

Only when he wanted something, Marti thought.

"We fell in love."

Marti didn't believe it, at least not on Peter's part. Rachel-Anne, Winter, Philippa—the one thing they had in common was Peter used them all to get what he wanted.

"When RachelAnne left him, it was our chance to be together. I was willing to forgive him for Winter. She had her uses. I went to see him." Philippa paused.

"Um, why?" Marti said. Interrogation wasn't her strong point. Good thing Philippa didn't need much encouragement.

"We needed to make plans. Plans for our future together. I thought he'd be happy. I found him smashing things with a hammer. RachelAnne's things. I tried to calm him down. Said she wasn't worth it. I offered to make RachelAnne disappear if he wanted. I have connections who can do that."

"This witch needs to be the next one tossed into that hole," Grandma said.

Marti seethed. She clenched her jaw to keep what was in her head from coming out of her mouth. She'd never thought about RachelAnne being in danger.

"Just keep her talking," Dmitri said quietly.

"What...what did he say to that?" Marti tried to keep her anger out of her voice. She wasn't successful.

Philippa didn't seem to notice. Or care. "He turned on me. Said both Winter and I were insane if we thought he'd leave a real live Mickkleson for either of us."

Now that she was wound up, Philippa couldn't stop talking.

"He said I might be a big-time lawyer, but who was I in the end? The adopted daughter of a cut-rate high school teacher. Who were my people? Where did I come from? RachelAnne gave him standing, and sooner or later, Queen Margaret would kick off and she'd have money too. More than I would ever have."

"Peter always was a snob. Or a wannabe snob," Marti said.

"Adopted," Philippa said. "I never knew, but it explained a few things from my childhood."

How had she not known? If Peter knew, it must have been common knowledge.

"He laughed at me." Philippa spat the words. Her face flushed. The barrel of the rifle shook.

"What did you do?" Marti knew what came next, but Philippa had to say it.

"He dropped the hammer. I picked it up, and that was the end of Peter."

"How did you get him here? You couldn't have done it by yourself."

"Harold Binks. I told him he wasn't the only one who could talk. He likes his job at the bank. Now you two shut up. I need to think. If it's murder-suicide, he'll have to go first." She pointed the rifle at Dmitri.

Harold wasn't Winter's alibi. She was his, but that was something for Big to sort out.

"I don't like it, but I'll sacrifice your young man to save you," Grandma said.

"Don't you dare," Marti said.

"Like you have anything to say about it," Philippa said.

Marti didn't want to give Philippa time to think. Philippa thinking would only lead to bad things for her and Dmitri. Now that she'd heard Philippa's confession, she'd run out of topics for conversation. Dmitri was a man of few words, but it was time for him to chip in and start talking.

"Hi, Dmitri."

Marti hadn't noticed Oliver creeping up on them. Neither had anyone else.

Dmitri groaned. "Give me strength."

"You're pretty snotty for someone with a rifle pointed at their chest," Marti said.

"What is this, a party?" Philippa said.

"Dmitri, man, everyone's looking for you." Oliver wiped his nose on the sleeve of his parka.

"Oliver, shut up," Dmitri said.

"Ms. Berryman, you forgot this." Oliver held up a cell phone in a bright green case.

"This could be the distraction I need," Grandma said.

"That's mine," Philippa said. "How did you get it?" She kept the gun leveled on Dmitri.

"You dropped it at the cabin," Oliver said. "I made a call. I hope you don't mind."

"You don't have the password, and what were you doing at my cabin?"

"I sleep there sometimes."

"I keep it locked." Philippa's attention was on Oliver, but her aim was still on Dmitri.

Grandma moved closer to Philippa.

Sirens wailed in the distance. The barrel of the rifle jerked.

"There's a key inside the butt of that plastic deer out front. You really should be more security-conscious. You never know who's hanging around." Oliver pulled his other hand out of his pocket. A key dangled from a loop of string. "Oops. I forgot to put it back."

The sirens stopped. Light flooded the Hollow.

"Give me that!" Philippa dove at Oliver.

Grandma made her move. The gun went off.

"You don't need a password to call 911," Oliver said.

By the time Big and his army reached them, Philippa was shivering on the ground. Marti had grabbed the rifle and thrown it out of reach.

"Everyone okay?" Big asked.

"Everyone's vertical. Other than Philippa. I don't see any blood," Dmitri said. "We're all good."

"Speak for yourself," Grandma said. "That woman is toxic." She spat on the ground. Or would have if she could have. She did a good imitation of it.

"She killed Peter," Marti said.

"So I hear," Big said.

Rodney rolled Philippa over and cuffed her.

"Y-y-y-you h-h-h-ave n-n-n-no p-p-p-proof-f-f-f."

"Au contraire, mon ami." Marti retrieved her phone.

"What's that all about?" Dmitri said.

"I read a lot of Hercule Poirot. I've always wanted to say it. Now seems like a good time. I may never get another chance. Did you get it all?" The last was addressed to Big.

"Yeah. As soon as you said 'Dmitri', the county dispatcher called me. The whole thing's recorded."

Before setting her phone on the ground, Marti had given the side button five quick presses. The line to emergency services was open the whole time Philippa talked.

"What took you so long?" She'd begun to worry she'd only clicked four times.

"We'd finally got the tracking set up on Oliver when your call came in. It took us a while to pinpoint your location. The technology in this county needs updating."

"I'll expect a grant application on my desk ASAP."

Rodney and another cop helped Philippa to her feet. Grandma gave her a good poke, and she shivered again.

"Just for good measure," Grandma said.

"Are you okay, Ma'am?" Rodney asked. "Do you need a doctor?"

"I-I-I-I'm n-n-n-not t-t-t-talking w-w-w-without m-m-m-my l-l-l-lawyer-r-r-r."

"Maybe you can call Terrance Appleby," Marti said.

"Nope," Big said. He told them Appleby'd been hauled in for questioning about his involvement in Peter and Winter's financial fraud. State investigators were on their way. Rumor had it the Feds were interested too.

Marti shivered. She wasn't ghost freeze cold, but she was tempted to ask Oliver for his parka. The only thing stopping her was the snot-on-the-sleeve thing. "Can we finish this somewhere warm?"

"Oh, we're all going down to the station. It's getting pretty crowded, but we'll make it work," Big said.

The adrenaline had worn off. Marti was so exhausted she didn't care where she went. Anywhere but Henrietta's Hollow was good with her.

"Is anyone going to untie my hands?" Dmitri said.

CHAPTER
TWENTY-FOUR

RODNEY DROVE her and Dmitri home. The TT was still at the Hollow. Mom wouldn't be happy, but Big promised to send someone to retrieve and deliver it.

It had to be near dawn. Marti was sure they'd been at the station all night, but when she checked the time, it was barely past her bedtime.

Rodney dropped her off first. She assumed he didn't want to be alone with her. Frankly, she didn't blame him. She was tired, cranky, and had had more than her fill of peopling for the day. Maybe the week.

"I'll talk to you tomorrow," Dmitri said.

"Oooo. He's talking to you again," Grandma said.

"Sure," Marti said. She had questions. A lot of questions. Big took their statements separately, and even Grandma couldn't be in more than one place at a time. She still had no idea how he and Philippa came to be at the Hollow.

He probably had questions for her too. Or not. Big may have filled him in on her statement. The chief sent her home after he asked why she'd gone to the Hollow and she answered, "Looking for ghosts." Some people just couldn't handle the truth.

Rodney and Dmitri sat in the car and watched until she unlocked the back door and waved.

"He could have walked you to the door," Grandma said.

"And what? Given me a kiss good night?"

Back door, open. Back door, open.

Harriet was the only one to greet her. Bickle House was dark. No one waited up for her. No one had called to check on her when she didn't come home. Marti was developing a bad case of the nobody-loves-me blues. She should feel like a hero. She saved Dmitri. She caught Peter's killer. It was time for bed before the nobody-loves-mes turned into the I'm-gonna-eat-some-worms.

One light was still on in the dining room. The dinner dishes remained on the table. A large note was propped up against the water pitcher.

You promised.
But we saved you some dessert.
It's in the fridge.
XXOOXX

The note was in RachelAnne's writing and decorated with kid-drawn hearts and flowers. In the kitchen, she found a large bowl of chocolate pudding next to a can of whipped cream. One of her favorites. Comfort food.

"They do love me," she said.

"Of course they do."

Marti slathered her pudding in whipped cream, grabbed a spoon, and headed upstairs. The dinner dishes could wait.

"MARTI. WAKE UP."

She pulled her blanket over her head and ignored her great-grandmother.

"Listen. I wanted to let you sleep in. You earned it. But you need to get down to the kitchen."

"Just a little longer." She felt like she had a hangover without any of the fun of earning a hangover. It wasn't fair.

"Get up. Your sister needs you."

Marti stuck her head out. "Not another murder. Tell me it's not another murder. No more dead bodies, please."

"Worse." Grandma's voice held the same cold rage it held when Philippa mentioned taking out RachelAnne.

Marti crawled out of bed and grabbed her robe. "Are you going to give me a hint?"

"Just go to the kitchen."

RACHELANNE SAT at the kitchen island as usual. Unusual was the large blanket she was wrapped in.

"Are you okay?"

"I might be coming down with something. I froze all night. Every time I started to get warm and fall asleep, I got cold again. Really cold. Teeth-chattering cold. Maybe there's something wrong with the furnace?"

Grandma's rage was nothing compared to Marti's. If Powder-head Doody-pants wasn't already dead, she'd take him out herself.

"Where are you going?" RachelAnne said.

"To check on the furnace."

"Why are you so angry?"

Marti didn't answer. She didn't trust herself.

"How much does he know about how things work?" she asked Grandma as soon as she was out of RachelAnne's earshot.

"Probably not much," Grandma said. "It's not like he's had any contact with someone who could tell him, and he hasn't had time to figure it out himself."

"So he only knows the stuff he's seen in movies?"

Grandma snorted. "Like that stuff's true."

"Exactly," Marti said.

Grandma's smile grew as the light dawned. "I'll go round up reinforcements."

"I'll get supplies."

In the kitchen, Marti searched for what she needed. The cupboards were better organized when Mrs. Partridge or Myrna Ward was in charge, but she was sure she'd find everything. If not, she'd fake it.

"What are you doing?" RachelAnne said.

"Fixing things."

"The furnace needs salt?"

Marti pulled a small jar from one cupboard and a bowl from another. She jerked the junk drawer open and rooted through it. "There must be a lighter in here somewhere."

"A lighter? Marti, what in the world—"

"Ha. Success." She pulled out a long lighter, the kind used for lighting BBQ grills, and clicked the trigger. Flame shot out. "This'll work." She gathered her arsenal and left.

Maya waited in the hall. The little cat took a few steps forward. She turned and meowed.

Marti didn't need to speak cat to know what she was supposed to do. She followed Maya all the way to the attic.

Edwards, Amity, and Grandma had Peter backed into a corner. An outside corner. Marti hoped he was confined to the house proper. Edwards and Amity had run of the grounds, but no one, dead or alive, had seen Peter anywhere outside the house. This would be easier if he couldn't escape.

"Woooohoooo. Booogity wooogity wooogity." Amity stuck out her arms and did a weird thing between jazz hands and lobster claws.

Peter shrank into the corner but not through the walls. One good sign.

Marti strode across the room. "You need to leave," she said.

"Y-you can see me?"

"And hear you. Trust me, not because I want to."

"Who are they? Can you make them go away?"

"Nope. Not even if I wanted to. It's time for you to leave."

"Skedaddle," Amity said.

"Scram. Vamoose. Cheerio, daddio," Edwards said.

Peter looked from Marti to her three companions and back again. "I'm dead, aren't I?" His ghost shimmer grew stronger.

"Yup," Marti said.

"Boo!" Amity jumped at him.

Peter ignored her. "What happened?"

"Don't you remember?"

"Last thing I remember is drinking in the Starlite Lounge. Was it a car accident?"

"One of your girlfriends got fed up with you." Of the few ghosts Marti had watched cross over, one faded away after learning the details of his death. She told her late brother-in-law exactly what had happened to him and hoped for the same.

Peter didn't fade. He grew stronger, more solid. "On the bright side, I finally made it to Bickle House."

"You need to go. As they say, I don't care where you go but you can't stay here."

"I like it here. My family's here. I think Maggie can see me. I believe I'll stay. Watch my little girl grow up."

"The best thing you can do for that little girl is leave her alone. For once in your life, do the right thing."

"But I don't have a life anymore, do I? No, I'll stay."

Marti produced an exaggerated sigh. "I didn't want to do this, but if you insist." She flipped the spout on the canister of salt and poured a line from wall to wall, trapping Peter in the corner.

"What are you doing?" Peter said.

Grandma, Edwards, and Amity all took three steps back.

"Is she going to do what I think she's going to do?" Edwards asked.

"Yup," Grandma said.

"If he wasn't such a rotter, I might feel sorry for him."

Her supporting cast was doing their job. Marti hoped her performance lived up to theirs.

"What are they talking about?" Peter said.

She opened the jar of dried Albanian whole-leaf sage and dumped it into the bowl. Not quite what they used in movies, but it would have to do. She put the bowl on the floor inside the salt line, clicked the lighter, and set the flame to the sage.

Nothing happened. She tried again. No luck. On her third try, the sage began to smolder and smoke. She hoped the smoke alarm didn't go off.

"Persona non grata. Sine qua non. Amo, amas, amat." She wracked her brain for more of her high school Latin. When she ran out, she made up nonsense words.

Behind her, the ghosts wailed and moaned.

"W-what are you doing?" Peter's confidence waned. His form grew thinner, translucent.

It was working.

"It hurts!" Amity screeched.

Marti almost believed her. "Voulez-vous persimmonly gazpacho."

Peter's eyes grew wide. He flickered. He shrank so far back into the corner, he filled it. Marti could see straight through to the wall behind him.

"Be gone," she shouted.

The smoke alarm shrieked, and Peter was gone.

"It worked," Amity said.

"Like a charm," Edwards said.

"Is he really gone?" It was almost too easy. What's more, it was fun.

"He's crossed over," Grandma said.

"Gone like yesterday," Edwards said.

"You're sure?"

"Ninety-nine point nine-nine percent sure, which is as good as I can get without going after him," Grandma said. "And before you ask, no. I won't."

"Maybe I am some kind of ghost whisperer after all."

"Let's not get carried away."

"You had a lot of help," Amity said.

Marti's phone rang in her pocket. The ACS office. The smoke detectors were wired into the security system. She answered.

"Don't worry. It's just me burning sage."

"Dare I ask?" Dmitri said.

CHAPTER

TWENTY-FIVE

MARTI STARED AT HER PHONE. After they'd gotten the smoke alarm situation settled and she'd convinced him there was no need for the fire department, Dmitri said he'd text her later. He didn't specify how late "later" was. She hadn't heard from him.

Big came to the house and officially informed RachelAnne that Peter's killer had been arrested.

"Philippa. Winter. I wonder how many more are out there?" RachelAnne looked numb. It could have been lack of sleep, but Marti was afraid it was shock at how much her late husband had hidden from and put over on her. The realization her whole marriage was a lie had to be devastating.

Big patted RachelAnne's hand and offered awkward reassurances.

Marti didn't want to think about that. "Don't you need to go?"

"Would you like to stay for lunch?" RachelAnne said.

"I do need to go," Big said. "I have a press conference this afternoon."

"Press conference? Not about Peter?" RachelAnne was alarmed. Marti didn't blame her.

"No," Big said. "The reappearance of Bicklesburg's most famous missing person."

"Just keep me out of it," Marti said.

"So now you want to stay out of things?"

"Huh?" RachelAnne said.

Marti pressed but couldn't get more than an "I'll try to keep you out of it" from Big. He left. She filled her sister in on Susan Silliphant. She downplayed her part and didn't mention Lilith. Most of the story was on a need-to-know basis, and RachelAnne didn't need to know. She had enough to deal with.

Still no text from Dmitri.

They watched the news conference. Neither Big nor Susan mentioned her. Big announced the identification of the remains found in Henrietta's Hollow as Charlotte Monahan. He didn't mention her part in that either. He also didn't mention Philip Berryman. Something to ask Dmitri about since he seemed to have an inside line to Big. If she ever heard from him.

The sun was setting by the time she received his text. *Meet me out front.*

SHE AND DMITRI sat on the front steps. Why they sat on the steps with a whole porch behind them, she didn't know. Other than it was what they'd done the first time they shared a beer after her return to Bickle House, and it felt right. Like that first time, Dmitri pulled two Coronas and a bottle opener from a brown paper bag. Unlike the first time, he also had a small plastic bag with two slices of lime.

"I'm getting better at this," he said.

"He likes you. Be nice," Grandma said.

"Did you see Big's news conference?" He handed her a beer. "Congratulations on solving the Susan Silliphant mystery."

He could have only heard about her part from Big. She needed to be careful what she said. The information pipeline flowed both ways.

"I didn't do anything. Susan came here intending to come forward. And, if you ever tell anyone I played a part in it, I'll have to hurt you."

"You know, that scares me more than it should."

Was he flirting again? She never could tell. "Since you seem to know so much, any leads on how Lili—Charlotte Monahan ended up in Henrietta's Hollow?"

"You don't know?"

She knew more than him, but admitting it wouldn't do her any favors. "Not a clue."

"Susan Silliphant had some ideas. Big's trying to locate the men in that photo you gave him. At least three have passed away. They're still tracking down the fourth."

"The fifth?"

"Philip Berryman, but you knew that."

She saw no reason to deny it. "What's going to happen to him?"

"Probably nothing. He took a turn for the worse when they told him about Philippa's arrest. He hasn't spoken since Big said the name 'Charlotte Monahan.' They don't expect him to last long."

Marti's feelings were mixed. She wanted Berryman to pay for what he'd done. She wanted the world to know. Too many feels to deal with now. She'd sort out her emotions later.

"Any more questions?" Dmitri said.

She had a million. "Why was your car at Henrietta's Hollow? And how did you and Philippa end up there when I found you?" She knew why they were there. Philippa made that clear.

"It's complicated."

"Tell me. I'll do my best to follow along."

"The short version. I went to the Hollow to meet Philippa Berryman. She stuck a gun in my back and forced me into her car.

We went to a hunting cabin just outside of town. When we went inside, she hit me over the head, and when I came to, I was tied up and had duct tape over my mouth."

"I know the feeling," Marti said.

"When it got dark, she took me back to the Hollow. You showed up. Oliver showed up. You know the rest."

Marti shivered.

"You okay?"

"It's too cold to sit out here. I could use Oliver's parka. Especially that nice new one. Any idea where he got that?"

Oliver'd shown up a lot lately. More than a few of those times were connected to Dmitri.

"He must have friends. Anyway, it's not that cold." Dmitri slid closer to her.

His nearness didn't do anything to warm her up on the outside. She didn't want to think about what it did to her insides.

"How did you end up at the Hollow? And don't tell me you were ghost hunting," he said.

"Okay."

Teen-Dmitri had believed in her ability or pretended he did. She didn't know where Adult-Dmitri stood on the subject. She didn't know where Adult-Dmitri stood on a lot of things. "More important question. Why did you go meet Philippa at the Hollow in the first place?"

"Do I have to tell you?"

"Well, you could tell me where you disappeared to for months."

"It was only six weeks. Philippa called and said you were in trouble."

"He does care," Grandma said.

"You didn't think to call me and check?"

"I lost my phone."

"Where?"

"If I knew that, it wouldn't be lost."

"He has a point," Grandma said.

Marti gave Grandma the evil eye. The one she'd learned from Grandma.

"I'll just leave you two alone. But you'd better fill me in on any good stuff." Grandma went inside.

"You just texted me," Marti said. Something didn't add up.

"Jeeze Louise. I went and got a new phone today."

"You could have called from the ACS phone."

"I was worried. I got out as fast as I could."

"You must have been some sort of serious worried."

"You do have a knack for getting yourself in trouble."

"I could point out that you were the one in trouble this time, but I won't."

"Thank you for that." He moved closer. Any closer and he'd be sitting in her lap. "So." He cleared his throat. "Would you like to go to dinner or a movie or something sometime?"

Dinner or a movie or something? That sounded like a date. He couldn't be asking her out on a date. They hadn't gone on dates when they were an item. Just sort of hung out. Like they were doing now.

"Marti? I'm asking you for a date. I mean, I understand if you don't—"

"Yes." Where did that come from? She'd meant to tell him she'd think about it. "You know, men involved with Mickkleson women haven't had a great amount of luck. The Judge. Peter. Almost you." She didn't point out the first two brought it on themselves.

"Big already mentioned that. I told him I'm not worried. Not much, anyway." He put his arm around her.

This was pleasant. Comfortable. Almost like a snuggle. It had been a long time since she'd snuggled with anyone. Anyone she wanted to admit to. She leaned her head on his shoulder.

"So, tell me. Just where *did* you disappear to?"

About the Author

Kay Charles is the much nicer, mystery-writing alter ego of dark fiction writer Patricia Lillie (author of *The Cuckoo Girls*, a 2020 Bram Stoker Award® finalist.) Like her evil twin, Kay grew up in a haunted house in a small town in Northeast Ohio, earned her MFA from Seton Hill University's Writing Popular Fiction program, teaches in Southern New Hampshire University's MFA in Creative Writing program, and is addicted to coffee, chocolate, and cake. Both their lives would be much easier if one of them enjoyed housework.

Visit her on the web at kaycharles.com.